Rise of the Pale Moon

Rise of the Pale Moon

PATRICIA BRANDON

PALMETTO
PUBLISHING
Charleston, SC
www.PalmettoPublishing.com

Copyright © 2024 by Patricia Brandon

All rights reserved
No portion of this book may be reproduced, stored in a retrieval system, or transmitted in any form by any means–electronic, mechanical, photocopy, recording, or other–except for brief quotations in printed reviews, without prior permission of the author.

Paperback ISBN: 9798822958579
eBook ISBN: 9798822958586

To Sasha,

Who has given me a much deeper
appreciation for the measure of freedom.

Spasibo

To Corinne,

My amazing and wonderful friend,
my fun partner in crime.
I miss you so much.
We had quite a ride in this life, didn't we?
May you rise like the pale moon, always!

ACKNOWLEDGEMENTS

Rise Logsdon, you are an amazing editor! Thank you so much for all you did, despite my massive technical deficits!

To my CotA Coffee Friends, thank you for all of the encouragement and support! What a wonderful bunch of friends!

To Alice Youngblood and the DAR-SC, thank you for the wonderful information on Emily Geiger! I've also discovered a family relation to her! What a gift!

To my wonderful daughters, McKenna and Gracyn, thank you for believing in your 'ole mama! You two are my greatest and most loved accomplishment in this life! I am so proud of the women you have become!

AUTHOR'S NOTES

This is my third historical fiction novel, and it has been the most difficult to research, thus far. Set just before and during the American Revolution, I discovered that, while there is plenty of research about the war itself, there is much less information about general daily life – routines and what their lives were really like in the colonial South. There is even less similar information about Native Americans, indentured servants, and chattel slaves during that period in history. What a tumultuous and complex time!

South Carolina history has always fascinated me, as has the history of slavery and other states of bondage in both our own America, and in the rest of the world. To truly understand the breadth and depth of slavery and man's inhumanity to man, across all races and creeds, it is best examined in that comprehensive context. Conversely, and thankfully, the same might be said of the side of humanity that holds fast to compassion, understanding, and hope.

The context of this research also reminded me that the birth of any nation is often fraught with conflicting and complex beliefs and attitudes, and issues to overcome. Understanding and full acceptance- changing society mindset- takes decades, even centuries, to resolve in the embracing of true freedom for all. It is my hope that this novel, this story, pays homage to those who lived during those times, and that it stirs in all of us the desire to understand our history and to learn from it, and to always help our world to begin again!

There is a cameo appearance by Thomas Paine, a Founding Father of this country, though he was from Great Britain. His legacy to our United States is grossly underappreciated in general, to my mind. He stirred the souls of many toward the Patriot cause. This novel largely adheres to his true political leanings and reflects possible relevant-like conversations he might have had, and what is known about his personality and interactions. An admitted disclaimer for the sake of the fictional side of the story: Thomas Paine did not attend a meeting in Charlestown in 1775, though he was immensely instrumental in advancing the cause for American independence. He did eventually become an aide to General Nathanael Greene, who also has a role in this story, as does General Thomas Sumter, the "Fighting Gamecock."

Emily Geiger, another South Carolinian, is said to have made a legendary ride to deliver a crucial message from General Greene to General Sumter. I have paid close attention to the many variations of her story and used an amalgamation of all to portray her journey and interactions with my fictional protagonists. Apologies in advance for any part of this novel that may not be totally correct – it is, after all, a work of fiction, though I have tried to remain as historically correct as possible, and to pay homage to the strength and character of both the slaves and the many tribes of natives indigenous to our country. Some names, terminology, etc., may not be entirely from the Catawba Nation, but hopefully reflect accurately on the overall spirit of native peoples.

Finally, I was amazed to discover a family connection to Emily Geiger! In 1736, Conrad Kunzler emigrated from St. Margrethen, Switzerland to then Charlestown, South Carolina. Along with the Geigers and Schellings, they were part of the Rheintal group who settled into the Congaree/Saxe Gotha area, on the northwestern edge of the township, on the frontier among the Indians.

Conrad had four sons, the eldest named Herman Kunzler (*anglicanized to Kinsler, from whom I am descended on my mother's side*), who also had a grandson named John Herman Kinsler. As an aside, John became a member of the House of Representatives from the Richland District (1850-18520, was elected to the Secession Convention, and later signed the Ordinance of Secession.

Herman Kunzler (*my ancestor*) had a brother named Johannes (John) Kunzler, who had a daughter named Dorothy Kinsler.

Emily Geiger's grandson – Maj. Jacob Herman Geiger, married Dorothy Kinsler after the death of his first wife. After his death, Dorothy married his first cousin, Maj. Abraham Geiger.

A little complicated, but I love the family connection! I'm so glad to have discovered a small piece of my heritage, and so much more about our South Carolina history!

> *"He that would make his own liberty secure, must guard even his enemy from oppression; for if he violates this duty, he establishes a precedent that will reach to himself." - Thomas Paine*

CHAPTER ONE

London, 1774

"For heaven sakes, don't leave him there!" Lady Carrington shook the dirt from the hem of her fine dress, then wrung bejeweled hands together. A mixture of dust and remnants of bricks blackened the polished floor in the meticulous home of Lord Carrington, a member of the King's Privy Council. Her shrill words chastised the Master Sweep and might have been interpreted as caring, until she complained.

"The filth is everywhere, and this ruination must be repaired at once!"

Ten-year-old Vieve Whittier stiffened, clenching her fists, and staring at the broken soot-covered body of little Simon. Her sweep-apprenticed brother, one of London's climbing boys, would never reach seven years of age. Like many of London's poor, Simon was made a climbing boy as soon as he became five, laboring for hours daily in the dirty chimneys of the affluent. On this day, the Master Sweep had selected him to attend to the chimney in the Carrington residence. Now his lifeless body, covered in bruises with skinless patches of raw redness, was a twisted mangle from entrapment within the narrow stack, having been forced to maneuver through a flue and chimney to clean with a scraping brush The immensity of grief was more than Vieve could bear, and the hot tears flowed down her cheeks unrestrained.

"I sent for his mother, as you requested, Milady, where she is on market errand. Word has been sent to Lord Carrington, as well. The boy moved too slowly. Rendered himself stuck, he did. I lit a torch underneath to hasten him along, but to no avail. A most unfortunate occurrence, but not unheard of, with these young waifs. Be assured that repairs will commence forthwith."

But her brother could never be repaired. Vieve fought to escape the reassuring grip of the beloved housekeeper, who tried in vain to comfort her as she lunged with all her might toward the Master Sweep. The anger, seething inside beneath the overwhelming grief, burst forth in an explosion of pain and loss.

"You killed him! You killed my brother! I hate you!" She continued to struggle against the firm grip of the elder housekeeper. Her simple blue dress, worn thin by daily wear, had torn across the bodice in the attempt to restrain her. Dark hair escaped the large, braided strand and fell about her face, clinging to soft wet skin. Lady Carrington made a strategic step in front of Simon's body to face the young girl, who fought to break free.

"Genevieve!"

Lord Carrington's wife rarely used her given name unless there were distinguished guests about, or admonishments were to be meted out. She spoke with a forced calm, but Vieve could sense the underlying layer of condescension.

"I will forgive your unladylike outburst because you have lost your kin." Addressing the housekeeper, she nodded, "Take her upstairs with the children until her mother returns."

Never relinquishing the hold on the distraught girl, the housekeeper whispered soothing words while guiding her away from the macabre scene and up the great staircase. Outside, worried voices in the street grew louder with the sound of footsteps scurrying up the brick portico. The front doors to the massive townhouse were thrown open by an almost delirious and wild-eyed Claire Whittier, followed by Lord Carrington, whose face was set in a stoic and grim manner beneath the top hat. Vieve could hear part of the raucous exchanges taking place below, even as the housekeeper struggled to restrain her mother, though she could not understand all that she heard.

"Where's my son? Where is he? Simon!"

"Claire. Claire, listen to me." Lord Carrington's deep and somber, yet gentle and sympathetic, voice rose above hers.

"Oh my God, Simon! Why is he lying there like that? A physician needs to be summoned, please, dear God! Simon!"

"Claire," Lord Carrington's voice wavered. "He's dead, Claire. I'm so sorry." He reached for her shoulders, but Claire Whittier escaped his grasp and ran to her son, weeping with abandon and rocking the battered body in her arms.

"Well, I must say," a stone-faced Lady Carrington stood in uncomfortable closeness before her husband, arms crossed, head held high; her whispered words wreaking of sarcasm. The scowl on her face deepened to rage. "I've always thought the boy favored you, but in death, the wretched resemblance is even more so. And what matter of convenience, that you and the scullery maid should arrive here together." Lady Carrington could no longer hide the rejection and embarrassment, knowing her place in society would forever change if the truth became widespread fodder for London gossip. She spat the next words between gritted teeth.

"Unless you want all of London, King George, and your children to know about any of this, get rid of her and the girl. Send them far away. Immediately, unless you want your coveted position as the next Chancellor of the Exchequer to become an impossibility. My father still has a considerable audience with the king, you know."

Trying to retain a measure of dignity, she spun away from him and ascended the staircase without looking back, her intentions set. Though her own marriage to Lord Carrington had been arranged for the demands of society, she had expected her husband to honor the union as she had. She would see to it that these peasants were banished from all of England, never to be seen again. Opening the door where Vieve and the children were sequestered, she pressed a hand against her cheek, as if to wipe away the indignity of what had just happened.

"My loves, I'm afraid we must say goodbye to Vieve." She forced a smile at her confused offspring, who huddled around their grieving friend, then stared at Vieve, the disdain in her voice now evident. "Pack your belongings. You and your mother will be returning to Covent Garden immediately. A carriage will take you to Drury Lane." She hesitated, her tone softening in the afterthought. "May your brother rest in peace, despite the destruction he caused. I pray you will learn to know your place in this world, Genevieve. Hopefully, better than your mother."

The words stung much as the frosty bite of London's coldest winter mornings. Whatever had transpired between her mother and Lord and Lady Carrington, Vieve knew one thing with certainty: Claire Whittier loved her children more than anything and had worked as hard as she could to maintain their care, despite not having a husband. Vieve had always been told that she once had a father who had died from the deadly Scarlet Fever just before Simon's birth, but she had no memory of him, nor knew his name. Claire was then left to make her own way with two children to raise.

For as long as she could remember, Vieve and her family had lived at the place called the Bawd House on Drury Lane, with the other ladies, many who were in much the same predicament as her mother. Claire had worked a coffee house, peddled flowers on the theatre streets, and on occasion, had provided what she referred to as "companionship" to a variety of gentlemen. She was an exquisite beauty when well-rested and groomed, despite her simple means. Her dark hair, fetching green eyes, and well-proportioned feminine pulchritude had been passed on to Vieve, who relished the strong resemblance to her mother. Though not fully aware of Claire's true profession, she understood that her mother's place was considered beneath that of London's finest ladies.

"Sometimes, men need someone to talk to and share some happy times," Claire had explained to Vieve, "and some will pay well to do so. It helps me to take care of all you need, so I don't mind. You must remember to never discuss my work with anyone. It's better for us that way. Some of the men are boorish oafs, but some are higher-born, pleasant sorts, and kind to me. Some even pay more than five shillings."

Lord Carrington had been one of those men. Vieve had heard the chatter among the other women in the Bawd, that he had talked often with her mother in the coffee house, given her small trinkets or gifts, and made Claire smile. When Simon was no longer a baby, Lord Carrington had provided her with work as a scullery maid in his home. When Vieve was eight years of age, she too was given work as a helper for her mother and a companion for the Carrington children, even sharing in some of their tutoring. How thrilled Claire had been when Vieve could read for her. Lord Carrington, and even Lady Carrington, were delighted when Vieve read stories for the youngest children, who loved her as a sister.

But now, Vieve clutched her mother's hand in the dim chill of the late afternoon outside the fashionable home, as they awaited the carriage that would take them to Drury Lane. Claire's eyes were red and swollen with unimaginable sorrow. Vieve squeezed her hand.

"Will Lord Carrington still visit with you, even though Lady Carrington no longer wants us here?"

"No, my sweet," Claire could not force a smile. She bent low to hold her child. "No, he will not be with us anymore. But he has said he will help us to bury our Simon and find a new place for you and me. Something better. We can start over in the colonies."

"The colonies? Is that far away? What will we do there?"

"Yes, very far. A long ship ride away. We will travel across the sea, Vieve, imagine that! To a place called Charlestown in The Province of South Carolina. And we will build a better life together, you and I, in a beautiful new land. A good and happy life for us. Let's try to be thankful for that, even in this terrible sadness." Claire's eyes clouded once more.

Vieve glanced up at the pale moon, just beginning to rise in the deepening gray sky. She remembered her mother taking her to church one day, sitting in the very back with those considered beneath the more affluent, and listening to a fiery reverend rail about the light of the moon shining in the darkness. A symbol of hope, he had raged, even when mankind shunned the Son, Jesus Christ, and chose their evil, dark ways instead. Vieve wondered at the soft light emanating from the celestial realm. On this night it seemed hope was all that was left.

CHAPTER TWO

Atlantic Ocean, 1774

In the steerage bowels of the ship destined for Charlestown, South Carolina, Claire Whittier struggled to hoist herself up on the dirty mat where she had been relegated for much of the voyage to the colonies. At nighttime, her wheezing became more intense, and she now struggled to breathe in the dank, dark surroundings. Like some of the crowded passengers who had perished from sickness, her skin was sallow and pale, and her once vibrant eyes were now dull and sunken into a thinned face. Vieve felt her mother's hands, then forehead, and frowned at the cool, pasty texture. The fever had burned for hours, but now her body shivered in relentless waves.

"Mama. Mama, can you hear me?"

Claire tried to motion for her daughter to lean closer, her hand brushing Vieve's cheek, then dropping to her side. There was no more strength left.

"I love you—my precious girl," she whispered in sharp, staccato phrases that matched the labored breathing. "Promise me—you will—never—give up." Her body shook in uncontrollable spasms, her voice barely audible. "Promise—me."

"Mama!" Vieve squeezed her mother's hands together, trying to will the life back into her wracked and withered body. "Mama don't leave me! I love you so much! We are almost to the end of our journey! Mama don't go! Please!" Vieve felt the tears cresting in her own eyes, the terror of being left alone in this desolate place was drawing nearer, more overwhelming.

"Promise—me," Claire gripped Vieve's arm, her eyes opening wide, then closing for a moment, before taking in the frightened child who struggled to hold the tears back for her only parent. "You will—see me—in—the moonlight—always—my sweet—girl," she breathed. "Never give up. Say—your prayers. Promise—me."

"I promise, Mama," she whispered, the understanding and unrelenting grief once again seeped into her body like the wretched sickness that had overtaken her mother. "I will never give up, never. I love you so much, Mama."

Vieve held Claire's feeble hands until they relaxed with her last breath. Her mother's lifeless eyes remained frozen in their loving gaze until she stroked them shut with her hand. Now the tears fell in violent waves of sobs, moistening the skin on Claire's sunken cheeks, and releasing the massive grief and fear that had lurked in the stillness of impending death. Vieve knew she was forever alone in every conceivable manner, trapped in a desolate place on a journey to a home in which she had never been. She felt the walls of trust and safety crumbling in merciless heaps around her. In the wreckage of her soul, only despair and fear remained. Vieve held Claire's hands in hers and laid her head on the chest that no longer rose and fell in labored breaths. She would spend one more night with her cherished mother.

The hours until first light passed in slow, painful roils, with only intermittent sleep and tearful prayers; the loving memories of her mother and Simon providing moments of respite from the demons of the unknown.

"Miss?" A female steerage passenger gave her arm a gentle shake.

Vieve sat up, still beside Claire's lifeless body.

"Miss, I've sent someone for the captain. Your mama was so sick. She has died now; may God rest her poor soul. Is there anyone else here with you? Anyone at all?"

Vieve shook her head, not speaking.

"Would you like me to stay with you?"

Vieve stared past the kind woman, into the dreaded unknown. There was no one to trust now. The woman remained standing in quiet contemplation before placing one hand on the child's shoulder and raising the other to cover her own face, the tears threatening to fall.

"I'll leave you be then, Miss. I'm so sorry."

Vieve felt the rocking lull of the great ship, creaking in the throes of the mighty Atlantic. Claire would never know how this journey would end. Vieve wished the vessel would burst into pieces, taking all who remained onboard into the cold deep. At least there might be a chance she could quiet the storm of immense grief inside. She closed her eyes, praying for the soul of her mother and the strength to carry on her own life without the loving care that Claire had provided.

"Genevieve Whittier?" The captain, grizzled and exhausted from the grueling passage to the colonies, spoke in a tired but commanding voice.

Vieve opened her eyes and nodded. He pointed toward Claire.

"This is your mother? Claire Whittier?"

Vieve nodded her head again.

"You came aboard only with her, is that correct?"

Vieve nodded once more.

"I am sorry for your loss. I will make the necessary arrangements for you when we reach Charlestown. For now, we must see to your mother. I will have the passenger who found you keep an eye on you for the remainder of the journey."

Vieve never left her mother's side. Not when they rolled her body up in the tattered blanket she had shared with Vieve, nor when a brief prayer was offered. She had watched, overcome with despair, as Claire Whittier was shoved, in an uncelebrated heave, over the edge of the ship into the dark waters below. Vieve fixed her gaze on the white splashes her mother's body had made, watching the rise and fall of the foam as it disappeared, melting into the vastness of an unforgiving ocean. With Claire gone from view, there were no more tears. At least for now. Vieve thought for a moment of jumping from the vessel.

Falling to her mother. The woman who now looked after her on board might have sensed as much, as she placed a firm hand on the poor girl's shoulder.

"Miss, I know your mother loved you very much. She was happy to be on this journey with you. We never know about our numbered days, I suppose."

No, we don't know. And I don't care anymore. But I promised I would not give up. I will keep going, even if I have no desire to do so. Because I made that promise.

Vieve stared skyward. A sliver of the moon appeared pale but glistening in the morning light. *I love you, Mama. Always. Somehow, I will keep going.*

Voices rose from the captain and another crewman standing nearby, who spoke in lowered tones, but their words drifted to her, nonetheless.

"No, only her and the woman. To be indentured, the lot of them, to whomever will pay. The girl should bring something. A comely little thing, she is. Smart. Curious. Asked lots of questions about the ship and the journey. Read stories to other little waifs on board, sang with them, too. Knows her manners, this one. Someone will pay."

The captain studied the young girl huddled against the wall of the ship, staring across the horizon, no doubt afraid. He smiled at his crewman.

"The Province of South Carolina is one of the wealthiest of the colonies. The planters and merchants in Charlestown, especially, possess a strong governing class, though there are many loyalists. But also, many leaders who want independence and have set down roots there for which they will fight. Despite Lord North's stabilizing the colonies after repeal of the Stamp Act, both he and King George remain stubbornly fixed in their belief in the right to tax them. The conflict there is only just beginning to rise, to be sure. Regardless of market conditions, the girl should bring a decent sum from Loyalist or Patriot. I care not which one."

Vieve did not turn to look at the men but considered their strange words. At least the place where she would be sounded like people of means lived there and would care for her. But she wondered at the exact meaning of *indentured, Loyalist, or Patriot*, and if the referenced conflict that was escalating would threaten her in any way. It did not matter. There were no other choices left.

CHAPTER THREE

Charlestown, Province of South Carolina, Summer 1774

"Her mother died enroute to Charlestown, God rest her. A prostitute and scullery maid for a member of the King's Privy Council, she was. Signed on as a free-willer, she did, not a King's passenger or redemptioner. The child's got no one, poor soul. An exception, this one. Got some education and manners about her. Years of servitude are negotiable. You did mention that you have a daughter about her age, is that so? This one could be a fine companion for her and a big help to the Mistress of Montague."

Elias Montague studied the dirty, destitute child before him. Given a proper cleaning and garment, she would indeed appear to be a suitable servant for the house, and a desirable companion for Lucy. Even with limited tutelage, she would be more refined than the Negroes at Montague Hall. She would also be a welcome help for Elizabeth. He smiled momentarily, thinking of his wife's pleasure at having a servant who could be made to appear more refined. Perhaps a proper companion and servant for Lucy would encourage Elizabeth to further embrace her stature as the mistress of one of the most notable rice and indigo plantations in the colonies. He knew that the life Elizabeth had anticipated as the wife of a prominent lawyer was more in keeping with that of the Charlestown aristocracy, but she had been dutiful in her acceptance of the move out of the civilities of town to the untamed land along the Ashley River. While he knew she shared in his desire to expand both wealth and position, she was growing weary of the daily rigors and loneliness of plantation life. Elias knew she craved the now limited amenities of more social surroundings, having been raised in Charlestown and used to all the trappings of gentility.

He motioned the girl toward him and bent low to see her face. He could see the path where tears had made their way down dirt-laden cheeks.

"What is your name?" His firm voice was commanding, but low, even soothing, as Lord Carrington's voice had once been. The girl remained silent. "I know it has been an unpleasant journey for you," he said in a softer tone. Please tell me your name."

"Genevieve," she whispered back, an almost inaudible response.

"Genevieve." Elias repeated, smiling, and dropping one knee to the floor while pushing his tricorn hat away from his face and loosening the cravat at his neck. He was a tall, solid-built man whose manner also reminded her of Lord Carrington. "Genevieve is a French name. It means 'of the race of women, of purity, grace, and beauty. God's blessing.' Did you know that?"

"My mother called me Vieve," she said without a smile, but searched his brown eyes for any sign of trust. Elias Montague relaxed, sitting back on his heels as he regarded her. Vieve studied the smooth black boots that matched the darkness of his hair. His fair skin had a darkened tone. She surmised he had spent considerable time in the bright sunshine that was said to be indigenous to this land.

"Then I shall call you the same as your mother did. Tell me about your training, Vieve. And what you like to do." Vieve stared hard at Elias Montague, saying nothing, then whispering once more.

"We lived with Lord and Lady Carrington. I learned to read and to write there. I read stories with the children, sang songs, and said their prayers. I learned with them."

"What else did you learn?"

"Some mathematics. My mother and Lady Carrington made the market list. Lord Carrington and the butler taught me to count. I helped my mother with housekeeping."

"And the tasks you performed?"

"I can mend, polish, and brush the floors. I can cook some. I helped to empty chamber pots a little. I most liked to sing with the children and to read with them and with my brother Simon."

"Where is your brother?"

"He died before we came here. He was a climbing boy." Vieve paused, then let the lancing of the secret wound open. "The Master Sweep killed him. He was not even seven."

There was no hate or vengeance in the voice of the young girl. Only grief, still raw and fresh. Elias Montague frowned, then smiled at her, a hint of both sad concern and promise present in his voice.

"I am sorry for the loss of your brother, and your mother as well. How would you like to come live and work at Montague Hall? Help my daughter and my wife? The terms would be approximately seven years or so to earn your keep. And you must work hard. After that time, you will be free to go wherever you would like. Or you could remain there at the plantation if you have done a suitable job and wish to continue."

"I have nowhere else to go," Vieve looked directly into the eyes of Elias Montague. "I promised my mother I would work hard, wherever I may be."

"Then it is settled. The captain will procure the appropriate papers and I will see that you wash in the river before we board the flatboat for Montague Hall. You will need suitable undergarments and shoes. We can wait on a coat. You are filthy and your clothing is wretched. The washroom slaves will clean what you have on with a good battling stick the next time garments are done, so bring them with you. At least they are not full of holes and may be salvaged. For now, I will take my leave until you are prepared."

Elias Montague turned with abruptness to finish his duties while Constance, who had watched over her since Claire's death, escorted Vieve to the nearby water's edge. This Charlestown appeared cleaner than the streets of London, but it bustled with the same activity.

"Stay in front of me, Miss, and you will have more privacy. Use the lye all over and these strips of cotton and hemp cloth to dry yourself as best you can."

Vieve did as instructed, fighting the immense embarrassment of her nakedness. With thanks, she noted that the people close by went about their business with little regard for her or anyone else who might be bathing in the designated area. The bracing chill of the gentle waves lapping against her skin was a refreshing and welcome respite from conditions on the crowded ship. Vieve held her breath and slipped beneath the shallow edges. She could feel the soft mud under her feet and marveled at the quietness of being submerged. She wondered if her mother could feel her presence in the water and smiled. Perhaps this strange place would not be so bad, or so lonely.

When she rose from the river to dry, Vieve saw Elias Montague regarding her with nonchalance and tossing a pair of brogan shoes, stockings, and a white shift dress to Constance.

"These should fit, I think. Finish dressing. I must see about final arrangements for a horse for my youngest son. I will return soon for you. Be ready. We have a journey ahead of us before sundown."

CHAPTER FOUR

Along the Ashley River, Charlestown,
South Carolina, Summer 1774

Seated on the wooden floor beneath the sails of the flatboat barge, the long journey up the scenic wilderness of the Ashley River was both captivating and overwhelming for Vieve. The sweaty and stalwart workers who helped muscle the vessel upriver with the tide mostly conversed with Elias Montague and the other men, laughing as they toiled and discussed events of the day. As the only female and the only child aboard, she was ignored, except for a muttered instruction or two when they needed her to move out of the way.

The vast expanse of land and river stretched for miles, with few meager dwellings scattered about, mostly those of poor farmers, who waved as the small party made their way upriver. Endless thick woods teemed with vibrant forest green, even up to the water's edge, and the soft sounds of nature floated through the air. Wildflowers meandered along the way, the intoxicating trumpet honeysuckle and jessamine underscored clean wafts of pine and a pungent smell of plough mud. An occasional white water lily patch peeked from around the still inlets. Tall pines towered overhead with grand cypress and water oak dotting the landscape. An occasional blue heron, or a smaller egret, flew above and graced the lush landscape when they landed on the river's marshy shores. Spanish moss hung, plentiful and mysterious, like long tendrils of thick gray hair, as the warm sunlight glistened and played among the floating mounds of gray. Having never been outside the crowded, dirty streets of London, Vieve was captivated by the life of this strange, but pristine land.

"The Indians call that *gray hair* or *tree hair*," Elias Montague stood next to her, motioning toward the moss in the trees.

"It's alive," she said, staring up at the massive trees and taking in the surrounding scenery. Elias smiled, amused at the fascination of the young girl.

"The tree hair? No, not alive. We pull it out of the trees to make mortar and plaster. It is often woven into horse blankets and baskets, and in some bedding."

"No, Sir. Not just the tree hair. Everything. It's like it's all breathing. All the land."

Elias sat beside the pretty young girl, crossing sturdy legs, and imagining what it might be like to be in such a strange wilderness as this, with no one to care for her. She was an inquisitive and bright child with a positive spirit, especially having just lost her family. Despite being the daughter of a lower-class woman, she might one day do better for herself. This would be a good time to prepare the young girl for her duties and station in plantation life. Elizabeth would most certainly expect her to know her place.

"Perhaps now I should tell you about Montague Hall."

"Is that where you live, Sir?"

"It is one of the most productive rice and indigo plantations in the colonies, though it is not the largest. I run an efficient and profitable business. I was a lawyer in Charleston. I still am. But I decided to venture into the business of rice and indigo that we export. My father left me this land. He came here from Barbados. I am the Master of the plantation. You should always refer to me as such. Likewise, my wife, Mrs. Montague, is the Mistress, which you should also call her. You will refer to my sons as 'Master Mal' and 'Master Oliver,' and my daughter as 'Mistress Lucy.' You answer to me and Mistress Montague first, then assist them. Do you understand?"

"Yes, Sir." She looked down at her hands once more. "I mean, yes, Master Montague." Vieve winced, noticing the growing formality in his tone with every word he spoke about Montague Hall. The further their journey endured, the more she noted the subtle tenseness in his demeanor.

"You will be assigned tasks by Mistress Montague. Mostly, you will be a companion and helper for Lucy. Mistress Lucy, that is. She is perhaps close to your age, a bit older, I think. My sons are each a few years older than you, also. Malachi, or Mal, as we call him, is the oldest, and Oliver is two years younger than he, I believe. The Overseer, Mr. Bennett, looks after the workings of the plantation, particularly when I am attending to other tasks there. He manages the slaves and has a Negro foreman to assist him, but my family is ultimately responsible for how the entire business is run."

"Slaves?"

"The Negroes I own. Their slave ancestors were also brought here. Some I bought at the market in Charlestown. They work the fields and perform labor as instructed. I own you, as well, but not for life, as I own them, although I am at liberty to sell or trade you, or them, if the need arises. You are bound as an indentured servant, to the terms of indenture, regardless of for whom you might work. As for the slaves, I have sixty, at last count. They work in some capacity all year round, as rice and indigo require intensive and constant labor. My sons and I work with them most of the time. Although you will help primarily in the house, Mistress Montague might have you also assist any of the slave women and children, as she sees fit."

"There are slave children?"

"Yes, there are not many at Montague right now, and most are quite young these days. One or two are closer to you in age. They are born here, also, which makes them mine, as well, for life. We do not teach them to read or speak educated English, as you know how to do, as they are quite simple beings and only need to focus on their given tasks. You may play with the children, especially when Lucy might do so, but otherwise those requirements stand. Do not educate the slaves, otherwise."

Vieve looked down at her hands, then out across the calm river. An uneasy feeling took root in her stomach and chest. She had heard

Lord Carrington, during one of their lavish dinners with aristocratic company, mention British slaves in the Caribbean colonies. She had even seen Negroes on occasion on the streets of London, dressed as she had been, but knew nothing about their lives either in this place or back in England.

"How many colonies are there? Are there slaves in all of them?"

"There are thirteen. You are in one of the southernmost of the colonies. But all of them, even the northern industrial ones, have some form of slavery. We need slaves here the most, of course, as we are a growing agricultural society. Our soil and land conditions are perfect for producing rice, indigo, and tobacco, which are the mainstays of life here. We cultivate rice and indigo for export, though there is a small tobacco patch. Thus, the need for cheap intensive labor, which slaves provide for us."

"Where do they come from? Do they like it here?"

"Primarily from the western coast of Africa. It does not matter whether they like it here, or no. This is the task for which they were purchased and born. They are given clothes, food, shelter, and taught their place and the ways here. Their lives are better here, given their obedience and compliance in the work needed. They get fresh air, not like the slaves in the northern colonies."

"Where do they live?"

"They live in cabins built for them to share. They have their own small garden to plant and harvest what they will and are doled provisions when suitable to do so. You will see that Montague Hall is its own village. We have a cook and smokehouse, a washhouse, as well as blacksmithing in the carriage house, a milkhouse, and of course the mill itself for winnowing, threshing, pounding, and preparing for shipping. There are other cabins, as well, for various needs. The privies, of course, are away from the mill area or where food is prepared."

"Where is the church?"

Elias Montague furrowed his dark brows only for a moment and stared into the waters of the Ashley before looking skyward beyond the tall pines.

"There are churches in Charlestown proper, but very few in these parts. Here in the backcountry, we do not have the luxury of churches. There is an outside covered area of sorts, that we use for chapel or for merriment, in the rare event that we have a number of guests here. An occasional priest travels through on the way to Charlestown or back to the northern colonies. If he takes his respite for the night at Montague Hall, he might be allowed to preach to them. Otherwise, Mistress Montague or I, or the Overseer, read a passage or two from the Bible to them on most Sundays. A White adult must be present when they gather for church or anything else."

"Why is that so, Sir?" Vieve wondered aloud.

"It is beholden upon us to see that they are assembled in such a manner as to best help and guide them, just as a parent once guided you in learning. And to teach them obedience."

"I went to church with my mother. We sang hymns and learned about God."

"You will continue to learn with Mistress Lucy, as she is schooled. If you wish to attend a worship time with the Negroes when it is provided otherwise, that would be permissible, unless you have conflicting duties. Mistress Lucy likes to sing. Perhaps you and she might sing the hymns you have learned, also. She has an affinity for music."

"Yes, I would like that."

"Vieve," he regarded her in a serious manner. "You must always remember to use the utmost of care and manners when speaking to Mistress Montague and my children, or any important guests we might have, though visitors are infrequent. Unless you have a clarifying instructional question, wait to speak unless spoken to. Always respond with their proper titles and a pleasant voice, and you will do fine at Montague Hall for as long as you are there. Do you understand what I'm saying to you?"

"Yes, Sir." Elias remained expressionless, saying nothing, but his eyebrows arched in a questioning glance. Vieve lowered her gaze away from him. "I mean, yes, Master Montague."

"Very good. We have just a little way further before our journey to Montague Hall is over. It won't be long before you are at your new home. It will be quite different from your London, to be sure. You will find there will be many tasks to learn at Montague Hall, but I think you will find it both challenging and rewarding. With care, your life will change for the better, also."

CHAPTER FIVE

Montague Hall on the Ashley River, Summer 1774

The horseback ride from the small farm, where they had disembarked to retrieve both Elias's horse and a fine quarter horse for his son, to the grounds of Montague Hall was as intriguing to Vieve as the scenic flat boat journey had been. She sat side-saddle in front of her new master, atop a massive black stallion, with the smaller horse in tow behind them. She had seen many horses before on the streets of London but had never been fortunate enough to sit on the back of such a magnificent creature as this. She felt almost regal and more at peace than she thought possible, basking in the early evening twilight that bestowed a soft glow to all around them.

Unpopulated and densely wooded land stretched as far as she could see, with only an infrequent meager cabin or primitive written sign, visible along the dirt pathway. The coastal forest, like the river edge, was also stocked with massive trees of pine, cedar, cypress, and water oak, interspersed with lush green low foliage, and the strange tree hair was scattered in abundance throughout the thickness of the landscape. The solitude of it all, in addition to being secure in the arms of Elias Montague, lulled her into a state of welcome serenity. How very different this Province of South Carolina was from the squalid streets of London. Here was an untamed and magnificent land brimming with natural beauty. The quiet hum of indigenous wildlife, the muscular, rhythmic strides of her first horse ride, and the undulating leaves amid warm humid air was a soothing balm for her troubled soul.

"This is Montague Hall." Elias Montague interrupted her reverie. "All around you is part of my plantation. You cannot see much of the rice fields and the indigo grounds from here, especially with the impending darkness, nor the shared estate garden, but they are behind the courtyard area. The slave quarters, washhouse, the cookhouse, smokehouse and storehouse, the blacksmith and carriage house, barn, and stables, and of course, the privies are all back there in the courtyard."

He gave her arm a gentle nudge while reigning his horse to a momentary stop at the brick-columned gated entrance. A wide pathway before them diverged to two separate paths that each weaved their way to either the front or rear of the plantation home. They had passed a view of Montague Hall on the flat boat, but Vieve had fallen asleep and missed the opportunity to observe it, along with partial views of the slave quarters and the various outbuildings situated in the long courtyard behind the main house. She gaped at the welcome display of familiar grandeur in such a remote wilderness as this.

The stately country home, made of black cypress wood and shuttered at each window, was situated beneath towering oak trees in a slight diagonal from the landing on the Ashley River. The front facade loomed visible and accessible from the landing on the water, while the back of the home would be more readily viewed from the path behind it. The sprawling white clapboard structure stood two and a half stories tall, crowned by a dormered hip roof and chimneys on the sides of the house that reached skyward. A double-tiered verandah with six squared columns, reminiscent of West Indian architecture, graced the entire front of the house, which rested on a raised solid brick foundation, with wide- railed brick steps centered before the doorway. As if he knew her thoughts, Elias pointed to the steps and foundation.

"See the bricks all around? They were all made right here, along with the clapboard for the house. Clay was mixed with water, rolled in sand, then packed in a wooden mold. Then fired and ready to be laid with mortar as the foundation. There is a cellar there, as well, where the house slaves also sleep."

"House slaves?" Vieve wondered aloud, recalling her tenure in the Carrington home.

"The slaves who work the fields are field hands, or slaves. Those who work and maintain the buildings and task areas in the courtyard have their own assigned responsibilities. The house slaves work inside our home, serving meals, cleaning, tending to the fires, and doing the daily necessities there. You will see them all."

Vieve looked across the grounds of Montague Hall. Scattered throughout were magnolia, tea olive, and camellia trees, and a variety of low flowering shrubs. Vieve had seen similar homes before in London, but never anything as isolated, set in such pastoral beauty, as this.

"I love it," she breathed, smiling. "Everything smells so fresh and alive. I like to watch the tree hair move."

"You will see more of Montague Hall on the morrow, including the slaves and such, and begin learning your tasks. For now, you will meet the rest of my family, have a morsel or two, and get a reprieve from your long journey here."

"Master Montague?"

"Yes?"

"Where do all the other people live?"

"The other people? Whom do you mean?"

"In London, there were buildings and so many people. Like in Charlestown, but dirtier and more crowded. Where are all the people?"

Elias relaxed in the saddle, gazing at his land as far as could be seen. This was indeed a curious and intelligent child, almost to a fault. How unfortunate, her circumstances.

"Very few people are out here in the backcountry. Larger plantations, such as this one, are few and far between. Fewer still are larger than ours, though some are. Most folks out in these parts are just small farmers, with no slaves, keeping their families alive."

"Where are all the people who live here? The slaves?"

"Tending to their evening duties, as they should. Preparing for the work at daybreak. You will meet a few who work in the house shortly."

The front door of Montague Hall burst open, and two boys clattered down the brick steps.

"Father! You are home!" The smaller of the two shouted, looking up at Elias, then at Vieve. "Who is that?"

"Good evening, my sons. I see you have helped manage in my short absence. Go fetch your mother and Lucy if they are about, and I will tell you all."

The boys rushed back inside as Elias bid them, racing to see who would reach the entrance first. The front door opened once more, this time with deliberate hesitation. A tall woman, likely Mistress Montague, with blonde hair bound at the nape of her neck and wrapped and pinned in a soft bun, followed by a girl with light brown braids also wrapped into a bun with a white cap. Vieve surmised her to be Mistress Lucy. The woman and girl made their way to the top step but did not descend. Both were dressed in blue gowns, simpler than the ladies strolling about in Charlestown, but something about Mistress Montague, the commanding way in which she carried herself, made Vieve feel small, even inferior. The boys gathered around Elias, grabbing hold of the reins of his horse. Elias removed the tricorn hat, dipping his head in deference to his wife and daughter.

"Good evening. Elizabeth, my love, you look beautiful, as always. It would seem you have all managed splendidly today."

Elizabeth Montague crossed her arms, then reached to brush a hand over the head of her daughter.

"I'm glad you have made it safely back. Yes, we have worked hard in your absence." She stared at Vieve with a chilly indifference. "Who is this you have brought to visit with us?"

Elias dismounted and lifted Vieve from the saddle, setting her on the ground beside him.

"This is Genevieve Whittier. She is called Vieve, and she is an indentured servant, not a visitor here. Her former employer, and that of her mother, was Lord Carrington, from the King's Privy Council. She is here to assist you, my dear, in any way you see fit, and to be a more suitable companion for Lucy, as such are not often available to us. She can read, do household chores, and more. A much-needed helper and companion for our daughter, I think."

"Why are you here alone? Where is your mother, your family?" Lucy spoke for the first time, frowning. Vieve looked up at Elias, not knowing if she should respond to the girl.

"You may speak when addressed, Vieve. Just remember the rules as we discussed them."

"My mother died on the ship," she murmured. "I have no family and nowhere to go. Master Montague gave me employ."

"Hello, Miss," the younger boy spoke up. He smiled as if he meant it. "I am Oliver. My brother and I can tend to your horse if you'd like. She's a beauty."

"Oliver, you may indeed tend to this horse. She is yours. A present for your twelfth birthday. She has not yet reached full growth, but no doubt will be a fine companion."

Oliver stared wide-eyed at the well-built animal, stroking her with firm, gentle hands and whispering in a soft, unintelligible, but loving, tone.

"Thank you, Father!" His excitement gave way to an unrestrained smile. "I will take very good care of her, I promise. I will have to think about a suitable name for such a fine horse. He turned to Vieve. "Welcome to Montague Hall, Miss Vieve."

Vieve returned his smile. She could sense an easygoing way about this son.

Elias placed a hand on Vieve's shoulder, then gestured first to the oldest boy, who regarded her with detachment, then to his wife and daughter.

"My oldest son, Malachi. We call him 'Mal.'"

"Good evening, Master Mal." She looked into his eyes but unlike Oliver, could not discern much about his nature. His hair, like that of the younger Oliver, was dark and secured at the back of his neck.

Both boys were of a solid frame, sturdy and tall like their father. Unlike Oliver, Mal did not respond to her in any way.

"This is Mistress Montague and Mistress Lucy," Elias said, nudging her arm again.

"Good evening, Mistress Montague, Mistress Lucy. Thank you for having me."

"Well," Elizabeth Montague raised her eyebrows. "I see she does know some manners. Where is she going to sleep, Elias? Only adult Negro women, and several men, are in the cellar. I do not think those would be suitable quarters for her."

"I think the attic might do for now," Elias mused aloud. "There are a few unfinished room spaces up there and the slave access stairs go there, as well. It will keep her close to Lucy and us, if her services are needed, but she will be isolated from the adults in the cellar. Oliver, Mal, please have Ashwiyaa and Big Zeb in the barn assist you in preparing a pallet for Vieve. She will need a blanket for when the weather is cooler. Then take care of your horse for the night, Oliver. When you are done, you can take Vieve's pallet to a suitable location in the attic."

Both boys scurried to do their father's bidding. Lucy and Mistress Montague continued to regard Vieve with mild disdain, looking down on her from the verandah.

"Where are your belongings?" Mistress Montague asked.

"I have a bag with another set of clothes, but they have not been washed since the ship's journey," Vieve offered. "And I have my mother's Bible."

"That's all?" Lucy was incredulous.

"Yes, Mistress Lucy. That is all."

"Lucy, take Vieve to the washhouse and leave the clothing for Evaline to wash the next time washing is done. Then bring her back to me and your mother." Elias was firm in his direction.

"Come on, then," Lucy frowned, walking to the bottom of the steps, and heading behind the house. Vieve followed, glancing back in time to see the scowl on the face of Mistress Montague as she expressed displeasure in not being consulted before the arrival of a new servant. Vieve winced, a measure of the overwhelming sadness returning once more.

The wash house, like all the outlying buildings in the courtyard, was of simple construction, with a fireplace at one end, iron pots for washing and rinsing with battling sticks and other tools, and drying racks set at the other end.

"Evaline!" Lucy called out. "Where are you?"

"We's in the cookhouse, Mistress Lucy!"

Vieve followed Lucy through the narrow walkway into the next building, which was also finished in sparse detail. Another fireplace laden with lidded cooking pots, two large tables, and a variety of cookhouse accouterments hung on the otherwise bare walls. An open, but covered, walkway ran from the cookhouse to the main house at Montague Hall. By the door closest to the walkway, a Negro woman, scarf wrapped and tied around her head and her dirty apron still on, appeared welcoming, rubbing ebony hands together and smiling. Beside her was a similarly dressed young girl, also with hair wrapped in a red scarf and dirty apron.

"Good evenin', Mistress Lucy. We's jes' 'bout finished up cleanin' in here. Who dis you brought wid you?"

"This is Vieve. She's from London. She's our new servant. She's mostly mine." Lucy's eyes narrowed as she turned to face Vieve, watching her discomfort.

"Well, Vieve, thas' a purty name and we's happy to see you. I'm Evaline. I takes care of the cookhouse and washhouse mostly. This here my chile, Maybelle. You look 'bout her age maybe."

Vieve smiled at the Negro girl her size. The girl smiled back. Her teeth gleamed white in the dim light of early evening. Vieve liked the lilting way in which Evaline spoke and sensed a semblance of connection with the dark woman and her daughter. She had never spoken with the few Negroes on the streets of London.

"Good evening, Miss Evaline and Miss Maybelle."

"Just their names," Lucy instructed with glaring condescension. "They are slaves. You are, too, just not for life, like they are. None of you have titles."

Your brother, Oliver, was much more pleasant and kind, Vieve thought to herself.

"What can I do for you, Mistress Lucy?" Evaline emphasized the word *mistress* which Vieve thought was amusing. She suppressed the urge to smile.

"These filthy clothes of hers are all she's got. They need washing and mending, next time around."

"Why yes'm, I thinks we kin git that all done fo' next time 'round. Some being done tomorrow." Evaline gave a broad smile to Vieve.

"We need to get back to the house," Lucy spun on her heels, not waiting for Vieve to follow.

"Good night then," Vieve nodded toward the pair. "Thank you for helping me."

"You come on back anytime. Maybelle and me, we learn you the ways 'round here."

"I would like that."

Vieve smiled and waved at the mother and daughter, while rushing to catch up with Lucy.

"I'll show you where the barn is and see about your sleeping pallet," Lucy said, her voice devoid of kindness. "Then you can help me get ready for bed before you rest up for the morrow."

Vieve followed her to the barn at the end of the courtyard. There was also an area for blacksmithing, with stables close by. She stared, in the deepening twilight, past the end of the courtyard to the far fields where stalks of blue seemed to sprawl all the way to the horizon. Many dark-skinned people were making their way out of them. Those must be the Negroes finishing for the day. Some carried work tools, wiping their brows, and moving with slow but deliberate strides toward the small cabins that must surely be the slave quarters. Others rode in the back of a large wagon driven by another Negro man with a White man beside him.

"Those blue plants are indigo. Those slaves work the fields. The rice fields are beyond that, closer to the river. Never mind for now."

Lucy motioned for Vieve to follow her inside, where Mal and Oliver, and a hulking Negro man were almost finished packing stuffing into a sack. The most unusual looking girl Vieve had ever seen stood beside them, with mounds of the tree hair from the oak trees in her hands. She was taller than Vieve, with straight hair, as black as the soot her brother Simon had been forced to clean, that was woven into two long braids. Her skin, not as dark as that of the Negroes, was a deep golden reddish-brown, like a wild ripening berry. She wore a simple cloth garb, with a woven belt around her waist. A hunting knife hung at her side; the wooden handle worn smooth from use.

"Hello, again," Oliver smiled at Vieve, and reached for some of the tree hair that the black-haired girl held. "We are almost finished with your pallet. This is Big Zeb, he manages the barn and blacksmithing, and that is Ashwiyaa. She helps Big Zeb and is teaching us how to scout, make canoes, shoot with a bow and arrow, and helping us learn the ways of planting like the Indians. Everyone, this is Vieve, from London."

"She's a servant," Lucy added, with little expression.

"Good evening," Vieve smiled. "I'm glad to make your acquaintance." She wondered what an *Indian* was exactly, and how the girl came to this place. Was she a slave, like Maybelle? "That is tree hair, is it not? Master Montague told me about it."

Big Zeb smiled back at her, but the Indian girl remained expressionless while considering the newcomer.

"Itla-okla," the girl said, now frowning.

Vieve looked to Oliver for help, sensing a measure of animosity from the girl.

"That's an Indian word for *tree hair*," he grinned at her. "Ashwiyaa taught us."

"Itla-okla. It is a lovely word. Thank you for sharing it with me." She smiled at the striking Indian girl and wanted to know more about her; why she was at Montague Hall. "Perhaps I will learn more from you, too."

The Indian girl chose to ignore her but handed the remaining tree hair to the Negro man called Big Zeb. Her lips and dark eyes were set in defiance. Vieve decided to focus on the others. "Thank you for making the pallet for me."

"Ticking here has feathers, straw, hay, corn husks, tree hair – whatever we done got dat been washed and dried out." Big Zeb smiled again at her. "'Dis here be a nice pallet fo' you, Miss."

"A bundling bag was all that we had for now," Malachi finally spoke with a bit of formal courtesy, "but it will work for you, if you take care of it."

"I will, Master Mal, I promise." She surmised him to be around fourteen.

"Once we's tie it all up here, we git it to yo' sleepin' place," Big Zeb patted the stuffed sack.

"Mal and I can take it up for her, Big Zeb," Oliver said. "You and Ashwiyaa can finish tidying up for the night."

"Yassir, Master Oliver, we do dat." The big man hummed under his breath while he worked. He seemed a happy sort, like someone Vieve would like to get to know.

"I'm going to take my leave now. Come, Vieve. Goodnight." Lucy moved toward the barn doors.

"Thank you, again. All of you." Vieve waved, as she exited the barn to go back to the main house with Lucy. She had a feeling that there was much to learn at Montague Hall.

CHAPTER SIX

Montague Hall, The Main House

Vieve had so many questions but decided to heed Elias Montague's warning about not speaking unless spoken to first. Lucy had proven to be not as welcoming as her brother, Oliver, had been. She followed Lucy up the right side of the curved stairwell that graced both sides of the back portico of Montague Hall. Inside was as beautiful as the outside; fine furnishings and accouterments befitting a home of gentility, but not as ornate as the London Carrington home had been.

"Unless you are with me or someone else in the family, you use those stairs there." Lucy pointed to a dark, narrow stairwell off the large hallway between the back and front of the house. "That goes up to the attic where your quarters will be and all the way down to the cellar with the house Negroes. But for now, you can go with me to my room upstairs so you can help me to prepare for sleeping."

Vieve glanced around the sparse but nicely appointed bed chamber. The room, a shade of soft blue that was almost gray, contained a fireplace, a sturdy four-postered bedstead and elegantly stuffed pallet, with a step stool and chamber pot that peeked from underneath the bed. A large wooden dresser, a vanity and chair, a trunk, and a small nightstand were beside the bed.

"Help me get undressed, then fold and place my clothes in the dresser, and brush my hair," Lucy commanded.

Vieve complied without speaking, placing the folded dress in a drawer, and accepting the hairbrush that Lucy thrust at her.

"Be gentle with my hair," she warned, running slender fingers through the mass of unbraided softness, and smoothing her bed gown, "and do not brush too hard if there is a tangle."

Vieve obeyed, once again without speaking, brushing the long, pale hair with learned skill and precision. Many times, she had brushed her mother's hair. She felt oddly at peace with this familiar and cherished routine.

"You have done this before," Lucy regarded her with a measure of care for the first time. Vieve noted the change in her demeanor, even her appearance. The long tresses fell about her shoulders in gentle waves and softened her face.

"Yes. I loved to brush my mother's hair. She was beautiful, as you are, Mistress Lucy."

Did your mother take sick on the ship? I would be lost without my mother, I think."

Vieve smiled, thinking of Claire with fondness and glad to be able to speak of her. How she missed her mother and Simon. Not having a family intensified the feelings of loneliness in this strange land.

"She became quite ill on the voyage. Many passengers did. She so wanted to come to the colonies."

"And what of your family? Your father or brothers and sisters?"

"I never knew my father. My brother Simon was a climbing boy. He was only six. He died also, right before our journey. The Master Sweep forced him into a chimney to clean where he could not breathe or move." Vieve prayed for the emotion not to be overwhelming, as she now thought of her mother and brother, and the stark sadness that engulfed her at barely ten years of age. Her eyes welled with tears, but they never fell. Lucy sat in quiet contemplation on the edge of her bed, studying the indentured servant girl.

"I'm sorry for you," she said, her voice just shy of real empathy. "You must miss them terribly."

"Yes," Vieve whispered. "Do you need anything else, Mistress Lucy?"

"No," Lucy regained her incivility, as she climbed into the bed. "That's all for tonight. You can go wait in the hallway for my brothers."

"Goodnight, then. Sleep well." Vieve blew out the candle beside Lucy's bed and made her way back to the slave stairwell entrance. Moonlight shone through the large windows and cast calming shadows on the massive walls. Elias Montague was waiting for her.

"I trust you are learning your way, Vieve. Mistress Montague was tired and has retired for the evening but will instruct you further at daybreak. In the meanwhile, you will need a good night's rest. Would you like a morsel to eat? The fare we had in Charlestown has likely long past its duty in easing the hunger, but I can have some bread procured for you."

"No, thank you, Master Montague, I am not hungry."

"Very well. I see Mal and Oliver returning with your pallet."

Vieve watched as the boys balanced the pallet between them, above their heads, and made their way up the dark slave stairwell. Mistress Montague had left strict instructions to take the stuffed pallet up by way of the slave stairs. Vieve and Elias followed behind them to the attic landing above the second floor.

"Father, where shall we place it?" Malachi looked at Elias while pushing the door open.

"Place it against the chimney wall, where it will stay warmer in the winter, cooler in the summer. Then open the window there so that the night air might keep the room cooler. Vieve, you can close it in the morning, to keep the heat at bay. Where is her blanket?"

"Father, I left it downstairs. I can fetch it." Oliver volunteered.

"Show her how to latch the window when done," Elias instructed. "Good night, Vieve."

Vieve gazed around the wooden beams of the attic space, void of all but her pallet and small bag that contained her mother's bible. The light of the quarter moon through the small window cast a peaceful sheath of dim light in the darkness.

"Master Montague?"

"Yes?"

"This is mine?"

"The room? Yes, meager as it is. But better for you here than in the cellar."

"No. No, I love it, I truly do. I've never had my own place to sleep."

Elias Montague smiled before taking Mal and Oliver and leaving her alone.

"Get your rest. You will need it. Goodnight."

"She likes the horribly bare attic?" Vieve heard Mal whisper as the door closed behind them. "She must have been very poor indeed."

Vieve went to the tiny dormer window that Mal had opened, propping her elbows on the inside ledge. An ethereal light bathed the front grounds of Montague Hall in quiet serenity. The waters of the Ashley River sparkled in the pale moonlight, giving the thick tree hair an almost mystical dimension. Her mother would have loved the beauty of it all. She felt the tears rising at the thought of life without her. This time, the many tears fell without reservation.

I wish you could see this, Mama. I miss you and Simon so much. A gentle knock on the door displaced the mournful memory, at least for the moment.

"Vieve, it's me, Oliver. I have your blanket." Oliver opened the door and made his way to her, placing the warm woven blanket in her hands. "You might need this now at night, but the weather here will get much hotter and oppressive as the summer months arrive. And this is for you—to welcome you to Montague Hall."

Oliver placed a plucking of tiny, fragrant tea olive branches in her hand. Vieve inhaled the intoxicating freshness.

"Thank you, Master Oliver."

"I don't much like being called that," he frowned. "It sounds like I'm my father. Call me 'Oliver,' please."

"Your father said that is how I am to address all of you. I can't disobey."

"Then, just call me by my name when no one else is around. That's not disobeying, since I'm telling you to do so, is that not so?"

Vieve could see his broad smile in the darkness, feel the friendship he seemed to offer.

"Very well. Thank you again for these, Oliver." She held the flowers up to him. "It smells so sweet and beautiful. My mother—her name was Claire—would have loved these very much. You know what these smell like?" She breathed in the heady scent once more. "Hope. This is what hope smells like." Oliver shoved his hands into the pockets of his breeches.

"I'm sorry for your loss, Vieve. Truly."

"The Bible says that we're supposed to give thanks, no matter what," she tried to smile at him. "Well, maybe not those words, but that's what we're supposed to do. So, I'm thankful to be here. And thankful for you being so nice to me."

Before he left, Oliver showed her how to latch the window during the day and walked to the doorway.

"Remember, you'll want to secure the window when you leave in the morning. Then you can open it once more at night to let the cooler air in. Good night, Vieve. I'm glad you're here."

"Oliver, wait. How do I know when to rise in the morning and where do I go for my duties?"

"You will know," he gave a soft laugh. "The rooster will wake you. And you will hear voices and more. Then, a loud bell. But I will come to your door if you are not awake on time. You will learn. Goodnight."

Vieve gazed out her window once more before removing her work dress and smoothing her bed gown. It had been a long day. The quietness of the night, the soft scent of tea olive, and the warm memories of her mother and brother lulled her into a peaceful reverie. Tomorrow she would learn more about Montague Hall and the life that she would soon begin as a servant. Perhaps she would find a way to be friends with everyone in this place. At least that was what she hoped. Hope—sweet hope—was what would carry her through. She placed the tea olive branches on top of her mother's Bible that rested on the wooden floor beside her pallet, said a quick prayer, and let her eyes close at last. Sleep would soon overtake the rush of memories, the exhaustion from the journey, and the rigors of the day that had taken their toll. She knew tomorrow would bring even greater challenges—the immensity of which would remain to be seen.

CHAPTER SEVEN

There was more dark than light when the loud crowing of the rooster roused Vieve from sleep. She sprang to the open window, taking in the early dawn freshness of the wild land as the first vestiges of sunlight seeped into the dim sky. A mixture of voices rose from the rear of the house and wafted up the slave stairwell and through the open window. Directions barked out, tools clanked against boarded wagons, and the sound of horses, cows, and working slaves pierced the morning air. Donning the work clothes and stockings that had been folded and placed beside her pallet, Vieve laced the leather shoes and tied them more tightly than usual. She ran fingers through her hair before creating one long braid, then retied the frayed ribbon around it. The dim light was not suitable for Bible-reading, so she offered a quick prayer, asking for strength to manage the day, then latched the small window as Oliver had shown her.

"Vieve?" Oliver called to her from the slave stairwell. "Are you awake?"

"Yes. Yes, I am ready! I am coming down now."

A resounding bell clanged in loud intervals from outside the house. She met Oliver, clothed as he had been the night before, at the bottom of the stairs.

"What is that bell for?"

"The morning call to work, for slaves to report as assigned for their duties." He smiled at her. "Did you sleep well?"

"Yes, very well. A good night's rest."

"There you are," Mistress Montague attempted a sliver of a smile as she rounded the corner from the family stairs. "See to Lucy's needs and wait here for further instructions." She gave a dismissive wave toward the upstairs bed chambers, then made her way out the back entrance to the courtyard.

"Where is she going?" Vieve raised questioning eyes to Oliver.

"She makes her first rounds through the courtyard to see that everyone is in place, especially in the cookhouse and washhouse. I will join my father and Mal outside to check the trunks for flooding the rice fields and assist the blacksmiths and coopers in preparing the barrels for shipments of rice and indigo. We will also work the indigo fields."

"Vieve!" Lucy's shrill call wafted down from her bed chamber. "Where are you?"

"Go," Oliver whispered. He placed his tricorn hat on his head, tipped it toward Vieve, then started toward the rear door before turning to her once more. "Lucy can be most demanding."

"So, I see," Vieve mumbled to herself, as she made her way back up the slave stairwell to Lucy's room.

"Good morning, Mistress Lucy. What do you need for me to do?"

"Be here promptly!" Lucy pouted, as she secured her shoes and reached for her white mob cap. "I need my hair brushed and braided. Where is your cap?" She frowned at Vieve.

"I'm sorry, I do not have one."

"I think I have an old one you can have. It might need mending." Lucy eased open a dresser drawer and tossed Vieve the extra cap, this one more worn, and came with ties. "There. Now you will look more presentable for a house servant."

"Thank you," Vieve offered. "It is kind of you to share it with me." She placed the cap on her head, leaving the ties to hang, as Lucy had done, then accepted the brush and comb held out to her, as Lucy seated herself in front of the vanity.

"I would like two braids today. Do not make them too tight."

Vieve complied as she made meticulous and slow brushes through Lucy's hair, before creating the requested braids. *What must it be like to have someone do whatever you ask?* She imagined herself with a servant.

Lord Carrington had servants back in London, but no Negroes like there were here.

"Don't you have any questions about all that you will do?" Lucy's voice took on a condescending and critical tone once more.

"Yes, I have many questions, but I knew you would tell me as I need to learn it. I do want to learn it all. May I ask now?"

"You may."

"What will I be doing on most days?"

"It depends on what is needed, or the season. You will work with me with my reading, singing, and Bible reading during the summer, when the indigo and rice are growing, up through harvest. You will be fortunate to learn also. My father gave my mother a lute and she is teaching me to play now. We tend to the estate garden, as well, shelling corn and beans, and helping with preserving food, washing, and mending clothes, churning butter and cheese, soap and candle-making. During the winter months, we weave more."

"There must be much to do to keep Montague Hall functioning as it should," Vieve responded with care." What about Master Mal and Master Oliver and their schooling?"

"Mal and Oliver receive schooling in the colder months when harvesting is done and before planting again. They learn all about how to manage the plantation, and perhaps learn a trade. Mal wants to be a lawyer in Charlestown, so he will be apprenticed when it is suitable. I think my mother still wishes she could go with him. She does not like having to manage the slaves."

"Might the slaves manage themselves?" Vieve asked.

"Of course not. They are not that wise."

"Could they learn to do so?"

"That is not their place, Vieve. That is why they are slaves. Don't you know anything?" Lucy's mouth twisted into a snarl.

"I do not know anything about plantations or slaves. But I do know about housekeeping and such. And I can read and sing. Lord and Lady Carrington taught me, as did the tutors for their children."

"Perhaps one day, when you are free, you can marry and have a small home to manage, like I will manage a large home, hopefully in Charlestown."

Mistress Montague appeared in the bed chamber doorway, wiping her brow, and pushing a lock of hair under her white ruffled mob cap.

"Good morning. Lucy. We need to practice your lute. Your father and brothers have consumed most of the bread and small beer and are now out with the slaves until supper. If you and perhaps Vieve wish a morsel, some may be left on the dining table. Otherwise, Big Zeb is attending a small pig on the spit and Evaline will see it is prepared with vegetables for when it is dinner time."

"Vieve," Mistress Montague made a direct address to her. "You are to go to Evaline today while Lucy practices her lute. She will begin to show you how food is prepared for us and for the slaves, and how the washing is done. I will be out there later. When it is supper time, later in the day, you will be shown how to serve the prepared food and proper ways to attend to us at dining time. You may leave now."

"Thank you, Mistress Montague."

Vieve followed Lucy down the house staircase through the drawing room, to the dining room. Two large chunks of bread were on a serving plate and a tankard of small beer sat beside it. Vieve chewed one of the pieces of crusty bread and gulped down the warm beer drink, as Lucy consumed the other. The sitting room reminded her somewhat of the Carrington home, though not as well-appointed. A gray print sofa and red and gold wing-backed chairs brightened the room, with gray floor-to-ceiling drapery covering the windows. Candle lamps were placed in strategic areas on a wooden book stand near the fireplace and on the small table near the sofa, as well as on a small chest of drawers. Portraits, perhaps of Elias Montague's parents, and of Elizabeth Montague and the children adorned a wall, and pastoral paintings completed the room. The ceilings boasted of hand-carved molding, and the floors, of random-width heart-pine boards. Vieve noticed placements of round holes scattered about the black cypress walls that faced the outside of the house, each plugged securely with painted wood of the same type. She had noted them in the dining room, as well, and wondered if they were in every room, or only those on the main floor of the home.

"Mistress Lucy, may I inquire as to the purpose of those?" She pointed to the plugged holes.

"Goodness, you don't know?"

Vieve shook her head.

"Those are firing holes. Should the house ever need to be defended from those who would do us harm."

"I do not know about those," Vieve stared at the scattering of the walled oddities.

"In case we are attacked by unfriendly Indians, or perhaps even Tories."

Vieve's eyebrows knit together in confusion.

"Oh, my goodness, you are ignorant. The holes are unplugged to allow for long rifles or muskets. There are attacking tribes of Indians here, such as the Cherokee. They captured Ashwiyaa from the Catawba Indians and traded her to my father for some rum and other goods. Savages, the lot of them. They mostly fight among themselves."

"And Tories?" Vieve asked.

Lucy's eyes narrowed.

"Colonists who favor the rule of the British Crown. My father says that the King taxes the colonies too much. He says there is conflict brewing. What about you, Vieve? You are British, are you not?"

"Yes, that was my home. But now I am here. I'm afraid I do not know all about these things you talk about just yet."

"You are not expected to know. You are just a servant." Lucy lifted her chin, looking down at her yet once more.

"If it is important to everyone here at Montague Hall, it will be important to me. I have no other home."

Lucy waved her hand toward the back entrance, then took the last bite of the crusty bread.

"You may go now. We will send for you when you are needed again."

For now, Vieve found her way back to the cookhouse, where Evaline and Maybelle had laid freshly picked and washed vegetable roots on the large table. Muffled sobbing came from the area of the pantry and storehouse, and a loud male voice cried out in agony, as a crack of a whip could be heard coming from the area of the barn and stables.

"Evaline? Maybelle? It's me, Vieve. What is happening?"

The sobbing stopped momentarily.

"We's comin'," Evaline's sad words were weak and frightened. Vieve followed the sound of the lowered voices until she saw Evaline seated on a small wooden chair beside sacks of flour, and Maybelle, with her arms wrapped around her.

"I did not mean to interrupt. I—I hope you are alright?" She wrung her hands together. Evaline was distraught, her shoulders shaking. "Miss Evaline, I am sorry," Vieve whispered.

"Ain't your fault," Maybelle said in soft spoken words as she held her mother's hand. "The Overseer, he done hobbled Henny for trying to run away."

"Hobbled? What do you mean by that?"

Maybelle gave Evaline a hug and motioned for Vieve to come closer.

"Hobbling. They do it to horses when there ain't nowhere to tie 'em up or they wants to teach 'em to stay in one place. If'n a Negro tries to 'scape, and he's catched, then da Overseer hobble him too. A horse gets his legs tie up together. But a Negro gets a beatin' on his back or 'cross his feets, maybe both, then the leg irons is put on 'im so he can't run no mo' fo' awhile. That's what happened to Henny. He our friend, he good to me and Momma. Always helps us in the garden when he don't have to."

Tears rose in Vieve's eyes. For a moment, she could not find the words to express the disdain that she felt. This made no sense, the cruelty of it. Once more, she envisioned Simon's body, twisted and covered in soot, and thought of the heartless Master Sweep.

"I'm so sorry," she repeated. "Why did he run? And why is the Overseer so cruel?"

"Henny got separated from his momma and papa 'while back. They was sold to someone goin' up the road a long way. But he was needed here. Henny jes' got full with the sadness and missin' his people. Ain't no one wants to be no slave no how. He tried to 'scape last night but done got hisself caught and brought back here. Now, he bein' punished."

"Does Master Montague know about this?"

"He sho' do," Maybelle replied. "He don't do much beatin' or hobblin' hisself – he have the Overseer do it – but he know it go on. He nice, otherwise, most times. But he know. He mostly care 'bout the rice and the indigo. That's how the Montagues is so rich. He used to work right by de slaves ev'ry day, til he got so rich, he don't have to now. He still do some. And he teachin' them boys how to do it all."

"What about Mistress Montague and the others? Do they hurt people?"

"The Mistress, she's a hard one. She can be nice, but turn herself 'round and be mean, too. Seen her slap someone hard when they ain't done a task right and she had to be fixin' it. She ain't always been like that, Mama say. Used to be nicer, kinder to us."

"And the Montague children?"

"Master Mal, he like to boss around, too. He can be nice, but not so much. When he in a good mood, mayhap. Mistress Lucy, she like her mama. Spoiled and all. We thinks Mistress Montague want to go back to Charlestown fo' good. Mistress Lucy, too. Master Oliver, he nice, so far. Don't know how he might be, good or bad. But he kind to us for now."

"There is so much here I don't understand." Vieve attempted a smile. "Please tell me how I can help you."

"Well," Evaline straightened her back, facing Vieve. "Ain't this somethin' here, now? We gots a new helper and here we sit. Time's a wastin'. We gonna learn you how to wash the clothes and how we cook and serve the food. So we's best be movin' along, now. We keep Henny in our prayers and we tend to 'im later when we can."

Vieve reveled in the opportunity to be kept busy. From the soaking, or bucking, of clothes in ash lye and animal fat, to the agitation and washing of them in the tubs with the battling sticks, and using a rock and a board to scrub out the tougher stains, she relished the hard work. It seemed to draw out a portion of her own grief and worry. The camaraderie, the constant chatter, the lilting voices of Evaline and Maybelle, and another older female slave named Hannah were soothing and full of comfort. Though Evaline would look to the stables and barn area for signs of the slave, Henny, she kept the all-day washing process going. When the last of the clothing was moved from the rinsing tub to the drying racks, she wiped her brow, collapsing onto a chair for a moment of rest.

"Well done, Vieve. You is a fast learner, yes you is!"

Vieve smiled, exhausted but happy. She relished the open friendliness of these Negroes when none of the Montagues were present and was happy to be without the presence of Lucy for a major part of the day. After the brief respite, she watched as Big Zeb helped tend to the pig, long roasting on the outdoor spit, while she and Maybelle assisted in preparing the vegetable roots of potatoes, carrots, turnips, and radishes, with a mess of picked green beans. She would learn about the drying, canning, and storing of food for the storehouse in the days to come and looked forward to the time spent with these women, who matched her own mother's gentle care and nurturing.

"What is each day like here?" Vieve inquired. "Is it like today?

"Folks git up early and work from day clean to first dark," Maybelle grinned, her white teeth gleaming. We say 'from the time you can see til the time you can't.' Ev'ry body eat dinner in the middle of the day, during the hottest part, during summer. That's the biggest meal. Then all work til dark, eat a little bit of leftover food, then sleep. Git Sundays off to tend to our own chores and garden, mostly. Sometimes prayin,' singin,' Bible-readin' if Massa or Mistress say it's alright. When it ain't so hot, we might work longer 'fo we stop to eat. So even in the big house, they got leftover food, come supper time. Days is mostly like that."

"The big house is where the Montagues live?"

"Thas' right. You in there, too." Maybelle smiled. "With a few other adult slaves what sleep down in the cellar. Where you stay?"

"I have a space in the attic. Nothing up there but my pallet. Just me. It is so quiet at night, with the window open so the cool air can come inside. I mostly tend to Mistress Lucy."

"You miss yo' mama?"

"So much it hurts sometimes. And my brother. But I'm glad I have you for a friend now."

"I glad too. Ain't had no White friend. No friends, much. Ashwiyaa ain't friendly with 'nary a soul 'round here. It's almost dinner time, so we's best be gittin' along."

Vieve marveled at the easy, quiet spirit of her new friend, Maybelle. The girl and Evaline loved to sing and laugh, as she did, and never once fussed or taunted her for not knowing how a particular task was carried out. When the Overseer or one of the Montagues were not around, the atmosphere was almost one of enjoyment. In these people she found solace and contentment. Perhaps even family.

CHAPTER EIGHT

"Oliver, have you chosen a name for your horse?" Elias took his plate from Dumplin, one of the more rotund house Negroes, and picked at the roasted vegetables and a chunk of pork, sopping up the pot liquor gravy with warm bread.

"Yes, I have," he smiled, chewing a large bite of potato. "Her name is Remiel."

"How did you come to choose such an odd name as that?" Elizabeth Montague motioned for Vieve to come away from her assigned post by the dining room door to serve more bread. Oliver looked up at her and smiled, as she held the plate of bread close for him.

"Remiel is the Archangel of Hope," he said with pride, glancing for a moment at Vieve, who blushed under his gaze. Elizabeth Montague took note of the exchange, frowning. "Remiel guides the souls of the faithful into Heaven. Those waiting to be judged. This angel guides people on the right path. I figure it's a good strong name for a horse who will guide me as well."

"Enough about your horse," Mal chided. "Father, is there any news of the Intolerable Acts that were made into law by the king?"

"Indeed, there is," Elias sat back in his chair. "The king wishes to quell the unrest in Boston after all of the tea was dumped into the harbor. He has closed the port there and established martial law. The Colonial Sons of Liberty have called for a boycott. It remains to be seen how the Continental Congress in Philadelphia will choose to respond in September when they will meet."

"Who destroyed the tea?" Oliver asked.

"Narragansett Mohawk Indian impersonators, I'm told, made their way on board three of the ships to stop the delivery of the tea, as it has been unfairly taxed by the British to pay for the war with the French and the Indians. I'm also told that Washington himself was against the action of those who destroyed the tea. Now, the British have extended the Quartering Act in Boston, in addition to taking away any form of colonial self- government."

"Will we fight, Father?" Oliver placed his fork on the table, looking to Elias for answers, who hesitated before responding to his son.

"I don't know. I pray it does not come to that. War is not what anyone should want. I suspect that there have been many attempts thus far to assuage the Crown to find reasonable solutions."

"But war would only be fought up there in Boston?" Lucy chimed in, interested in the first time in the discussion of politics.

"No, my sweet. If war is to be fought, it will be throughout the colonies."

"That's enough, Elias, please, this talk of war." Elizabeth Montague was insistent. "No one knows if that will come to pass. We should not let it consume our thoughts."

"Then we will no longer receive goods from Great Britain?" Lucy was incredulous.

"Lucy!" Elizabeth's raised voice pierced the air as her hands were placed flat in a firm stance on the table. "Vieve, take Lucy's plate to the washhouse and come back for the rest. Then you will help Dumplin clear the table. Lucy, it's time for your lessons. Vieve can join you when she is finished. I will take my leave to prepare. Please excuse me."

Mistress Montague did not wait for a response from anyone but moved toward the staircase without looking back. Lucy rose to follow her. Vieve removed Lucy's plate and started toward the back door when Oliver called out to her.

"Vieve, I'm finished as well. May I give you my plate also?"

Vieve complied without a word, taking the plate and utensils from him.

"Do you like the name of my horse? I thought you might." He smiled at her.

"Yes, Master Oliver, I like it very much." She returned his smile but found him sullen once more, as she turned from his gaze, making her way toward the back door to the washhouse.

"Oliver is sweet on the little servant girl," Mal looked first at Oliver, then Elias, his facial expression one of disdain, rather than brotherly mockery. "You should know your place, brother."

"Mal, hold your tongue," Elias wiped his lips with his hand, and rose from the table. "We need to keep Montague Hall running as smoothly as possible, for the sake of everyone here. No discord between family should intervene in those endeavors. Ever. Let your behavior be always honorable. Back to work, gentlemen."

Elias headed toward the privies outside before the late afternoon work resumed. Mal followed his father, ignoring Vieve as she passed him while returning to the dining hall. Vieve took instructions from Dumplin, who she found to be rather jovial when not in the presence of Elizabeth Montague in particular. Oliver pushed his chair underneath the large wooden table and turned to face Vieve.

"You know I do not like being called 'Master.'" He waited once again for her response.

"I cannot call you anything else when around your family, when I have been told not to do so." Vieve was mindful of Dumplin listening to every word. "And I do not want to be different from everyone."

"Vieve, you are different. You are the only servant or slave here who is not a Negro."

""There are no others?"

"No. not at Montague Hall. Elsewhere, yes, are some. They are mostly white men from Ireland, Scotland, and Great Britain. Indentured who serve as slaves until they have repaid their debt for safe passage here."

"Master Oliver," she looked at him while gathering the remainder of the utensils. Dumplin smiled at her insistence to use Oliver's title.

"I want to be your friend, as you wish. But I also want to be the friend of all at Montague Hall. And I cannot break the rules."

"I just want a friend. That's all." Oliver crossed his arms, his words softer.

"And I don't want to be afraid of being beaten or hurt if I make a mistake."

Oliver stared at her; his brows knit together in confusion.

"Why would you think that?"

"I have heard it happens. I have to go now. I don't want to keep Mistress Lucy and especially Mistress Montague waiting long. Good day."

As Vieve mounted the slave stairs, she heard Dumplin's firm voice, responding to what must have been a whispered question from Oliver.

"No Massa Oliver, you is kind to us all, and help us, too. But you ain't one of us. That girl chile done had a hard time. She know she ain't like us and ain't like you. She different. Gonna make her own way, best she know how to do. Best not be makin' things hard on her. 'Ole Dumplin tell you straight."

Vieve let each word sink in, with every step up the narrow staircase. *That girl chile done had a hard time. Ain't like us and ain't like you. Different.* There had been many in London with circumstances similar to hers. She never considered herself apart from other servants. But this strange place was most different, indeed. Perhaps she was, as well. *She gonna make her own way, best she know how to do.*

Vieve stood at the top of the stairwell before entering Lucy's room. Something was indeed different inside her soul now. She had made it through the most harrowing of journeys, lost everything and everyone who had been an endearing part of her life. The sadness of that loss would always leave a gaping black hole. Yet, in the very bleakness of the loss, there was strength seeping in somehow. *Faith*, her mother would have said. *Never give up.* Vieve ran a hand along the length of the clapboard wall beside her. Smooth, yet rough in places, tiny invisible indentures of imperfection along the surface, all painted over and not readily visible to the eye. A wall that kept the weathering elements out, the safety of its contents secured within. She leaned against it, placing a hand on the firm surface. *I am indentured like you. I will be like you from here on out. Strong as I can be.*

CHAPTER NINE

Vieve had come to love the quiet coolness of the dark that engulfed Montague Hall at nighttime and the reverie from the cessation of the exhausting workday. She relished time spent with Maybelle and the other slaves who worked with determination and vigor in the hot and humid summers here. The weather had finally begun to show signs of Autumn relief from the intense humidity and heat. Though she was ten years of age, Vieve felt much older and more grown, perhaps wiser. Even Mistress Montague and Mistress Lucy seemed to regard her with less animosity, though it was always lurking underneath the civilities afforded her and the other house slaves. They had allowed her to accompany Lucy in singing, while the girl played her lute, which brought immense happiness to the hardest of days. Only Ashwiyaa, the Indian girl, remained distant from her and most everyone else, but Vieve was determined to find a friend in the reclusive girl who slept in the barn with the animals and kept to herself.

At the end of this day, when sleep was about to overtake her, she heard the soft but distinct drone of voices. The muffled tones of Elizabeth and Elias Montague were coming from somewhere below. But how was this possible? She rose from her pallet and crept along the path of the delicate sounds. They were arising from the opposite side of the dark attic. Vieve moved in silence, negotiating each step of her space as she inched closer. A speck of dim candlelight was also emanating from somewhere below. She wondered how the light had found its way to her isolated room in the top of the house. The voices were becoming more audible, the light, though miniscule, was brighter now.

Then she saw it. A round hole in one of the planks in the attic wall, the size of which could easily accommodate a rifle barrel. Placing her cheek against the wall, she slid into place so that she could see part of the sitting room below as it came into view despite the high-ceilinged walls. Only Elias Montague could be seen from her vantage point, as if she were seated in the great ceiling. Her bare feet brushed against a small object on the floor that moved when she touched it. Vieve knelt to explore the rough-hewn floor as best she could in the dark. Finally, she grasped a small round piece of wood and raised it to squinting eyes. In an instant recognition dawned and she marveled at the white-tipped plugging piece that had been meant to close up one of the firing holes. A section of board that must have originally been intended as an outside piece for the firing hole had been used instead to complete the massive wall below and the beams in the attic. The plugging piece had disengaged somehow, perhaps in the seasonal changing of house temperatures, thus allowing the firing hole to once again be opened. She peered once more through the hole into the candle-lit sitting room and strained to hear the conversation below.

"I have no answers, Elizabeth. Whatever is going to happen, will happen. As a planter, of course I do not want war. Everything we have worked hard to achieve will be destroyed."

"Perhaps we should leave here, go some place where we will be safer."

"My dear, there will be no other place that will be completely free of war violence, if war is to be in the colonies. The conflict may vary, in terms of who is fighting where and the strategy of battle. Rest assured, there will be no thoroughly safe place anywhere."

"What will become of us, Elias? Where will we go?"

"As I said, I have no answers. If war is waged, life as we know it will change most certainly. You want assurances I simply cannot give."

"Then go to Charlestown. Convince them not to fight. Better to live under the rule of the Crown than to lose everything."

Elias chuckled aloud, shaking his head, and quaffed a sip of something no doubt strong.

"This is not in my hands. All of the colonies are involved, why do you not understand? This is about economics, yes, and the unreasonable and punitive taxations and edicts from Great Britain. It is growing, Elizabeth, this desire for a country in which those who live here make the laws of the land and claim their God-given rights as free men. This is a country like no other in the history of mankind. The stakes involved are greatly raised. No one will be able to remain neutral. At some point, every sentient being will have to make a choice. God knows, even the Indians have begun to take sides, slaves as well, will choose the side that promises them freedom. Our home – as we know it – will be forever changed. If we even survive."

Vieve could not see Elizabeth Montague but could well-imagine her fears of impending war, especially in the manner in which Elias had just described it.

"I'm going to bed, as you should Elias. We will have to hope for the best. I am growing concerned about Lucy, by the way. She has fallen once or twice, over the past month, of no apparent cause. She complains of her hands and fingers feeling differently when she plays the lute. And at times she appears more cross with me. What do you make of it?"

"I don't know. I'm sure she will be fine. She's growing as she should. Perhaps some fresh air would do her some good. Have Vieve take her out for a walk on the grounds or in the garden."

Vieve plugged the firing hole once more and backed away from the view of the sitting room, making her way to bed, only to find that sleep was elusive on this night. Thoughts of war permeated her imagination, and she wondered if Mistress Lucy would be alright. She had only seen her stumble and fall once and had not given the event much thought. She closed her eyes, knowing that tomorrow would bring more work, more challenges, and perhaps more answers, if fate were kind. She decided, for now, to tell no one of her nighttime discovery.

When she awoke before the ringing of the bell, Vieve scrambled to ready herself in preparation for the day. The men folk, including Master Mal and Master Oliver, were outside in the courtyard preparing the wagons for the journey to the indigo and rice fields. She saw Maybelle making her way to the cook and wash houses. She called out to her friend.

"Good morning, Maybelle!"

"Mornin'!" Maybelle returned with a wave, then disappeared inside the cookhouse. Vieve saw Oliver looking up at her, tipping his tricorn hat when he caught her eye. She waved in silence back to him, then latched the window for the day. It was going to be hot and muggy once again. As had become part of her daily ritual, she went first to Mistress Lucy's room.

"You are here early," the girl announced. "Just in time to help me get ready. And Mama says that you are to accompany me for a walk in the flower garden before my lessons."

Vieve complied in the meticulous process of brushing and preparing her hair for the day and made the bed so that the room was presentable for the day. Lucy addressed her once more.

"My mother designed and helped to create the flower gardens. Have you seen them?"

"No, Mistress Lucy, not up close. I saw them from a distance when I first arrived here."

"You will walk with me in them shortly. Do not pick any of the flowers unless I tell you to do so. Understand?"

"Yes," Vieve winced at the condescending tone in the demanding voice and found herself wishing she could work with Maybelle and Evaline on this day, or assist Dumplin and her helper, Merrilee, in the house.

"Go and get a pail from the barn. We might need one on our walk," Lucy instructed.

Vieve did as she was told and found her way into the barn area where she saw a large pail hanging against the far wall of the building.

She lifted the handle from the large nail in which it was resting and brushed the remnants of hay out of the bottom.

"You cannot have that!" Ashwiyaa's angry voice rose above the hum of the morning activity.

"Mistress Lucy asked me to fetch a pail for her. She did not say which one. I meant no harm. Is there a better one to take to her?" Vieve returned the pail to its place on the wall.

Ashwiyaa frowned at her, pointing to another similar pail sitting on the dirt floor of the barn. Vieve retrieved the pail from the ground and faced the Indian girl once more. Ashwiyaa stood in a menacing pose, arms akimbo, and a hand resting on her hunting knife, as she stood between Vieve and the large entrance to the barn.

"Ashwiyaa, you do not like me, do you? I am different, as I know you are. I have made friends with Maybelle and wish to be your friend, as well."

"I have no friends."

Ashwiyaa stood in defiance before making an abrupt turn to exit the barn, leaving Vieve alone and confused. She felt sad for a moment, then pushed the feeling aside. *Never give up.* Her mother's voice echoed inside her head. She smiled at the thought. *Yes, I will win this battle with you, Indian girl.* Making her way back across the courtyard, she raised the pail to show Mistress Lucy and waved once again at Maybelle and Evaline, who were working hard to prepare the big meal for the day.

"There you are. Come with me. We will go to the shared garden first. Vegetables and fruit are there." Lucy pointed toward the path on the far side of the house to the designated area. "This garden is for us mostly, but we share sometimes with the slaves. They have a small garden near their quarters that they tend for themselves, also." She stopped walking and rubbed the tops of her legs, then faced Vieve. "Why do you want to be friends with the Negroes?"

"I want to be friends with everyone," Vieve replied, trying to hide the surprise at the sudden question. "They are quite nice to me, and I like the way they smile and try to be happy, even when they are working very hard. They are kind people."

Lucy stared at her, making Vieve even more uncomfortable in the rising heat of the day. For a moment, neither spoke.

"Do you find me unkind, Vieve?" Lucy's eyes narrowed.

"I think you are learning to be a mistress." Vieve prayed she had not given the wrong answer. "But kindness is an important virtue, my mother always said. Your legs, are they hurting you? I see you're rubbing them."

"They feel stiff. I do not know why."

"I have an idea if you wish. My brother, Simon, often needed his legs gently stretched after climbing in the chimneys. Do you wish me to see if that might help your legs?"

"What do you mean?" Lucy asked, still rubbing the front of her legs down to her knees.

"Hold onto that tree there with both of your hands. I will take each leg and stretch it for you. You can tell me if you wish the stretching to be more or no."

To Vieve's surprise, the girl complied with her instructions, as Vieve made slow, gentle, and deliberate motions in raising Lucy's foot behind her and pushing it toward the back of her leg. She held it in place for a brief moment before relaxing her hold. Lucy smiled.

"It does feel better. Do it more."

Vieve repeated the motion for Lucy's right leg, then her left, stretching each several times.

"I wish you to do this in the morning and at night before I sleep," she said, still embracing the tree trunk.

"Very well, Mistress Lucy," Vieve replied.

"And you will be my friend as part of your duties."

Now Vieve stared at the back of the older girl. This endeavor would be a challenge.

"Mistress Lucy, may I speak honestly?"

"You may. And keep stretching my legs."

"You can command me to be your servant. I am exactly that, I know. But a friendship is different. Each person must care about the other the same. As equals. Friends take care of one another. We are not friends, as I am but a servant."

"If I command you to be my friend, then you must."

"Friendship does not work that way, Mistress Lucy. If I am your friend, I do things for you because I wish to, not because you force me to do so. And if we were to be friends, you would do the same for me. That is how friendship is."

"Let's go to the gardens. I don't wish to talk about this anymore."

"Very well."

For the first time since arriving at Montague Hall, Vieve felt sorry for Lucy. How odd, to have no friends, or any idea about having a friend, when she could have many. They meandered through the gardens at a pace that Lucy could tolerate, picking small handfuls of the berries and fruit, and some of pungent herbs, as well as a few of the blooms of peonies, snapdragons, lilies, black-eyed Susans, and Queen Anne's Lace. After Lucy tired of the effort, Vieve carried the pail as they began their walk back to the house. When they reached the stairway to the back of the house, Vieve offered her arm to Lucy, who accepted without comment, as they climbed each step together. Once at the top, Lucy made her way to prepare for her lessons, while Vieve came back down the steps to take the remaining food items to Evaline, Maybelle, and her older sister, Jonsie, to help them with preparing for supper. She stopped at the barn, glancing for any sign of Ashwiyaa, who was nowhere to be seen. Placing the bucket back in its place, she left an assortment of berries and herbs for the Indian girl and said a quick prayer for her well-being and anticipated friendship. Her quiet gesture was interrupted by Oliver, who had carried an armful of tools into the barn.

"Hello, Vieve. What are you doing here?"

"Good day, Master Oliver. I was just leaving some items for Ashwiyaa, in hopes that she would be encouraged to be my friend."

"Please just call me Oliver, Vieve. It's just us in here. I hate being called the 'Master' part. You know I don't like it."

"Very well, Oliver, I shall try to remember to do so when your family is not around. But you know I must do their bidding otherwise. Please allow me some time to adjust to such."

"Very well, then. So how are you getting on with everything, and with Lucy?"

"I am learning all I can, and she and Mistress Montague are more tolerant of me these days." She smiled at him, thinking about Lucy wanting to force her into friendship. "I would like to know more about how the rice and indigo are grown. Can you tell me?"

"I can tell you a bit, yes." He returned her smile. "The indigo fields are prepared in March, followed by early April planting and weeding. Thankfully, indigo is very drought tolerant, so the care is important, but the crop is more adaptable to the heat here. Around July is the first harvest and continued weeding. A second harvest is in August or September, depending on how the crop progresses. After the indigo is cut, women mostly carry it to the vats to be processed for dyes and such. Soaked first, then beaten until the grains thicken, and that water then drained to yet another vat. Eventually it is dried, cut into squares, packed in barrels, and then shipped to market during the winter months. So the harvesting is continuing."

"And the rice?" Vieve asked.

"That is much more complicated. We grow the best. Carolina Gold, it is. The land must be leveled, the fields rolled and prepared, then flooded to suppress wild growth and to increase the nutrient content from the soil. It is planted in March, grown until about September, then harvested between mid-September to October, so, as you can imagine, the Spring planting season is most important. Again, harvesting is very soon."

"The fields are flooded, you say? How does that work?"

"That is a good question." Oliver smiled at her yet again. "Yes, they are flooded. About twenty years or so ago, a system of water gates called trunks were devised and forced open when the tides rose and closed when they receded. Using these trunks and levees along the river helps to catch the fresh water and use it to flood the rice fields. Individual fields may be flooded, and the water level adjusted independently of other fields. The rice mills are recently tidal-powered and more than one hundred barrels a day can be milled. Rice cultivation is mostly women's work, as the flooding times negate the need for excessive hoeing, and such. The men make the barrels and prepare for shipments to be made. It is quite the process. Montague Hall is well-located for the use of such a system and my father helped to build it here."

"I wondered about the gates, the trunks, that is, and how they work."

"I will show you sometime. You are very curious, for a girl. Lucy does not care at all about how the plantation operates. Just that it produces the means to buy whatever she wants."

"Can girls not be curious? I always like to discover about new things and learn, just so I know more and appreciate how things work for everyone."

"I suppose they can be inquisitive. But most seem to care only about female workings, and not men's work. They are not like you." Oliver gave her an appreciative glance.

"But you just said that women mostly work the rice fields. And doesn't Mistress Montague understand the workings of Montague Hall? I would think the women need to be very curious. And also, quite smart. Does your father know about how meals are prepared and how laundry is done – the more feminine tasks?"

"He does know. But of course, that is all turned over to my mother as a mistress."

"But he knows and understands the importance of these tasks here?" Vieve asked.

"Yes, my father is very aware of all that makes Montague Hall successful. Come with me, I have something to show you." Oliver motioned her around a corner into the woodworking and iron works area. He pushed open a door to a smaller storage area. On a table sat a large upside-down wagon, with four wood and iron wheels and a pulling handle made of the same.

"I don't understand." Vieve turned to him with curious eyes.

"It's for Lucy, mostly. To pull her when she is unable to walk. She seems to be weaker in the legs especially these days. I have seen her fall a few times and heard her complain about strange feelings in her legs and arms and hands, too. I don't know what to make of it but figured this would help her sometimes. Of course, you would likely be pulling it. Or perhaps you and Maybelle or Ashwiyaa. It is not quite finished yet but will be soon."

"How very thoughtful of you, Oliver. I know she will love it. I would love to take her outside in it." Vieve smiled, running a hand along a wheel rim, and pulling until the wheel spun in place. "I love being outside here and it will be most enjoyable to go exploring with her."

"If you wish, I will ask my father to consider letting Maybelle and Ashwiyaa assist when possible. It would be easier for you and perhaps Lucy would become more at ease with everyone."

"Oh yes, that would be perfect," Vieve laughed. "I think it would help her very much to become more acquainted and to laugh with others. Perhaps she would get better also, with some sunshine and fresh air."

"I would very much like to laugh more, also," Oliver offered. "I have a question for you, if I may ask it?"

Vieve nodded for him to continue.

"The other day you said that you did not want to be afraid of being hurt or beaten if you did something wrong. What made you think that?"

"I heard about the slave man, Henny. The hobbling of him."

"That would never happen to you, Vieve. You are very careful and caring and you would not attempt to escape. That's what Henny did. It cost him."

"Why should hobbling be done to anyone? And, if it is done to him, why would it not be done to me, if I were perceived to have committed a wrong? It is a most dreadful thing to suffer like that. I heard he was missing his family. How horrible for anyone to be torn away from their loved ones."

Oliver shoved both hands in the pockets of his work pants, looked down, then back at Vieve. His eyes reflected her confusion and pain.

"In truth, I don't know why it was done, that form of punishment. Henny tried to escape. He is a slave and is not free to go about his own way. He belongs to my father."

"And I belong to him, as well. At least I do until my keep is paid and my work time is over. Master Montague can sell or trade me, as well, or punish me, with no regard for my consent or my feelings on the matter."

"I do not care that you are a servant, Vieve. I like you very much and want you to be my friend. I would never hurt you, not ever, for any reason. I do not think of you as a servant at all."

"But I am a servant, and nothing more. You are 'Master Oliver' as well when your family is present. Make no mistake, Oliver. I may be your friend, but I am a servant first, and there would be no different treatment afforded any slave, even me, other than the time I must serve. It is not your fault. But it is the truth."

"I will never let anything bad happen to you." Oliver clinched both fists while searching her eyes.

"What might be done to me may not ever be up to you. I must go now. Thank you for making the wagon. I look forward to taking Mistress Lucy out in it. Good day, Oliver."

"Wait!" he called to her as she made her way to the barn entrance. "Please say you will meet me after the meal tonight, after you finish with Lucy. I will come to your room."

"Very well. I must go now before I am missed."

Vieve smiled as she made her way back to Mistress Lucy and Mistress Montague. She would look forward to time spent with her friend Oliver. He was becoming more special to her with each passing day.

CHAPTER TEN

"Father," Oliver finished chewing the remains of his supper time green beans and potatoes before continuing. "I have made something for Lucy that I think might help her. Big Zeb helped me." He smiled at Lucy, who gave him an appreciative glance. "It is a sturdy wagon that may be used to take her out and about on our land. The sunshine and fresh air might help her to be more well."

"A wagon for me?" Lucy smiled, taking in the family gathered around the dining table as Vieve and Dumplin observed and tended to the tasks at hand. "Thank you, Oliver! Where shall I go in it?"

"Wherever you like, I suppose. The gardens, all around the courtyard, the river dock. Father, what do you think of having Vieve and Maybelle and Ashwiyaa attend to Lucy's needs when they go out? Vieve cannot attend to her needs alone, pulling her everywhere, and there is safety in the number of those helping, don't you think? Especially girls."

Elias Montague took a hardy sip of small beer, made eye contact with his wife, and rubbed his chin before replying to his youngest son. Vieve noted Lucy's smile.

"That is a possibility, perhaps. If Dumplin or Merrilee can assist in the cook and wash houses some, I see no harm in it, after Lucy's lessons are done. Elizabeth?"

"Whatever you think best, Elias. Perhaps the outdoors would prove beneficial for her. They can also help tend to the shared garden and the flowers."

"It may not be a daily occurrence, but certainly it can be done with frequency and good care. Lucy, if this is acceptable to you, I think

Vieve, Maybelle, and Ashwiyaa can assist with this. You will need to remain out of the way of the other slaves working and to take the utmost of care. Vieve, you will oversee these excursions, with Ashwiyaa to make sure of where you are at all times."

"Yes, Master Montague, I will be most happy to help Mistress Lucy." She smiled at Oliver, who was pleased at her satisfied response. Mal, who had been quiet for the remainder of the meal, addressed Elias.

"Father, any news to share of late?"

"There is some, yes. As skirmishes continue across the colonies, I hear tell that January will bring about the First Provincial Congress in Charlestown, according to Henry Laurens. There will be much discussion and action regarding safety, militia development, and such, as the colonies continue to be faced with indignities from the British Crown."

"What kind of militia development?" Mal inquired.

"Training all landowners and the common men to be diligently dedicated in learning the use of arms and that they receive good and regular training at least once a fortnight. All in preparation for whatever is happening. Regiments will be organized, I feel sure."

"Does this mean that war is imminent, Father?" Mal's eyes narrowed in concern.

Elias Montague shifted in his chair, looking down at the table and making the task of chewing the last bite of roasted meat fraught with deliberate slowness.

"While I cannot say with absolute certainty, I do believe that war on some level will indeed occur. I no longer see peaceful resolution as an option. We will have to prepare with everyone else and do the best we can."

"I do not wish this conversation to continue, Elias." Elizabeth frowned, pushing a strand of hair out of her eyes. "No one knows for sure that war will happen at all."

"Elizabeth," Elias spoke in a firm voice, only mildly raised, but in stark contrast to the prior supper conversations in which they had discussed the issue before. "I'm afraid there is no avoiding such. Wise individuals would all do well to prepare for that possibility. Our children must also be prepared, and we must all act with utmost confidence in our best intentions and strategies, and with sound minds, as well. Let us put it aside for now."

The light evening repast ended sooner than usual. Vieve scurried to complete the supper chores and seeing to the needs of Lucy, who had become somewhat less demanding since their conversation about friendship in the garden. As she readied herself for sleep and a visit from Oliver, she thought about the time spent thus far at Montague Hall, and all that had happened since her arrival here. She hoped her mother would be proud of how much growing up she had done thus far. How she missed Claire Whittier and little Simon, too.

"Vieve?" Oliver's voice, muffled and low, came through the attic door, as the vestiges of remaining twilight vanished into the darkness. "May I come inside?"

Vieve opened the door, motioning him in, as she smoothed her night dress and went to stand by the open window. Oliver peered out, as well, silent for a moment before speaking once again. The soft moonlight played among the clouds and drifted through the hanging gray moss, giving an ethereal glow to the glistening ripples of the Ashley River in the purple hues of the warm night.

"I know this is not much of a room, but I truly think you have the best view in the house." He gave her a genuine smile, which she returned. "Are you glad about the wagon?"

"Very glad, yes, and happy that Maybelle and Ashwiyaa can be included. If I can just get Ashwiyaa to like me. She always seems angry."

"That is her way, to be guarded. She is like you in some ways. Different. She did not come here so willingly. She was captured by the Cherokee, who are enemies of her people, the Catawba. They traded her to my father for supplies and rum. She has been here about two years now. Mostly, she teaches me, Mal, my father, and Mr. Bennett, the Overseer, about tracking, shooting bows and arrows, Indian ways, so that we are knowledgeable about the land, how to scout, to successfully trade with them, and about how they work."

"She must miss her people very much. But she does not seem to want friends. Is she friendly with anyone around here?" Vieve asked. "She does not like me, I don't think."

"Give her time, she will like you," Oliver smiled again. "She wanted to sleep in the barn with the animals and that is where she is the happiest. She is nice to me but is not fond of Mal or Lucy. Truthfully, many are a little afraid of her because she can do so much and is fierce when she chooses."

"With respect, Mal and Lucy are not as nice as you are, Oliver. Ashwiyaa knows this. Perhaps they will be, one day."

"Vieve, give them time, too." Oliver rapped his fingers on the wood frame of the window.

"Maybe. Some people just do not care to try to like others at all. Even back in Great Britain, there are those who place themselves above others so that they feel they can treat them badly. But Mistress Lucy has been nicer to me, I will say that." Vieve smiled at him. "Has Ashwiyaa ever tried to run away?"

"No, never. She is treated well here—that is, mostly left alone with her chores or when we need her." Oliver smiled. "I think she knows she is safer here than out in the wild, where she could be captured again. Sometimes I think she would consider running away dishonorable, but she has never said that."

"Well, perhaps she will one day be my friend, I hope."

"About the wagon," Oliver added, "there are a few places to take it. Of course, the courtyard and the gardens. But I will tell you where to go that is even better." He leaned closer to Vieve and whispered. "If you follow the path that goes behind the house and toward the river side, there is a place where the river is shallow and mostly hidden. No one goes that far down the path, though it isn't really that far from the courtyard. I swim there and throw rocks across the water. I have fished there too. I have also built a fire there. The direction of the flow of the river and the breeze there keeps the smoke from traveling back toward the main house, if the fire is small."

"Oliver, why are you telling me this?" Vieve's eyebrows knit together in confusion.

"It would be a good place to take Lucy. And you all would like it too."

"What if she will not keep your place a secret, once we show her?"

"I have an idea about that," Oliver grinned again, this time even bigger than before, and whispered. "I will tell her of it, and it will be her idea to go, not yours. You just don't tell her you already know. That way, she will keep the secret and you will not be in trouble for taking her there, as she will demand to go."

Vieve laughed aloud, covering her mouth with a hand. Oliver's eyes widened.

"I think that is the first time I have heard you laugh so much," he smiled. "I like it."

"I do, too, Oliver. But for now, we must both go to sleep. Tomorrow will be here soon enough."

"Yes, it will," he sighed. "I suppose you are right. But Vieve – will you talk with me like this again?"

"Yes," she answered without hesitation. "I will. Because you are my friend. Goodnight, Oliver."

She decided not to tell him about her discovery of the firing hole in the board inside the attic, or about how the conversation below can be heard quite easily when one is still and quiet. For now, that would remain her secret.

CHAPTER ELEVEN

Montague Hall/Ashley River, Autumn 1774

"Today seems cooler, and the harvesting is going well," Elizabeth Montague noted during the mid-day dinner repast, "and Lucy wishes to take a ride in the wagon. Vieve, if you will go inform Maybelle and Ashwiyaa. You will take her after she has had a short rest."

"Yes, ma'am, Mistress Montague, I will do so at once." Vieve bounded out the back door of the great hall and found Maybelle first, who was helping Evaline to wash and wipe clean the utensils and cooking pots with the boiled water from the fireplace.

"She gon' let us take Mistress Lucy out de ride?" Maybelle's eyes grew wide, as she faced Evaline. "Mama, that be alright fo' you?"

"Mistress Montague done asked 'fo' it, then you gots to go, sho' 'nuf." Evaline smiled at Vieve. "You best keep a watch on 'em all, honey chile. Don't let nothin' bad happen to no one out in dem woods."

"I promise, Miss Evaline, we will take care. Ashwiyaa will be with us also." She flashed a big smile at Maybelle. "This could be a good day, indeed. Now I have to find Ashwiyaa."

Vieve made her way to the barn area in time to find the Catawba Indian girl taking care of the animals inside, managing the hay and buckets of water.

"Good afternoon, Ashwiyaa."

"What you need?" The reply was curt, with an edge of aggression. The Indian girl faced Vieve as if to dare her to come closer.

"Mistress Montague wishes for you and Maybelle and me to accompany Mistress Lucy on a wagon ride. It will be after she has a rest."

The Indian girl straightened to her full height, her dark hair hanging past her shoulders. She said nothing for a moment while regarding Vieve with disdain, as she brushed away the remnants of hay from her clothing.

"I not go with you. I am needed here."

"Mistress Montague wants you to go," Vieve said with as quiet and gentle a response as she dared. "Lucy has weak legs, and we will take her in a wagon. Maybelle is going too. It could be fun, you know."

"I not care about that. I do my work. My need is here."

Vieve folded her arms across her chest in a guarded response to Ashwiyaa's initial refusal.

"Look, Ashwiyaa. You can not like me or Maybelle if you want. I don't care. But we did not ask for you. Mistress Montague did. We are all here in this place, somehow. Can't we even just try to be nicer to one another?"

Ashwiyaa picked up a hoe and leaned against it, lifting it once to shove hard onto the dirt floor. "Very well. I go. But you are not a friend."

"I am glad that you will come. I hope you bring your bow and arrows."

Vieve exited the barn and skipped back to the main house to finish assisting Dumplin and Merrilee with cleaning up, then made her way up the slave stairwell to check on Mistress Lucy.

"There you are," Lucy said. " I wish my hair to be braided into one strand as yours is. And I need you to fetch my straw hat from the shelf of the closet. That way it will be more comfortable to wear with my hair."

Vieve complied without speaking, making meticulous strokes of brushing Lucy's hair, and weaving the requested braid. Lucy smiled at her.

"We are going to go to a special place today that Oliver told me about. My mother and father are not to know, for now. Do you understand?"

"Yes, Mistress Lucy, I understand. If you are sure, I will keep the confidence."

"Good," Lucy mumbled, tying her brogan shoes into meticulous bows. "I will ride there but get out of the wagon when we arrive."

The girls met Maybelle and Ashwiyaa outside in the courtyard, where Oliver was waiting with the wagon. He assisted in helping Lucy to situate herself in it while speaking to the group.

"I have made a small fire at the place I told Lucy about, on my way back from the fields and have left you some fresh corn cooking there by the coals. You will need to let it finish cooking for a bit before you rake it out of there with a stick. I hope you like it." He smiled at Vieve. "There is also a watermelon on the edge of the river. It should be chilled some when you wish to have it. I hope you all have an enjoyable day."

"Thank you," Vieve smiled at him and took hold of the pull handle on the wagon. "It will be a good day for Mistress Lucy, and we will see that she is safe as well."

"Off you go, then," Oliver waved them down the road before he headed back to the fields. "Lucy knows where to turn off the path, but I marked it with burlap, to make it easier to see. You should remove it when you reach there."

For the first few minutes of the journey, no one spoke. Lucy gripped the side of the wagon as it rolled over the rough path. Ashwiyaa moved to the front of the small group to establish her leadership as the scout without acknowledging anyone. Maybelle hummed a cheerful tune, oblivious to the underlying tension.

"What a beautiful day this is," Vieve offered. "It's not too hot and the sun looks so pretty the way it dances in the *itla-okla*. That's the right word for the tree hair, is that right, Ashwiyaa?"

"Yes," came the curt reply.

"I would like to wade into the water when we arrive there!" Vieve exclaimed, "and cool off my feet. I love the cool waters."

Maybelle hummed louder, finally breaking into singing "Wade in de water, children." It was a lovely, low, and deep-felt tune. Even Lucy did not dare to interrupt her until the final, "God's a-gwine-a trouble de water," though Vieve joined in with any of the repeated words she could recognize, and knew well the meaning of the words she sang.

"That is lovely, Maybelle. You sing beautifully," Vieve exclaimed. "Where did you learn it?"

"From my mama and others," Maybelle smiled. "Is jes' an old song, is all."

"Mistress Lucy, would you like me to sing a song with you? One we both know together from your lessons?" Vieve hinted. To her surprise, Lucy accepted the offer and began singing, "The Liberty Song," with Vieve injecting soft harmony into the words being sung. When they finished, Ashwiyaa spoke, her voice laden with heavy sarcasm.

"For which men, the freedom?"

"For the country. Our country," Lucy shot back.

"For my people? Her people?" Ashwiyaa pointed to Maybelle, then glared at Vieve. "What of your people? You have no freedom here. Yet you sing."

Vieve felt a wave of relief when the burlap sash tied to a nearby tree came into view.

"Look, here is where we turn," she interjected, pointing to the marking Oliver had left them. Ashwiyaa scowled, removing her hunting knife from its sheath, and tearing into the knotted cloth to remove it from the low branches. The faint hint of the fresh corn, roasted in the husks, drifted around the smoldering flames and down river toward Charlestown.

"Look, there is the river, just like Oliver said! Lucy's voice was playful and excited. "And there is the fire burning in the river rocks!"

"Ashwiyaa tended to the low flames, examining the husks of corn, and placing them next to charred burning pieces to finish cooking and stay warm. Maybelle and Vieve assisted Lucy in climbing out of the wagon.

"I wish to go down to the river with you and stand in the water," Lucy breathed with excitement. "Help me remove my dress and shoes and my hat."

Vieve and Maybelle exchanged questioning glances before attempting to help with Lucy's outer dress and shoes. Lucy stood only in her white undergarment and bare pale feet, squeezing her toes into the rich dirt beneath her as best she could.

"It feels good."

Vieve could not help but wonder at the widest smile she had ever seen the girl display.

"Mistress Lucy, hold tight to Maybelle while I remove my work dress and then you can take hold of me while Maybelle does the same." Vieve draped her dress over a nearby branch, removed the brogan shoes and took a firm hold of Lucy's arm while Maybelle also removed her own clothes. Vieve took note of the gentle shaking motion of Lucy's body as she tried to stand firm on the sloping land that graced the river's edge. Ashwiyaa had set aside her quiver of arrows and the bow, along with her sheathed knife. She walked along the waterline, untying her wrap skirt and mantle-type shirt which fastened at the left shoulder and left her right shoulder bare. She wore only a small deerskin loincloth otherwise. Her small budding breasts were left bare and red-tanned in the sunlight that sparkled the waters of the Ashley River. Vieve thought her rather beautiful when the façade of harshness was set aside. She watched as Ashwiyaa found the watermelon left between rocks and a log wedged together at the river's edge.

"Mistress Lucy, you's got to keep yo' feet planted right in this mud down here, else you gwine-a slip and fall." Maybelle instructed the girl how to step and move her feet in small, deliberate motions. Lucy maintained a firm grip on the shoulders of both Vieve and Maybelle as she ventured further into the water that swirled above their ankles. Ashwiyaa joined them, an amused smile tugging at her lips at the sight of the three struggling girls.

"Do not go more into the strong waters."

"Why not?" Lucy demanded, turning toward Ashwiyaa as she took another giant step. The twisting of her body at the same time she attempted a bigger step created enough imbalance between them that Lucy slid straight down into the chilly waters, bringing Maybelle and Vieve with her. All three shrieked in surprise as the water covered them and the river bottom undulated beneath, their bodies now sitting in the plough mud along the edge of the river. Ashwiyaa rushed to grab the back of Lucy's gown, pulling her above the gurgling water.

"That why. You no listen."

Maybelle and Vieve clung to Lucy and to one another. All were drenched from the fall, their gowns clinging to their youthful bodies now splotched with mud. Their hair was soaked with water that ran down their cheeks. The girls stared at one another, wiping water, mud, and pride from their eyes. Vieve was the first to laugh aloud, smiling and relishing the awkwardness of the moment.

"Mistress Lucy, you are very brave. That was so much fun!"

"Come in the water, Ashwiyaa!" Maybelle reached for the Indian girl, pulling her down beside them in the muddy river. She glared at Maybelle, then allowed a soft smile to spread across her face.

Lucy stared momentarily out into the vastness of the pristine river, still holding a firm grip on the slave girl and her indentured servant. Without warning, she threw back her head and laughed so hard that Vieve feared she would fall backward into the water once more.

"I do declare that is the most wonderful thing I have ever done! I want to sit a moment right here."

"Ashwiyaa, please," Vieve begged, looking into the dark eyes of the Indian girl, "tell us of this river, the land, and how you came to be so wise in all of its ways. I truly want to know."

Much to her surprise, Ashwiyaa spoke in a reverent, almost quiet tone about the harmony and balance in the great forces of nature, of the spirits that the Catawba believed inhabited everything, from the river and rocks to the stars, the animals, the air and fire, and the earth itself. Her Catawba Indians were river people, she told them, who created pottery, baskets, beaded work and more.

"The Great Spirit, *Wakan Tanka – He Who Never Dies* – is Supreme Being."

"*Wakan Tanka*. It is a good name, I think." Vieve thought aloud. " We believe differently, perhaps. I believe in God. Jesus Christ. My mother took me to church in London to worship. But I am most happy you are here with us and sharing about your people."

"Mama say that Jesus has him a plan fo' ev'ry kinda thing. That He much bigger than all of us down here." Maybelle smiled. "We done all waded in the water now. Maybe God gonna cover us and the water too."

"I think we should do some more covering too," Vieve grinned.

"What do you mean?" Lucy ventured.

"We should cover some too. Like this!" Vieve used both hands to splay them across the top of the water, making large splashes among the foursome and soaking them yet again.

The other girls joined in the revelry, splashing and kicking until they had their fill of merriment, before Ashwiyaa spoke again.

"Need to eat corn and watermelon, too, while we dry from water. I cut fruit now." With that, Ashwiyaa retrieved the chilled watermelon from the river, placed it on a flat piece of rock, removed her large hunting knife from its sheath, and divided the melon into four pieces. Vieve and Maybelle helped Lucy rise from her river perch and take cautious steps back out of the Ashley River to sit around the last of the fire, while drying out. Using the edge of her hunting knife, Ashwiyaa rolled each of the pieces of corn from the remains of the fire to let them cool while most of the melon was consumed, and their clothes finished drying in the warmth of an early southern autumn sun.

"Truly," Vieve breathed, after taking a bite out of the hot corn, "this is the best food I have ever had! And this is the best day ever!"

"I want to come back here again," Lucy smiled. "But you all must do something different." She looked at each of them, pleading with both her eyes and voice. No one spoke. Vieve, Maybelle, and Ashwiyaa exchanged questioning glances.

"Call me Lucy. At least when my parents are not around." Lucy looked at Vieve. "Oliver says you do it for him. Will you also let me try to be a friend?" She hesitated, looking once more at each of them. "Please say you will. I don't know about having friends much. But I would like to learn. You will have to help me."

"Only if you really mean you want to be a friend. A real friend."

"I do it, too," Maybelle smiled.

"Ashwiyaa?" Lucy raised her eyes to the Indian girl.

"*Wakan Tanka* say wise spirits should seek peace and healing. I will seek with you." She turned toward Vieve and Maybelle, not smiling, but there was no anger in her face. "And with you."

Vieve grasped the wagon handle and looked up into the sky to give one last gaze across the waning sunny blue that reflected in the depths of the Ashley River, while Ashwiyaa and Maybelle loaded Lucy inside the wagon. This had been the best day she had experienced at Montague Hall thus far. Even with talk of war looming, and the plight of the slaves, and even her own future as an indentured servant was most unsure, she remained hopeful. She wished, more than anything, that she could tell her mother all about what had happened in the days since her untimely death. Somehow, she knew that Claire Whittier would be immensely proud. But she would also worry about the days to come for them all. But this day had brought laughter and respite from all that divided them.

CHAPTER TWELVE

Even at a distance Vieve could sense the anger and frustration from Elizabeth Montague, who now stood stiff and erect, arms crossed upon her chest, in the courtyard near the barn entrance, as her daughter, smiling and bedraggled, now laughed aloud with the likes of the indentured and the enslaved. Oliver, Mal, and Elias Montague, along with Big Zeb, were unloading the wagon gear and preparing the tools for the next day of harvesting work. The late afternoon time had elapsed with greater speed than the young girls realized, as the harsh realities of plantation life now eclipsed the earlier merriment of the day. Vieve swallowed hard, glancing at Oliver, who grinned with unabashed pleasure at the sight of the girls approaching in their current state of disarray, their dirty clothing, unkempt hair, and traces of mud clinging to all. Mal smirked with open disdain, while Elias showed no emotion, but stared at Lucy, who was happier than she had been in months.

"Come here, Vieve!" Mistress Montague, her eyes narrowed, and lips pursed, issued the stark command. Vieve stopped pulling the wagon, dropped the handle, and peeked at her friends, who were all grim-faced and silent.

"Mother, we had so much fun!" Lucy made an attempt to appease.

"I will speak with you later, Lucy!" Elizabeth Montague hissed at her daughter, then turned her wrath toward Vieve.

"You were left in charge of this little excursion, were you not?"

Vieve hesitated, wanting to choose her words with care.

"Answer me when I speak to you!" Mistress Montague thundered, seizing the servant girl by the arm, and giving her a violent shake.

Tears rose in Vieve's eyes, and she struggled to maintain a semblance of dignity.

"Mother, stop!" Oliver cried out, taking a step toward them before Elias Montague held him back.

"I caused this, Mother!" Lucy gripped the sides of the wagon. "I insisted on going in the river. They did everything right for me. I caused this!"

"I'm so sorry," Vieve sputtered, "but Mistress Lucy was safe at all times. We held on to her. We never let go of her, ever."

"I see how you held on to her! Look at her, she's a filthy mess, as the lot of you all are!" The furious woman grasped Vieve's arm once more. "You will learn to mind me! No supper for you tonight!"

"Elizabeth, I ask you to reconsider." Elias Montague spoke with quiet calmness. "Vieve can only do what Lucy allows her to do. Lucy has expressed that she herself insisted on this action. No one was hurt, and a good time outside ensued for our daughter. Is that not what we wanted?"

"I expect my daughter to behave like a young lady at all times. Not like a common servant or slave, groveling in the mud."

"Mother," Oliver pleaded, "look how happy Lucy is! This was not a banquet gathering. No guests were present. It was good for her to be out there. I hope they can do it again." He smiled at Vieve. "And more."

All stood in silence for a brief moment. Vieve saw Mal brushing the hair out of his amused eyes and looking for a response from Elias, who remained calm and unmoved by the situation at hand.

"May I speak, please?" The words slipped out in a brave whisper. Vieve felt the courage to assuage the discomfort, to be the wall that kept the conflict at bay.

"You may," Elias Montague gestured for her to continue.

"Mistress Montague," Vieve faced her owner. "We care about Lucy – begging your pardon – Mistress Lucy, very much and we want her to be safe. We were happy to see her in good spirits. Please forgive me if I have disappointed you in any way. I did not mean to do so."

"A good and wise choice of words," Elias did not smile, but his eyes gave way to approval, knowing that Vieve's boldness, even in her naivete, had given his wife room to check her anger, save face, and keep the upper hand in delivering an authoritative response. "Elizabeth?"

"I will accept the apology. At least for now. Lucy and I will discuss particulars for future similar endeavors. And someone should know where she is at all times." She turned toward Ashwiyaa and Maybelle. "Please get Lucy out of the wagon and bring some warm water to clean her up."

"I fetch it fo' you right away," Maybelle chimed in, grinning sideways at Vieve, as she and Ashwiyaa assisted Lucy in exiting the wagon. Vieve gave Lucy her arm and held onto her as they made their way up the back steps into the great hall.

"I'm so sorry my mother spoke to you that way. She had no cause." Lucy whispered to Vieve.

"You did what a real friend would do, Lucy. You took responsibility for you, and you spoke up for us. Thank you. You can't take responsibility for what anyone else does or doesn't do."

"I did do that, didn't I?" Lucy beamed. "It just came out of me from somewhere inside. It felt right. I did not think about it at all. Does that mean I'm your friend now?"

"It's a good start." Vieve smiled back. "We will figure out the rest. After I get you to your chamber, I will go help fetch the water from Maybelle and Ashwiyaa and bring it to you."

"Vieve," Lucy took a deep breath when they reached the threshold to her room, "we are going to find more adventures. And now, I have something I want to ask you. It is no small thing."

"What do you mean?" Vieve replied. Lucy placed her hands on both of Vieve's shoulders and whispered in the lowest of tones.

"If you learn my lessons with me, we can teach Maybelle and Ashwiyaa also. We can also teach them to read."

Vieve stared at the young girl who seemed destined to be the mistress of a plantation like Montague Hall one day.

"I've never wanted anything more than this!" Lucy shook her head. "Never. Please say that you want to do this and that you will help me."

"You know we both could get into big trouble if we do that, don't you? Maybelle, Ashwiyaa, too. You say you want to be a friend, but what if you are angry with us, then what?"

"I can tell you why I might be angry, can I not? You can tell me, too. Yes, I do want a friend, very much. I didn't really care about having friends a lot until today. Truly, this feels right. Ashwiyaa and Maybelle are smart, don't you think? So are you. If we can all learn, how much more fun we could have, and there is so much we could accomplish for so many people. And they can teach us their ways, too. Vieve, if we help each other, we can make things different. At least around here. Honestly, I feel as if I have a whole new reason to live. It is a wonderful endeavor, is it not?"

"I will tell them that you said that." Vieve squeezed Lucy's hand after the bed gown was removed and Lucy sat wrapped in a dry cloth, waiting to be cleaned. "We will have to think on that with great care. I'll be back soon." She skipped down the entire slave stairwell, smiling to herself as she headed to the cook and wash house, while Mistress Montague made her way up the main staircase to Lucy.

"Guess what," she shook Maybelle's arm and grinned at Ashwiyaa, lowering her voice while delivering the secret plan of learning and sharing. "Lucy and I want to do it, too, and we want you to teach us your ways as well. We will find ways to do it. Sundays, most likely, when things are easier on that day, but we can do it every chance we get. What do you say?"

"Can't tell Mama. She can't know nothin' fo' now. They gon' beat her and all of us, if they think Mama know what we doin'. You, too, Vieve, if they catch you doin' it."

"Lucy said it felt right deep inside to do it. I feel that way, too. We want to do this. We have to. But of course, we will respect your wishes.

Ashwiyaa, you haven't spoken. What do you think?" Vieve faced the Indian girl, who met her gaze with a pensive, serious expression, her brows furrowed together.

"This could bring great danger to some." She gave a gentle smile. "But better good will come if it is done. I will do this thing you ask."

"What's wrong, Maybelle?" Vieve could see the expression on the slave girl's face hid something important. Maybelle stood more erect, even proud, as she whispered in the most exquisite and beautiful English that Vieve had ever heard.

"You cannot tell anyone that I already know how to speak as an educated person, though I do not know how to read. I am not the only one. I have listened to proper English all of my life and have learned how to speak it by paying close attention. I want Lucy to know, but I am very afraid to tell her. I want to speak as an educated person." Tears creeped into the corners of the dark ebony eyes. Maybelle's voice wavered. "I have a dream of being a teacher. It is not likely to ever happen, but I dream of it so many times. So now you know."

Vieve and Ashwiyaa stared at their friend, tears of amazement rising in both their eyes.

"Maybelle," Vieve clapped her hands together, "that is the most incredible thing I have ever heard. You are amazing, how smart you are. We must do this, we must!"

"She, who speaks with wisdom," Ashwiyaa raised both hands in the air, smiling at Maybelle. "May she always speak as such. And may Wakan Tanka grant her this wish, and ours, as well. I will learn to speak more, as well."

Carrying the bucket of warm water up the slave stairs in the great hall, Vieve glanced at the sliver of pale moon in the late afternoon light that had faded to a dusky gray. At least she could still hold fast to hope. And at least on this day, unparalleled joy.

CHAPTER THIRTEEN

Late 1774

From her perch at the firing hole, in the darkness of the attic, Vieve could hear the voices of Elias and Elizabeth Montague below in the sitting room once again.

"Henry Laurens is coming here to Montague Hall in February?" Elizabeth raised questioning eyes to her husband. "After the First Provincial Congress meeting in Charlestown? Why?"

"Laurens is one of the finest men in these parts. He was inclined to prefer supporting reconciliation with the British Crown at first, until he saw the deterioration of that effort. He is firmly behind the Patriot cause and wants to see South Carolina with a fully independent government now. He will be escorting a colleague of Benjamin Franklin, so we will have two guests for the night. Franklin founded the American Philosophical Society of Philadelphia, of which Laurens is an ardent member. Laurens will accompany a Mr. Thomas Paine, a Brit who is in strong support of our cause here, back to the Philadelphia area. This Mr. Paine believes that the colonies must establish a democratic government with a strong written constitution, so that we might gain the advantages of both free trade and emancipation from the prospect of being forced into European wars and further abominable taxation. This war here, however, is imminent, I'm afraid."

"What does that mean for us, Elias?" Elizabeth frowned; her hands folded in her lap. "And what of the children? Tell me the truth."

"Mal and Oliver are not old enough to fight, yet, to my mind, but Mal could. I fear they will be fighting, however, before it is all over with. Mal, especially. Before it is done, we will likely be facing the decimation of what we have built. We may very well be faced with starting over at another point in time in the rebuilding of Montague Hall."

"Or we could simply return to Charlestown and resume good lives there."

"Elizabeth, my dear, I don't think you yet understand how difficult this will be for us all, Charlestown included. There will be great destruction and chaos everywhere, regardless of the outcome. But we can pray to God Almighty that the Patriots prevail in endeavors to secure freedom. When we go to Drayton Hall in a few weeks for the wedding of John's niece, there will be much discussion by the men after the main merriment is over. But the signs are everywhere. War is coming. Hell is coming. And we'd best be as prepared as we can be for the inevitable."

Vieve plugged the firing hole once more and leaned against the wall, breathing with slow, visceral breaths, letting the air fill her chest into her belly. She allowed her cheek to rest against the cool roughness of the wood as she contemplated all that she had just heard. Closing her eyes, she remembered Maybelle saying that her father, whom the young slave girl had never met, had been sold to Drayton Hall Plantation. Was a reunion possible? How could she get Maybelle, or perhaps even Evaline, there? She reviewed the words of Elias Montague in her head, trying to remember the names and events he had mentioned, so that she could relay them to her friends.

A soft knock on her door interrupted her thoughts.

"Vieve, are you awake? It's Oliver. Can you talk?"

"Just a minute," Vieve whispered back, smoothing her sleeping gown, and running fingers through her hair. She opened the door for him, secretly pleased to see him. "Good evening, Oliver. Come in."

Oliver crossed the threshold, standing briefly by the open window then sitting cross-legged on the floor, motioning for Vieve to sit beside him.

"You look worried," he mused. "Is everything alright?"

"Yes. Yes, everything is fine." She decided to pursue her thoughts with careful intention. "It's just that there is something I have been thinking about very much."

"What is it? Perhaps I might help." Oliver rested his chin in both palms.

"I heard that – well," Vieve hesitated, looking into his eyes, "I heard that there was going to be a wedding at Drayton Hall. Is that a plantation here?"

"Yes, a very big and successful one, belonging to Mr. John Drayton. I think his niece is getting married there. It will be a celebration, of course, and there will be some fine Charleston families there. We will go, as well. Why do you ask?"

"Would you keep a confidence for me? Can you?"

"Yes, I can. Of course, as long as no one is getting hurt. What is it?"

Vieve took a deep breath, wringing both hands together and hesitating before she continued.

"I have heard that Maybelle's father was sold to Master Drayton. Do you know if that is true, or if he is still a slave there?"

"I believe that is true. I remember that. His name is Jude. A big man, more knowledgeable than many. Strong, too. I think that he is responsible for helping Mr. John Drayton inside the home and with managing his carriage and such. I know that he was traded for a hefty sum even for a slave, and a couple of field hands, as well. Why do you ask?"

"Maybelle has never met her father. And Evaline loved him very much. I know they were not married, but that Evaline had Maybelle after he was no longer here at Montague Hall. Oliver, please. If you can help in any way, could you? Would it be possible to take Maybelle to Drayton Hall? She could help while there. Perhaps she could see him, even have a brief moment with him? No one should be without their father, do you think?"

"You have always been without your father, have you not?" Oliver frowned. "And you are a well-spirited girl."

"I never knew him, or even his name. My mother raised me. But if I knew who and where he was, I would want desperately to meet him, to know who I was, where I came from. Would you not want to know the same, if you had never looked upon your father?" She pleaded with compassion, engaging Oliver with her eyes.

"I suppose I would, yes. But Vieve, you know it is different for slaves."

"Is it?" she shook her head back and forth in a soft, deliberate motion. "That is only so because it has been deemed that by those more powerful who look away from such a sad thing. No, Oliver, that is not so at all. They love their families, as you love yours. All people do. I saw my mother face terrible circumstances that tore her apart, just as it must have crushed Evaline into a thousand pieces when Jude had to leave. I hear that he was distraught as well. Would you not be devastated if someone you deeply cared for was taken from you?"

Vieve studied Oliver, watched the tension of his fists, the way he ran his fingers through his dark hair, looking down, as if trying to remove the unpleasant thoughts from his head. When he returned her gaze, Vieve thought she sensed the heightened emotion on his face. Were those tears in his eyes?

"Maybelle knows he is her father," she ventured, " but she has never met him or been able to see who she came from."

"You want me to see if Maybelle can go to Drayton Hall with us? Is that what you are asking?"

"Yes, it is. I want it for Maybelle very much. Do you think it even possible?"

"In truth, Vieve, I do not know." He tapped his fingers on the side of his chin. "But if it will make you happy, I will try. You cannot say anything about this, you know. Not to my family. They would not want to stir anything up. I would like it if you could attend, as well, to help Lucy and keep a watchful eye for any sign of difficulty, to ensure that such a meeting does not get noticed by anyone."

"Yes, yes of course I would do that, Oliver. And I know that Maybelle would be most careful too. She could help me care for Lucy, and also to help Mistress Montague. Thank you for agreeing to try to find a way to help. I am grateful. Maybelle will be thankful, as well."

"I will let you know what I find out," Oliver smiled. "If it can be done without drawing undue attention."

"Thank you, Oliver! So much." Vieve hugged his neck, surprised when he grasped her shoulders to return the embrace. " I will repay the kindness somehow, be assured."

"You have already, by being my friend, Vieve. I hope you are always my friend, no matter what is happening."

"You mean, like war?" Vieve removed her arms from him.

"Yes, that, of course. If we should ever be separated because of war, you are my friend, and I would find you. I will always be your friend—even if we should disagree on anything. Such as the appropriateness of Maybelle on this trip." He smiled at her.

"Oliver, I am scared of war. I don't want it to happen."

"Nor do I. But my father says it is most likely, and that life, as we know it, will change, good or bad, because of it. Montague Hall might change, or we could even lose it. My father could lose his life, as he supports the Patriot cause, as I do. But he is not foolish and will take every precaution to take care of Montague Hall, especially."

"Does your mother support the Patriot effort also?"

Oliver winced, running fingers through his dark hair once more and folding arms across his chest.

"I'm not sure exactly how she feels. In truth, I don't think she understands her own feelings. She loves my father, but I know she misses Charlestown and her parents, her old life there, very much. She has always wanted to go back to the more genteel world. Life here is hard. Whether she believes in the cause of the Patriots or the authority of the Crown, I am not sure. She supports my father in all that he does, but I do not know of her true inclinations. She keeps those to herself. Of course, if there is war, Charlestown would not be spared either."

"We should both sleep," Vieve offered. "Tomorrow will be a busy day."

"Indeed," Oliver smiled. "Let's hope that the morrow brings good things for all. Goodnight, Vieve." She watched as he peered out the window once again, then closed the door behind him. She had grown fond of Oliver, finding solace in their friendship, and wondering if it would stand the test of time as he said. Would any of them withstand the ravages of a war that threatened to destroy everything? What would life be like here if the colonies won their freedom? What would happen to those who disobeyed the Crown, if the Patriot cause was averted? Vieve looked for the moon on this night, but it was nowhere to be found.

CHAPTER FOURTEEN

Drayton Hall was massive in appearance; a three-story brick plantation house with two wide and steep steps up to the second level. Vieve marveled at the simple and sturdy elegance of the plantation home. Oliver had told her that rice and indigo were also grown here, along with the pigs and cattle that they raised for market. At some point, there had been thirteen indentured servants there, as well as the many slaves, all of whom had helped to build the plantation.

The day, temperate and pleasant, with soft sunlight peeking through the layers of clouds, made a perfect setting for a wedding ceremony. Meticulously groomed shrubbery and pots of festive flowers adorned the property. From the covered area where the ceremony would take place, she heard wafts of violins and perhaps flutes.

Slave workers scurried about to finish readying the lush site for the solemn affair, as guests arrived on their horses and in carriages and wagons. From their perch in the rear wagon, Vieve and Maybelle whispered to one another, while watching the Montague family in the front carriage.

"You think they have forgotten about my father being here?" Maybelle leaned close to Vieve. "How are we going to know where he is?"

"I'm not sure," Vieve whispered back. "But we will find him, Maybelle, we will."

"Does Lucy know about this? About him?"

"No, I have not told her. Oliver knows. He helped make it so for you. I wanted to tell Lucy, but I did not want to put her in an awkward position. I also could not get her alone long enough to be sure we were not overheard. If we need to tell her, we can. Mistress Montague has kept closer to her than usual, of late. I do trust that Lucy would help us. Oliver, too. Mal, not so much."

"He's a snake, that one," Maybelle mumbled beneath the hand cupped around her lips. Vieve suppressed a giggle. "He is not the nicest person. He and Mistress Elizabeth are a lot alike."

"I'd like to kill him, if I had half a chance." Maybelle glared toward the carriage in front of them.

"Maybelle! I've never heard you say such. Why?"

Maybelle rubbed her hands together, her eyes narrowing. She moved even closer to Vieve so no one would hear the whispers.

"My sister Jonsie and Mama say Jonsie is with child." Maybelle spat the words out. "His."

"What?" Vieve stared at her friend. "Are you sure? He forced her?"

"You know he did. She had to do what he demanded. She could not refuse him. She does not want this baby to be a slave. And Mistress Montague could easily sell it if they find out it's his child. Jonsie doesn't want this baby at all. Right now, no one knows but us." Maybelle lowered her voice. "Ashwiyaa and Dumplin will see Jonsie and Mama today to help figure out what to do. If she gets rid of it, and they find out, they will beat her. That's money lost for another slave. She loves her baby. Loves it enough to not want it born into slavery."

"My God." Vieve shook her head. "Maybelle, are you saying she would end the baby's life? How does Evaline feel about this?"

"She is so sad right now. I worry about her. She's sad about my sister. Sad about her grandbaby. Sad about Jude and not having him in her life. She's happy that I am going to see him, though. She asked me to give him her best regards and to kiss his cheek for her. She also sent this." Maybelle pulled a long, tattered gray piece of cloth from inside her weathered rucksack. "Jude gave it to her to wrap her head on the hot days in the field when she was out there. It was his. He told her to think of him whenever she wore it. She wanted him to see just how much she had worn it and thought of him. Said to tell him to remember her. Even if he had a woman by now. She won't ever forget him."

Vieve reached to touch the cloth. How hard it must have been to lose a love like that. And at the whim of those who thought slave lives meant nothing. She thought once again of her own mother's body, wrapped in an old blanket they had shared and shoved overboard, and of poor little Simon's battered body.

"Some things I just don't understand." She looked at Maybelle, her face brightening. "But today will be a good day. We will find Jude and find a way for you to speak with him."

Invited guests made their way to the privies, or to partake of a morsel and drink before the ceremony began. Vieve and Maybelle attended to Lucy while the rest of the Montague family offered pleasantries to other arrivals and made their way toward the honored guests. It would be a day of merriment before the ride back to Montague Hall. Vieve smoothed her simple gown and gazed at the surroundings, looking for signs of the slave known as Jude, as she and Maybelle walked with Lucy to a privy and retrieved a rum drink for her. Before long, the wedding guests were making their way to a covered area close to the Ashley River, where a priest and noted Charlestown people were already waiting. Oliver approached the girls, offering his arm to Lucy, but speaking to Vieve.

"I think I should escort my sister, perhaps. Would you all please help tend to the horses with the livery servant over there? Maybelle, perhaps you could tell him whose carriage this is and offer him a greeting from me? I believe that he was one of our slaves at one time. He is the one in the dark livery suit, turned up with green, and a waistcoat."

Before Vieve could respond, he made a hasty exit with Lucy, holding and guiding her to the wedding party area. Vieve stared at the Negro man in the fancy suit, assisting the remnants of arriving guests with the carriages and wagons, and instructing a cadre of male slaves as to where all should go. She reached for Maybelle's hand. It was trembling. Maybelle bit her lip, staring at the big Negro man.

"Go to him," Vieve whispered to the slave girl. "This is your chance, Maybelle. I can guide the horses to where they need to be and help care for them. Oliver has helped us find a way to do this." She watched as Maybelle crossed the carriage path and stood before this stranger, her father. Thinking better of the moment, Vieve decided to give her friend the dignified privacy she deserved and turned her attention to the horses.

"Good day, Sir. Is your name Jude?" Maybelle spoke in a hushed, reverent tone. She had envisioned this moment in her head many times, but now found herself lacking in the right words to offer.

"Good day, Miss. I's Jude. How might I help you?" The man spoke with a rich, deep voice. Maybelle pulled the long gray cloth out of her rucksack, staring at him and smiling. She had his big round eyes.

"Someone sent this for you, Sir. And she hopes that you remember her."

Maybelle placed the cloth in his hands and waited.

The man before her stood tall but seemed to crumble beneath the weight of unexpected emotion. His fingers made gentle stroking motions over the worn cloth, then his fists, weathered from the work at hand, closed in a fierce grip around the faded cloth.

"Evaline," he breathed, raising his eyes to Maybelle. It was a statement rather than a question.

"Yes, Sir, Evaline. She thinks of you most fondly."

From a cherished place far back in time, the tears rose in Jude's eyes, and he held the cloth to his cheek, breathing in the scent of the woman he had loved. He studied Maybelle with heightened intensity, a measure of understanding beginning to dawn as he studied the young slave girl.

"And who are you?" The man saw a younger vision of Evaline standing before him. Her ebony skin and soft, bright eyes made the breath catch in his throat. His voice shook, as did his sturdy shoulders.

"My name is Maybelle. I am her youngest daughter. You know she had one daughter already when you knew her. Her name is Jonsie. That husband, Jonsie's father, died before you were around, of course. There hasn't been anyone else in her life. Except you, Sir." Maybelle watched Jude's face melt into a myriad of emotion as he shook his head and acknowledged her once more.

"Then you are…" his voice trailed into oblivion as he smiled at her through tears.

"Yes," Maybelle smiled back. "I am your daughter."

From a distance, Vieve gazed once again at the man and Maybelle, now embraced in the warmest of affection. Tears crept from the corners of her eyes, and she smiled watching the blissful reunion, wishing that Oliver could see it, understand the enormity of what he had helped to do. She looked for him among the wedding guests and saw him speaking with a finely dressed and beautiful girl, who smiled, touching his arm as they spoke, laughing at whatever he was saying. As for her part, Vieve felt the strange uncomfortableness of jealousy, an emotion with which she was unfamiliar when it came to boys. She turned her attention back to Maybelle and Jude. Today was indeed a good day, bittersweet, to be sure, filled with grace and mercy. But most of all, with hope. She would focus on those things and not the strange feelings she felt about Oliver. She smiled, knowing what today had meant to Maybelle.

From across the manicured grounds of Drayton Hall, Vieve missed the appreciative gaze of Oliver Montague. Frowning, Elizabeth Montague, who had been watching her children, comparing each with others of similar pedigree, did not miss the open display of affection her youngest son directed toward the young servant girl. Mistress Montague kept her eyes on the pretty indentured servant who her youngest son favored with great affection. She would have to find a way to dissuade Oliver from such an inappropriate choice. She and Elias would speak with him about his misplaced romantic feelings, and his duty to choose a more suitable match for him.

The carriage and wagon ride back to Montague Hall in the late afternoon, as twilight clouds of pale summer colors etched across the sky, soothed Vieve's mind, as did Maybelle's head resting on her shoulder. In truth, she had never seen Maybelle so happy. It had been a most fulfilling day.

CHAPTER FIFTEEN

In the darkness of her attic room, Vieve heard the commotion below, even before she had removed the firing hole plug. Mr. Bennett, the Overseer, was speaking with Elias and Elizabeth Montague in the sitting room. His tone was serious.

"I hated to tell you this evening, after your busy day at Drayton Hall, but another slave got wind of it and snitched on her. They know I provide something worthy if they keep me apprised of such. Jonsie is definitely with child and talk is that she will ask Ashwiyaa and Dumplin to help her get rid of it."

Vieve's lips parted in surprise, as the name of Maybelle's older sister was mentioned. The remainder of this day had just turned sour.

"She's early along, maybe. Not quickened. Nothing has been done yet, likely, I don't believe. I got this information early."

"Good job, Mr. Bennett. You think my son has fathered this child?" Elias's words were tired, a tinge of frustration in his voice. "He is becoming of that age, I suppose, at fifteen now, and the slave girl is of ripe child-bearing age."

"I do not want it here, Elias." Elizabeth Montague spoke with authority, glaring at Mr. Bennett. "Sell it. Get rid of it. Jonsie, too. She's a field hand who can be replaced. That one is a bit lazy anyway. Has Dumplin or Ashwiyaa helped her with this matter at all yet?"

"No, Ma'am, not to my knowledge. At least not yet, I think. Nothing been done just yet, far as I know. But that Indian girl and them Negroes know how to try to stop that slave from being born, they surely do."

Vieve winced, hearing the unborn baby already being referred to as a simple property investment.

"What do you want me to do? I say I make an example out of her for any of them who might be considering the same or offering to help her get rid of it."

"I want that girl gone, Elias. Gone. No dark baby to look like any of us. Take Mal into Charlestown, if need be, to quench those needs. Or tell him to find Vieve when he desires such."

Vieve felt the blood drain from her face, her breath making a momentary stop in the back of her throat. How could any woman be so cold, so viciously cruel, in meting out such to any female? She knew now, with painful awareness, of how little she meant to Elizabeth Montague. Mal would never be responsible for his reprehensible behavior toward someone he considered beneath him in any way. She leaned harder against the firing hole wall, straining to hear. Elias Montague reproached his wife.

"Vieve is not yet of mature age or body to interest Mal. You know that."

"Does it really matter? She is a servant, and she is like us. At least that baby would be fair, not dark-skinned. No grandchild of mine, slave or no, is going to be a Negro. No one else needs to know if Vieve should become pregnant. We can even send her away for a period of time. Or trade her, I don't care."

Elias Montague pressed his fingers together, tapping gently and staring into the fire in the great hearth. For several moments, silence prevailed.

"Punish Jonsie in the morning. A few licks, not enough to incapacitate. I need her working for a while longer. Be sure everyone hears and knows, especially Dumplin and Ashwiyaa. We can trade her away for a bit, or sell her, procure another. She's young enough to provide more years of good service to us or elsewhere and can have more babies."

"I do not want that girl here, Elias, another minute." Elizabeth Montague was beyond distressed. "At least grant me that much! I am retiring for the night. It has been a most exhausting day. Goodnight to you both." She rose from her seat to mount the staircase. Vieve listened until the horrific conversation had been terminated, and all had left the sitting room. She let herself sink to the floor, leaning back against the cool firmness of the wall and staring up and out of her room window into the deep evening sky. She had to find a way to let her good friends know. She closed her eyes only for a moment, checking to be sure her brogans were still secured. She would remain in her work clothes on this night, and find a way to communicate with Maybelle, Ashwiyaa, and Dumplin. But how? *Think! Think, think…what to do now?*

Vieve did not know how much time had passed when she woke from her brief respite. The darkness was more intense, quiet, with no signs of anyone stirring inside or out. It was still the deepest of night. Slipping in silence through her room door and down the slave stairwell, she moved with slow, deliberate stealth to the grounds in the courtyard below and found her way to the tiny primitive cabin that belonged to Maybelle, Jonsie, and Evaline. Glancing right, then left, she made soft taps on the wooden door. Evaline appeared, rubbing her eyes.

"Evaline, I'm so sorry to wake you." Vieve could see Maybelle and Jonsie rising from their pallets.

"Gracious goodness, chile'. What in the world brings you here this time of night?" Evaline ushered Vieve inside, peeking out behind her to be sure no one was there.

"If anyone comes here, say that I came to you because I felt sick and did not know what to do. At least, that is mostly true, anyway. I have bad news, I'm afraid."

Vieve relayed all that she had heard, watching the faces of her friends take on troubled, serious, and pained expressions.

"Sweet Jesus, help us," Evaline grasped Jonsie and held her close, her voice cracking with emotion. Jonsie began to weep.

"I done told you they was gone punish me," she moaned, "and make me birth this here baby – this child here, already a slave before being born, already gonna be taken from me, and sold for a price to do their bidding. And Dumplin and Ashwiyaa ain't even give me anything to stop it yet. Master Mal, this all his fault! Now, Mr. Bennett gonna beat me!"

"What can we do?" Vieve placed a hand on the backs of Evaline and Jonsie. She felt helpless and small. Maybelle paced back and forth in the one-room cabin.

"We need some help." She turned to Vieve. "Master Oliver, Mistress Lucy, you think they would help us?"

"How?" Vieve was incredulous. "What could they say or do to make a difference now? Someone has already betrayed this to the Overseer, who told Master Montague. And Mistress Elizabeth wants to get rid of Jonsie, too." Vieve did not tell them what Elizabeth Montague had said about her own potential fate.

"Vieve, can you get word to Ashwiyaa? We will take care of Dumplin. They was already plannin' to give Jonsie some black root and cedar root, but not many knew that. At least we thought no one else knew. But I s'pose the tongues of those who ain't really our friends is waggin' like a happy dog. We need to give her some potion right now, make her real sick, too."

"I don't understand how Master Oliver or Mistress Lucy can help, what do you mean?" Vieve asked.

"If one of them, or even both, can say they have seen Jonsie very sick and that they have seen her washing out her clouts recently when she was having her time – we can make them think that the baby didn't make it because Jonsie couldn't carry it. One of them can say that they done heard Jonsie say that she did not want to lose this baby but that she work so hard in the fields, that the baby just didn't live long enough to grow and be born. We just need for them to believe Jonsie wanted to keep the baby so they ain't punish her." Maybelle turned to Vieve.

"Can you talk to them? In the meanwhile, we got to give Jonsie more potion. And Ashwiyaa has to hide it."

"Clouts, what are those? I don't understand."

"They are just the old rags stuffed with feathers and washed moss and such when she has her time, when she's bleeding." Maybelle smiled. "You haven't had yours yet, have you? You'll find out when you start to bleed down there between your legs. Happens every now and again. When it does, you will be able to carry a child inside, if a man lays with you." Maybelle motioned for Vieve to lean close to her. "Ashwiyaa says that her people believe that a woman has more spiritual awakenings, like visions, when they are in the red tent. That's what they call it for where they go when they are having their time. They stay in a tent. Ashwiyaa did it for a bit, but she doesn't so much now that she's been here for a few years. Ashwiyaa told me she saw you in one of her visions. That a snake-like creature attacked you. She ever tell you that?"

"No, never," Vieve said. "What do you think she meant? Was she dreaming?"

"Who knows? I don't question it. I just listen." Maybelle smiled. "It's Ashwiyaa. She said one day we would all know what that vision meant. Guess we will just have to wait and see."

Vieve stared at the three before her. There was so much she did not fully comprehend. Even more that she found frightening.

"I can try to help," she said. "I will go right now. You want Ashwiyaa to come here tonight?"

"Yes, chile', this night. Fast as she can get here." Evaline continued to hold onto Jonsie. "Jonsie gonna have to be sick for a while, sicker than usual and much quicker. Now that some others know, we got to act, and while all others is sleepin'."

"Anything be better than a child of mine havin' to live this here way," Jonsie faced Vieve. "Go now."

Vieve crept through the quiet darkness to the barn where Ashwiyaa stayed. She was surprised to find her sitting on her pallet, awake and hoisting her hunting knife.

"They need me now, don't they?" She questioned Vieve while returning the knife to its sheath after digging the ground underneath her pallet.

"Yes. They do. Go to their cabin. Hurry, Ashwiyaa. And be careful!"

Vieve scurried out of the barn, taking care to leave after Ashwiyaa and returning to the big house by way of the privies, in case someone should be awake and near.

Safely back in her room, Vieve stood by the open window and stared at the area closest to Maybelle's cabin. She had to get Oliver or Lucy on their side. And she would have to trust them more than ever before. Would either agree to not tell Master Elias and Mistress Elizabeth the truth? She had already asked much of Oliver, though she believed he would help if he could. Sleep would be elusive or not at all on this night. Indeed, the coming days might be full of new, unimaginable worries. Vieve stared into the darkness. If only Claire Whittier was here to talk with her, to offer motherly advice. She would have to trust her own instincts, perhaps greater than ever before. And risk more than she ever thought possible.

CHAPTER SIXTEEN

Mr. Bennett's voice, booming louder than usual, permeated the still morning calm and woke Vieve from the remnants of needed sleep. Though she had heard no ominous sound of a cracking whip, nor Jonsie's screams or cries, his words left no doubt as to what had transpired. She stared at the window, taking in the darkness of the early morning hour. How awful it must be for the girl. First, Mal is cruel in his abuse of her, then she is forced to become sick and weak, only to be whipped afterward.

"You have no rights here, Slave! Let this be a hard-learned lesson to you and others. Do not interfere, ever. Do you understand me? Not ever! Lucky for you, Master Montague did not want you beat within an inch of your sorry life! Mistress and Master Montague will decide the fate of any slave baby here, born, or full-grown, or anywhere in-between, including your baby. Go, get out of my sight!"

The tears fell and great sobs erupted from deep within. Oliver's voice at her door sounded mournful and concerned.

"Vieve? Vieve, are you alright? Please, may I come in?" He gave a slight push to the door, which swung open to a view of Vieve, red-eyed and sitting upright on her pallet, her clenched hands covering her mouth. Her body shook with emotion. "You heard Mr. Bennett, didn't you?"

Vieve nodded, unable to speak, but her distraught eyes pleaded with the youngest son of Master Montague. Oliver stood over her, hands by his side, before reaching out to stroke the top of her head, then sitting beside her.

"Vieve, I'm sorry, truly. I did not know this was going to happen. Do you know if Jonsie is with child? Tell me, please." Oliver grasped her hand and held it between his.

"I have no choice but to trust you, Oliver. As my friend, I will trust you. Please do not tell your father and mother any of this. Please." Vieve poured out the predicament of Jonsie, only that she was indeed pregnant, and that the pregnancy had made her quite sick and weak.

"Now you must trust me, Vieve. Who is the father of this baby?" Oliver's voice softened to a whisper. "If you know, please tell me." Vieve pulled away from him, letting both hands drop in her lap, clenched and shaking. Her eyes closed, then opened, the tears returning, as she searched Oliver's eyes once more. She spoke in hushed, painful breaths.

"Your brother, Mal. He fathered this baby by forcing himself upon Jonsie." Vieve maintained her eye contact with Oliver, searching for knowledge of what he might think or do. In an instant his brows knit together in a fury of surprise and anger.

"Mal is the father. You are sure?" He watched as she nodded her head in a slow, deliberate motion. "When did you discover this?"

Vieve's lips parted in surprise at the question she was not prepared to answer.

"Tell me everything, Vieve. If I am to try to help – and I will – I must know the truth so that I can find the best way."

Without speaking, she rose and motioned for him to follow her to the now-plugged firing hole in the wall. His eyes widened, and he turned a questioning gaze to her.

"I don't understand."

"I discovered it some time ago. Unplugged, it allows for spoken words from the drawing room and stairwell to be heard. And sometimes I can see a part of what is happening in the room as well. Last night, I heard Mr. Bennett talking with your father and mother. Master Montague said for him to deliver only a milder punishment, so as not to hurt the baby if one was truly there. I went to Evaline's cabin afterward." Once again, Vieve kept hidden the feelings of Mistress

Montague in regard to the possible future actions of Master Mal. "That's when the plan was made for us to try to help her. Then, I went to fetch Ashwiyaa for help."

Oliver unplugged the firing hole, staring into the living space below, then returned the plug to the hole. He turned to face Vieve, whistling under his breath.

"No wonder you weren't sure about trusting me. I'm glad you decided to tell me." He smiled at her. "Rest assured, I want to help you and I will. Tell me the rest."

Vieve smoothed her work dress and fastened her brogans one more. Motioning toward the door to be sure it was closed, she told him all that had transpired during the night. His eyebrows furrowed together once more.

"You can see why Jonsie is so distraught, why we need your help. Oliver, you have already done more than I could ever ask of your friendship to me. Do you think it is possible to help them without damaging your relationship with your father and mother?"

"Maybe. Perhaps I can. I need to think some. But I cannot promise a solution that will work the best for all. But Vieve – I will do what I can. Thank you for trusting me. For now, you must go to the cookhouse immediately. Tell Evaline, Maybelle, and Ashwiyaa nothing more of my involvement after this and instruct them that they must never speak of me as a friend to anyone other than you. You must make them understand that. Tell me that you know what I am asking of you."

"I understand, Oliver. I will tell them this morning, rest assured."

"Go now but return with haste. I will inform Lucy and Mother that I sent you on a quick errand to deliver something to Big Zeb for me."

"I will go there now. And Oliver, thank you. Thank you most of all for being my friend. You are very special to me."

Vieve made her way through the stairwell and out the back door to the courtyard. She was oblivious to the tenderness in Oliver's eyes.

He watched her through her open window before latching it shut and heading downstairs to break the fast before another grueling day. All the while, he pondered on ways to save Jonsie from further physical punishment and keep the dark secret asked of him by Vieve. Saving the slave from the wrath of Elizabeth Montigue would be a more difficult matter.

CHAPTER SEVENTEEN

Once again, the night voices, soft and unintelligible, meandered through the quiet. Vieve unplugged the firing piece, pressing her ear to the now open hole. Mal's voice, irritated and angry, rose above the rest.

"I have done nothing wrong! Why the concern here? I am a master as well, am I not? That slave is nothing, nor is any baby. If anything, it will be another work hand for us, perhaps smarter than most."

"We must concern ourselves with rectifying this issue to the best interest of our family, personally and workwise." Elizabeth Montague was calm on this evening, not apologizing for her son at all, but neither showing overt approval, as Mal spoke again.

"If anything, that Negro should be severely punished, if she has attempted to kill our property."

Vieve covered her mouth, both in frustration at the callousness, and in an effort to conceal anger and surprise at his demeaning response toward his own flesh and blood.

"I believe that Jonsie lost the baby and was very saddened at that loss." Oliver's voice was reassuring in his defense of Maybelle's sister. "It is also true that Evaline and Maybelle work much harder than Jonsie, but they all have been dependable slaves. I think Evaline especially is saddened by what has happened. This is her daughter and would-be grandchild, to be sure."

"What makes you think that Jonsie merely lost this baby, and did not try to keep us from having another slave?" Elias Montague inquired of his youngest son.

"And why should we care at all about anything a slave thinks, if thinking is even possible for them?" Malachi glared at Oliver; his voice tinged with frustration. Oliver chose to ignore the outburst, his voice remaining calm.

"I have seen Jonsie crying, washing out her clouts some time before now. Evaline was there, too, and told her that she could one day have another, not to mourn this one so. Maybelle was providing comfort, too. Those are not the words one might hear said to someone who truly wanted to kill her baby. I think Jonsie was most distraught at the thought of losing her baby."

"It is not 'her' baby. It is ours! A Montague Hall slave!" Mal thundered at Oliver, slamming a hand on the back of a chair.

"Enough!" Elias's raised voice rang through the rafters. "I will decide on the issue at hand. In the meanwhile, I expect you both to conduct yourselves in the manner of gentlemen."

"Father, what has been done is not the conduct of a gentleman." Oliver said in hushed firmness, glaring at his brother. "While slaves are our property, yes, but even you have said that there should be an expectation of behavior becoming that of a gentleman. There are other ways to address certain needs."

"You are not old enough to fully understand, but you will be one day, little brother. Then perhaps you will feel differently toward our little indentured servant girl." Mal snarled, back, "Isn't that so, Father? He looked to Elias for support. "Then you will understand her place here. And yours."

"Enough!" The sound of Elias's hand crashing against the arm of his chair made its way to Vieve. "I will not say it again."

"It matters not to me what her intent was." Elizabeth Montague spoke. "Though if masters were more selective in satisfying their needs, or perhaps did so with their wives, such as this would not occur."

Vieve put a hand over her mouth in a sharp intake of breath. Was she referencing Elias, as well as Mal, or someone else? What a sad display of humanity. Elizabeth continued, when no one responded to her words.

"Elias, take Mal to Charlestown to address such needs of your son. Let the slaves create their own in their own likeness. As your wife, and the mistress here, that is a reasonable request. When Mal, Oliver too, are married, we will have appropriate grandchildren. None will have to be hidden or disguised for propriety's sake."

"And me, what about me?" Lucy's clear, mournful voice sounded louder than all others. *She's standing on the top of the stairwell.* "Does my honor and place demand better as well, or can wives be treated in such a manner as Mal has done? Mal, I love you. You know that. But I am most distressed."

"Lucy! What are you doing awake? This does not involve you! Oliver, go help your sister back to bed." Elizabeth Montague barked out instructions, noting Lucy's precarious perch at the top of the stairs, as she clung to the railing. Lucy ignored her mother and spoke in slow, deliberate measure.

"I was with Oliver, riding in my wagon. I, too, saw and heard Jonsie. She was very distraught over losing this child. I do not believe that anyone has helped her destroy it. What I did not know is that it was Mal's baby. Mal's child."

"I have done nothing wrong! Nothing but what many other masters have done at some time." Mal took a step toward the stairs, his voice more pleading with his sister. "Jonsie is our property, as is that dead slave baby. If anyone deserves punishment, it is she! Why is the concern here for anyone but our property?"

"So, it is acceptable for you to behave in such a reprehensible manner? Is it?" Lucy demanded.

"I said that is enough! From all of you! I will make the decision and you will all abide by it. The hour is getting late. Not another word. Go to your bedchambers now. Now! Goodnight."

Vieve felt her body sink to the hard floor, head in her hands, tears falling, as the long minutes passed. Oliver and Lucy had tried to help—more than she ever thought possible. The actions of these two Montague children were the most loving gesture she had ever witnessed. How could some people be so full of cruelty while others, even of the same family, be willing to embrace compassion? A sudden soft knock at the door roused her from the swirl of confusing thoughts. Oliver was here.

"Vieve," he said in hushed tones. "It's me. May I come inside? I need to talk with you. Although I think you know."

Vieve opened the door, motioning him inside and throwing her arms around his neck. He returned the affection before looking into her eyes, smiling.

"So, you did hear all? Even Lucy?"

"I heard enough, yes. How can I ever thank you? Lucy, too. I have never had such done for me. And I'm quite sure that Evaline, Jonsie, and Maybelle would feel the same. You are both my dear friends. I will never forget this, Oliver. Never."

"I hope that the news I have to share will also make you happy. I fear some might make you sad."

"What do you mean?" Vieve pulled away from him, her eyes filled with returning concern.

"I spoke earlier in the day with my father, while Mal was busy with other duties. He said that John Drayton, at Drayton Hall might take Jonsie, as he needed another female slave of child-bearing age. My father would trade for her to be sent there." Oliver noted the sadness in her eyes. "Vieve, I'm afraid I cannot undo that. But there is good news, I hope."

"I don't understand. What do you mean? Jonsie being taken away is terrible news."

"I know. Remember, I told you I might not be able to control the final decisions for all. My father said that Big Zeb is getting older, and in need of some help around the barn here and with the animals and carriages and such. He needs to help train another seasoned but younger slave to eventually assume these important duties. We have more than enough young male field hands. My father is considering a trade."

"I'm sorry, Oliver, I still don't understand." Vieve wrung her hands together. "Evaline will be crushed at losing a daughter, after losing a grandchild just so that it would not have to become a slave."

"Yes, I'm well aware of that." Oliver held her hand. "And I'm truly sorry. But what if I told you that the slave who might come here would make her immensely happy."

"What are you saying, Oliver?" She stared at him, eyes widening. "Are you saying what I think you are saying?" Vieve's hands rose to her cheeks. "Tell me!"

"I am, yes. My father is asking Mr. Drayton if he would consider returning Jude to us, for Jonsie and a field hand perhaps. And we could find word on Jonsie fairly often, I'm sure, as Jude would travel some when needed and now knows all in Mr. Drayton's purview. It's not the best outcome we could have, but it is something, is it not?"

Vieve's eyes clouded with tears once more. No, it was not what she had anticipated at all, especially for Evaline and Maybelle. They would have to say goodbye to a daughter and a sister. Jonsie would be thrust among people she had never known, to start another life, not of her choosing. *Like me.* Vieve let the tears fall in front of Oliver. The consolation brought no joy, though it was the best of all that could happen, if indeed it came to be. Evaline and Maybelle would be overjoyed at the return of Jude. There was only one looming fear in her head for the moment. Would Mal act on the idea given to him by his mother, and either condoned or ignored by his father?

CHAPTER EIGHTEEN

Deep woods somewhere at
Montague Hall, January 1775

Vieve smiled at Maybelle and Lucy, who held onto the handle of the wagon where she remained seated. Ashwiyaa's face was covered with a pasty white concoction, with what appeared to be the black head of a snake painted around her eyes, with the snake body that weaved in black and red around her cheek on both sides down to her mouth. Wisps of green, yellow, brown, and blue paint were brushed in small streaks on each side of her serious face. Feathers hung from the cloth band around her head of braided hair and protruded above the band like a thick crown of colors. She was garbed in her simple dress with black and white feathers and beads hanging from her neck. Small pottery bowls containing the colored paint, made from charcoal, ocher, plant leaves, and mixed with animal fat rested on a halved wooden log that Ashwiyaa had placed in front of her.

The chilly Sunday afternoon had arrived after the heart wrenching departure of Jonsie and the exuberant return of Jude to Montague Hall. Maybelle had taken leave after the welcome of her father, and gladly joined the gathering of girls so that Evaline would have extended time to be alone with Jude to discuss all that had happened over the years apart. Vieve noted the terrible bittersweetness of this day; of a woman faced with the loss of her daughter, yet also with the joyful return of the man she loved.

"Why do you wear such to cover your face and why are we here in the woods, Ashwiyaa?" Lucy brushed the hair out of her eyes, smoothed her dress, and looked around at the other incredulous faces.

"You have been very secretive indeed," Vieve smiled. "What is all of this about?" She waved an arm across the length of the wooden log plank that held the small pots.

"Sit, all of you. Lucy, stay in the wagon. For my people, this paint is spiritual and shows great power. The colors signify strength, unity, and vision. It is our way of asking for protection in a prayer to *Wakan Tanka*. We do this for special ceremonies, like naming, healing, and the preparation and return of great warriors when battle has occurred. Especially when there is a moon to see in the sky. To my people, the moon is a guardian spirit who guides, protects, and is the keeper of time, fertility, and of seasons. She is one of great transformation and insight. On cold winter nights, we call it the Wolf Moon and it signifies a time for great examination and letting go of the past and finding our way out of dark times."

"But what does all of this mean for us, Ashwiyaa?" Maybelle smiled.

"You need to learn to wait for blessing from the Great Spirit, oh Dark One," she chided Maybelle with a smile. Maybelle grinned at Vieve and Lucy, her white teeth gleaming in the shade of the dark woods. Ashwiyaa waved a hand over the bowls of paint in front of her.

"On this day, we honor and celebrate the unity of all gathered here. Each has acted to help another. All have been of noble service. Each has been of great courage. Everyone has earned the trust of the other. Together, we are stronger. We read. We sing. We honor that which makes us alike and different. We find our way through the troubles, with the moon that guides us to safety. Today, I will decorate you with war paint. We fight all evil together. We never stop fighting for good. We seek peace among all. We must promise."

"Will our faces look like yours, Ashwiyaa? Maybelle asked.

"Not like mine. No black snake on yours. The great warrior captains of my people wore them. But I give you the honor of each color.

White is peace and paradise. Black is the quiet of night; brown is of animals and death that comes to all; blue is wisdom, the sky, moon, and water; green is healing and endurance; yellow is the sun, wisdom, and the dawn; and red is the sunset, earth, war, and blood. Together, they signify great strength and life among us."

Ashwiyaa decorated the colorful faces of each with deft, angular strokes on each side of their faces. When she was done, all stood in solemn silence before her, with Vieve and Maybelle holding each of Lucy's arms. Ashwiyaa mixed the red paint with water from the Ashley River. Dipping her hand into the bowl, she gave a gentle spray to the faces of each girl.

"I cover you with the blood of all of our ancestors. May we never forget the battles they fought, the strength they showed, the good in them. May the Great Spirit guide us as sister warriors into the unknown of tomorrow, as it guided them, until that day when we each hopefully go to an honorable death after a wise and good life."

"And may we all rise in glory, as my God has promised in the Bible," Maybelle added, reaching toward the heavens with her right hand.

"Ashwiyaa, I want to ask you something. What does your name mean if it has a meaning?" Vieve asked. The Indian girl smiled, looking up at the sliver of moon that appeared between the clouds of the Southern winter afternoon.

"All of the names of my people have great meaning. 'Ashwiyaa' means "arms oneself" such as a great warrior. My father gave that name to me."

"I love your name." Vieve smiled. My whole first name is 'Genevieve.' Master Montague said that it meant, 'Of the race of women; the fair one.' My mother gave me the nickname of 'Vieve.' I'm going to give you a nickname too, because Ashwiyaa is sometimes a mouthful." Vieve smiled. "Your shortened name is 'Ash.' In our Bible, it is a reminder of our own mortality; of our life and the need to live with great meaning. It fits you. Now that I know you better."

"May we call you 'Ash'?" Lucy ventured, smiling at Ashwiyaa. "It is a good nickname for you."

"Ash," Ashwiyaa repeated. "Like the ashes from a great fire. Yes, you may call me that. I think it pleases *Wakan Tanka*. And me also. I am 'Ash.'"

"One more thing, Ashwiyaa. I heard you had a vision about me. Something about a snake-like creature attacking me. Do you know what it is?" Vieve asked.

"No. That is of the spirit world. But I know it means something. Just don't know what. One day we will know."

"It's getting late, and all will be expecting us." Vieve pushed the sleeves up on her work dress as she assisted Lucy in returning to the wagon. "At least we do not have to prepare the supper tonight, since Dumplin and Merrilee have done it for today. But we should get back before they miss us. We can wash off the paint by the river before we go."

Vieve stared once more at the painted reflection that returned her smile in the winter waters of the Ashley. How she wished her mother and Simon, and even Oliver, could see her now. She felt stronger than she had ever been perhaps in her entire life and marveled at the depth of friendship – sisterhood – that had been created through the efforts of each of these girls. Together, they had learned to read, taught one another the ways of each, laid aside the fear that had kept them apart, and forged the strongest of bonds. Even with war looming on the horizon, and the vast differences among them, Vieve felt genuine happiness on this day, though she knew that life, as they all knew it, would be challenged more than any could imagine, despite the strength of their friendship and the secrets they kept among them.

CHAPTER NINETEEN

1775

"Yes, there was a general meeting to elect a Provincial Congress during the months of last November and December." Elias Montague paused in his answer to Mal about the latest news, taking in the family seated around the table for a light repast of bread, roasted meat and vegetables on this evening. Vieve watched from her station beside the door to the preparation area as he imbibed a sizable swig of wine and wiped his mouth before continuing.

"On January 11, in Charlestown, thirteen men were elected to the Executive Council of Safety. My good friend Henry Laurens was elected as the president and Charles Pinckney as vice president. They were vested with the entire command of our military, the power to contract debts, to stamp and issue money, to liquidate and pay all accounts, and to sign all commissions for the army. The task at hand, of course, was the convincing of backcountry settlers of the need to join in overthrowing the royal government. There has not been much enthusiasm on their part for the need for independence to date.

On January 17, the Provincial Congress resolved that all inhabitants of the colony be strongly requested to train with the military of the province in the use of arms and such. The training and exercise will take place once a fortnight in various locations. It is hoped that by the end of February, every parish and district will have assembled extended regiments and companies to enlarge and strengthen our militia, although I am certain that they will be in widely varying stages of readiness for defense."

"So, war is indeed imminent then, Father?" Oliver raised questioning eyes to Elias, then made a passing glance at Vieve, who looked down at her hands folded at her waist.

"In all likelihood, yes. I see no peaceful resolution in sight, though one is always desirable. After the Intolerable, or Coercive, Acts were inflicted upon Massachusetts colonists last year for their actions in Boston, all of the colonies have reacted in indignation and outrage against the attempts by the Crown to take away the self-governance of that colony, to violate the colonial charters."

"But that is just the colony of Massachusetts, is it not?" Mal asked.

"The British had hoped that these punitive measures would create an example made of Massachusetts," Elias responded, "and reverse the growing colonial resistance to parliamentary authority. The result was quite the opposite, however, and has only increased Patriot resolve toward independence for all of the colonies. The harshness of these acts made it more difficult for moderate colonials to lend favorability toward Parliament. Thus, the colonies all sent representatives to the First Continental Congress in Philadelphia in September of last year." Elias wiped his mouth, then continued.

"It was decided that, if the Intolerable Acts were not dissolved, then all goods were to cease being exported to Great Britain. A pledge was also made to support Massachusetts in case of an attack there. Christopher Gadsden was ordered to return from the First Continental Congress to command our provincial troops in the event an attack on Charlestown was inevitable. To my mind, that has all but sealed the fate of the colonies in the likelihood of war, though I believe it will begin in Massachusetts. Rest assured, our Southern colonies and lands will feel the tremendous weight of a most destructive war."

"This guest who will be coming here with Henry Laurens in February, who is he?" Elizabeth Montague had laid aside any aversion to discussing war and now wondered aloud at its impact on them all in South Carolina.

"The man I mentioned to you once before, my dear, is Mr. Thomas Paine. I have invited him and Henry to dine with us before Mr. Paine makes his way back to Philadelphia. After the meeting in Charlestown, Henry decided that he should remain in South Carolina, instead of making the journey northward. After they depart from Montague Hall, Thomas Paine will travel back to Philadelphia to meet with Benjamin Franklin and his American Philosophical Society, and to resume his editorial duties. Henry will be instrumental in the patriotic efforts here, but with great diplomacy, as he is respected by the Crown."

"But what sort of man is this Mr. Thomas Paine? Is he from Philadelphia?"

"No. Interestingly enough, he is from Great Britain, and was brought to the colonies last year by Benjamin Franklin. He is an ardent Patriot who believes wholly in that cause. Quite an interesting man, this Mr. Paine. I am told that he favors separation of Church and State and believes that government should be based on reason, rather than faith. He has stated that he feels the only role of government in religious affairs is to insure the freedom of religion."

"He is a man of God, then?" Oliver questioned.

"No, he is the opposite as we perhaps see it. He is deist, however. That is to say that he believes in a god of some sort, but does not believe in the deity of Jesus Christ, as we do."

"Good heavens!" Elizabeth exclaimed. "How will he be received in any part of our society?"

"He is no doubt an exceptional orator and a convincing man, despite his disinclination toward the divinity of Christ. He is also a thought-provoking and passionate man who has given much thought to the Patriot cause. Indeed, he is a man of reason. His religious beliefs are not as ours. Perhaps that might change. It is said that he values intelligent conversation. Why, then, should we turn him away?"

"I would very much like to meet him," Lucy offered.

"Sister, you have been much more concerned with events other than fashion and trade, of late," Mal chided her. "Why don't you go back to your preoccupation with things more suited to your place."

"My place?" Lucy's voice raised above the clatter of her fork against her plate. "I cannot learn to be interested in the world around me because I am a girl, you mean?" She glared at Mal, then tore off a large chunk of meat to chew. Vieve tried to hide a smile, looking down at her hands.

"I meant no disrespect," he countered, an ingratiating smirk crossing his face. "Only that you have never cared much for the workings of any such besides what is important to you, such as merchandise you can buy. That has been your place."

"My place can change if I so choose," Lucy spat back at him, and risked a quick glance at Vieve. "My place is to grow and learn and be more accomplished and educated. I am doing so. What a shame if one cannot grow to be a proper citizen, regardless of being male or female, don't you think?"

"I think women should tend to womanly things and leave politics to the men, is what I think." Mal crossed his arms and looked to Elias for support. "Why should you care, you cannot vote, remember, as that is a man's duty."

"Is that very thing not what the colonists are striving for?" Lucy retorted. "To be able to have a voice. To self-govern?"

Vieve worked hard to suppress a smile. Lucy had grown so much in wisdom, stamina, and self-assurance, at least in her mental capacity, though her physical prowess was declining.

"What about the slaves, or the Indians, or the indentured?" Oliver intervened. All eyes turned toward him, especially those of Vieve and Dumplin, who stood in silence, looking anywhere but at the other Montagues, awaiting their instructions, and wondering what the response would be from the Master or Mistress.

"What about them?" Elizabeth Montague gave a stern glance to her youngest son. "Slaves are not free individuals. They have no say. Nor do the indentured, for as long as they are in servitude. They owe us for their existence here. And the Indians are but savages. They are not the same. Their task, regardless of station, is to do the bidding of those who are of higher place and have the means and power to run a plantation. We have provided for them all."

"With all due respect, who made that so, Mother, that any human is worth more than another? Is it not the desire of any man, any human being, educated or no, to be free, to live as one might choose? How would any of us feel if we were enslaved in bondage?"

"Oliver, you are weak," Mal frowned at him. "You have a God-given station, and we have an important business to run at Montague Hall. Do not get bogged down in buffoonery. All here know their place. Well, perhaps not Lucy." Mal gave his sister an evil grin.

Vieve let pained eyes wander to Oliver, who sat in quiet defiance facing his older brother. Oliver was the kindest, most generous person she had ever known. He had treated her with respect from her first day on the plantation. And now he dared to ask aloud the questions that had plagued her even when she was but a poor child of servitude in London.

"God-given station is what I have as a believer in Christ." Oliver said with slow deliberation. "That is given freely to anyone who truly believes, slave or free, is it not? And believers are told to go and make more believers as best we can, are we not so instructed? I would argue that any power over other human beings is not a God-given right at all, except for perhaps that of parent and child."

"I think that we have entertained enough discussion for one evening," Elias Montague intervened, placing his fork on a now empty plate. "The meal is done. Let us all prepare for rest and for a strenuous day, come morning. Vieve and Dumplin may clear the table now. Elizabeth, I would see you in the sitting room for a moment after all have retired for the night."

Vieve reflected on all she had just heard. She knew where she would be once her duties were done. Elias must have something important to discuss with his wife.

CHAPTER TWENTY

From her perch in the attic room, Vieve could sense the urgency in the tone of Elias Montague, even more so now in the serious silence of the night, when he was seated with Elizabeth. She could see Elias, but not his wife. She imagined the mistress, seated with an after-dinner libation, her haughty demeanor relaxed, but ever-present.

"There is something else that you are not saying, Elias. What is it?"

Elias uncrossed his legs, took another sip of brandy from his cup, and hesitated before answering his wife.

"Malachi," he said. "I think the timing is right to send Malachi to London to study, to learn parliamentary law and proceedings, while we still have the ability to send him."

"You would send him to Great Britain?" Elizabeth was incredulous. "Now? Why?"

"Yes, especially now. It may not be possible to do so later. It would be a trifecta of achievement if you will. He would be impeccably schooled, away from here for a good period of time while the ever-present possibility of war persists, as well as the likelihood of his having to fight. Oliver is more than capable of assisting here, especially now that Jude may be returning to help Big Zeb. Oliver is too young to fight, for now at least. With Mal gone, Oliver having to fight might be less likely, though every man may have to make such a decision as time goes by. Mal's presence in London might also give us an added layer of protection from the Crown, in the event of eventual war. Lastly, he would be more prepared for a suitable occupation, whether in Charlestown, here, or elsewhere, with alliances of his own. He can certainly sow his oats in London, as well. He would be a man in every way upon returning.

"How long would he be gone, Elias?" Elizabeth sounded worried for her oldest son.

"Perhaps as little as a year or two, or as long as three or so, depending on events here. He could also spend time apprenticing in Charlestown, where you could more readily visit with him, were things to work out for us."

Vieve could not see the face of her mistress but could hear the relief in her voice and feel the palpable thoughts that must be racing through her head. She had begged for Jonsie to be gone, and Elias Montague had acquiesced to that demand. In return, he had skillfully considered an option that would benefit all at Montague Hall, even Mal, while preventing more harm being done by his son. Vieve wondered whether Elias was truly displeased with Mal's behavior, or whether such was so accepted that he was merely attempting to look for business solutions befitting a wise plantation master.

"How soon would Mal be leaving us?" Elizabeth ventured.

"As soon as is reasonably possible I can make the arrangements. I could accompany him to Charlestown right after our guests leave."

"That soon?"

"Yes. If we are not too late as it is."

"Have you spoken with him yet?"

"No. I felt it important for us to be united in that decision. Are we?"

Vieve listened for the response from Elizabeth Montague that was not immediate in its deliverance.

"Yes," she offered after the notable hesitation. "Yes, of course. You have granted my request, for which I'm grateful, and you are taking care in protecting our son. How could I not agree with that decision, as difficult as it will be to see him leave us for such an extended period of time."

Vieve felt her entire body breathe in a mighty sigh of thankful resolve. Her worst fear, other than war itself, might be gone. Her fingers stroked the opening of the firing hole, the rough edges felt cool to the touch. A light sweat had crossed her forehead.

"You are aware that Henry Laurens returned in November from time in Great Britain. Quite an accomplished man, Henry Laurens is. He has notable British contacts, has educated his many children there—some are there still—and will make efforts on behalf of Mal for us. Though he now gives quiet support for the American position, as he recognizes the obvious British aggression, he is still trying to retain diplomacy and peaceful negotiations with the Crown. A precarious position for him. He also privately abhors slavery, has discussed the possibility of manumission of his own slaves, who I understand are quite fond of him. Yet, he continues to run several plantations, and created great wealth as a partner in Austin and Laurens, the largest slave-trading house in North America. With his political passion, and that of Thomas Paine, and our sons, I look forward to a most entertaining and informative evening when these two important men join us on their way to Philadelphia." Elias's voice had taken on a more jovial undertone.

"Also, my dear, would you assist Lucy, and also the servants with a more becoming choice of garb for the evening, and in overseeing the preparation of a sumptuous meal for the afternoon?"

"Certainly, Elias. I will also see that we have an appropriate amount of wine or shandy and perhaps a mincemeat pie in addition to a variety of meat and fish, if Big Zeb can catch some. Perhaps Lucy, with some help, can procure the greenery and foliage needed for the dining room, and help arrange it all with the candles. I will see it done as you wish."

"The discussion will be most lively, I feel sure." Vieve could hear the smile in the voice of Elias. "With the Provincial Congress meeting done in Charlestown, there will be much news, as it is. With the political and religious leanings—or lack thereof in one area—of Mr. Paine, along with the inclinations of Henry Laurens, it will be a most invigorating evening."

Vieve plugged the firing hole and made her way to latch the window before she snuggled onto the pallet on the floor. Tonight, her prayers would include thanksgiving for Mal's upcoming departure, the arrival of Jude, the safety of Jonsie in her new place, and the strength of the loving and loyal friendships with which she had been blessed. She looked into the dark sky for any sign of the moon. It was not visible among the dark clouds that hung thick in their Southern sky. But Vieve had faith that it was there, just the same.

CHAPTER TWENTY-ONE

Early February 1775

All of Montague Hall seemed to breathe in energetic bursts of activity on this day with the prospect of the important guests who would arrive in due time. Vieve could smell the heady warmth of the venison and duck being prepared with such care that she could almost taste the smoky meats that had been seasoned with rosemary, thyme, and sage, with the addition of peppers and salt. Though fewer vegetables were available during the brief winter season, Dumplin and others had prepared ample servings of cabbage, collard greens and kale, and made a large mincemeat pie. Evaline and Maybelle had overseen the baking of fresh bread and the pressing and fermenting of apple cider. Vieve knew that there would be rum, as well as a bottle of brandy that had been procured specifically for Mr. Thomas Paine, who she had heard had immense enjoyment of that spirit.

"There you are," Lucy smiled at Vieve from her bed, after one of the naps that she took with more frequency of late. "I have a dress for you if it fits. Mother has also seen to it that the house Negroes are more appropriately dressed today. And what do you think about you and I wearing our hair alike?"

"I can braid our hair the same, of course, if you wish. Everyone is talking about the visitors coming today. It feels like it did at Christmas time, with all of the meal preparations and excitement, even with all the talk of war everywhere." Vieve assisted Lucy in moving to the bench beside her vanity and began brushing her hair. "Even the slaves get a little time to themselves, since your father has seen to it that they will be finished with their field duties earlier than usual today. Oliver says that the preparations for the rice planting are going well, as are the preparations for indigo planting in March. All of the work at Montague Hall seems to be centered around our guests for now."

"Yes, it's going to be an important evening for sure." Lucy reached for the hand of her friend. "Vieve, I know you are aware of the plans for Malachi to go to London. Mal is my brother, and I love him. But I know he can be brutish sometimes, even cruel.

I hope that while he is gone, things will be better for everyone, and that, when he returns, he will have a change of heart, of sorts. Perhaps a kindlier manner about him. Please tell me that you don't hate him. I know that Maybelle and Ash are not fond of him at all."

Vieve hesitated before responding, once again brushing Lucy's hair with slow, gentle strokes. She knew she could be honest in her response, but also understood that Mal was family to Lucy.

"I don't hate your brother. Truly, I do not. But he is not my friend. Not like you and Oliver. I think he very much sees himself as a plantation master and he is trying to live up to that, and to please your mother and especially your father. It is natural to want to please one's family. Anything he does has nothing to do with how I feel about you as my friend. I would never hold you or Oliver responsible for what Mal chooses to do." She smiled at Lucy. "I will say that, yes, I am happy he is going away for some extended time. I hope, too, that when he returns, he has a more benevolent heart."

"I'm glad, Vieve, that you are going to be in the dining room this afternoon when our guests are here. I know you won't be participating in the discussion, but I will feel reassured that you are there and listening to much of it."

"Lucy," Vieve smiled, "I should thank you for being such a good friend to me. I know we did not start out that way. I was not fond of you at all. I didn't think I could ever be your friend, much less trust you." Vieve held Lucy's hand. "But you have shown such incredible strength and wisdom. Because of your change of heart, the four of us have become close friends now. I wish I could change many things. But not this. I love you and Ash and Maybelle so much, as if you were my sisters. I only had little Simon, you know, and my mother. You all have become my family, in a way. Oliver, as well."

"You think I'm strong and wise?" Now Lucy smiled, tears appearing in the corners of her eyes. "That's even better than just being a pretty girl who might be a plantation mistress one day, or perhaps married to a Charlestown lawyer. Especially now that I'm not so strong of limb these days. You know, I wish I could change some things, too." Lucy gave a sudden frown, pulling her hand away from Vieve's. "I feel guilty that I cannot change much, other than my own heart or mind, though. I think about it often, how it would be if there were more feelings of goodwill between all. I feel more powerful with that change of heart, truly, but I know that I am not."

"But you are!"Vieve exclaimed. "Lucy, you are more powerful and strong! Because of your courage, you have changed. We have all changed, because you saw us as friends, because you so wanted friends. Of course, we're the only ones around," Vieve smiled.

"That day in the woods, by the river, remember?" Lucy grinned. "That day has been the best in my life. No Charlestown society party could ever be as much fun as that. I never felt so alive. How could I ignore such? People change only when they are not afraid to look deeply into their hearts and ask the important questions. And then answer them in honesty. And you know what, else Vieve?"

"What is that?"

"God answered those questions for me. He whispered them to my heart. And now, I have no choice but to live for that as best I can."

Vieve held onto her friend, embracing Lucy in a burst of emotion. How she wished her mother could see her now. Claire Whittier would be so proud.

"Enough now," she wiped her eyes. "We need to get us both dressed and ready for what promises to be an evening filled with possibilities!"

CHAPTER TWENTY-TWO

From her place against the dining room wall for the meal held later in the day than usual, Vieve smoothed the soft pale green dress given to her by Lucy and brushed a lock of hair away from her face. Thomas Paine was, as promised, a most fascinating man. He was rather handsome with his head of dark wavy hair cropped beneath his ears. She surmised him to be in his thirties, a self-educated man, and his personality was both genteel and lively. He was of average height and sturdy build, with dark, piercing, and brilliant eyes, an aquiline nose, and a ruddy complexion, perhaps the result of the abundant enjoyment of the spirits. It had already been established that he was fond of music, singing, and was an expert horseman, though he espoused to be a lover of long walks. The initial banter around the table thus far had centered on the discussion of plantation business and life in general, with normal relevant pleasantries. Vieve caught a glimpse of Oliver smiling at her. Mal, too, was more jovial. He chatted amiably with all and smiled at her improved change of appearance. *I am not invisible tonight.*

"You are from Great Britain, Mr. Paine," Mal ventured, "is that correct? We have an indentured servant from London." He nodded his head toward Vieve, who blushed under the scrutinizing gazes. *Definitely not invisible.* "Her name is 'Vieve.' She was brought here after a series of unfortunate events. Your accents are similar." Mal's lazy smirk reflected his pleasure at the discomfort he had caused.

"And we are fortunate to have her," Lucy retorted, smiling, then directing a disapproving glance to her brother. Thomas Paine remained quiet while studying the young girl who held her place against the wall alongside Dumplin.

"Vieve. That is an unusual but lovely name. Perhaps a shorter nomenclature for 'Genevieve'?" He gave a genuine smile, which she returned, nodding her head.

"You may speak, Vieve." Elias Montague smiled also.

"Yes. My mother gave the name to me."

"She has no other family. We took her in." Mal added, the intent of his statement designed to both shock and elevate the benevolence of the master family at Montague Hall had the desired effect. Thomas Paine studied her once more, then raised his glass.

"Then, welcome to the colonies, Miss Vieve. Despite your meager beginnings, may you and all gathered here be blessed with opportunity and achievement, as befitting of a country so poised to lead the way to unprecedented freedom among the nations."

Lucy and Oliver raised their glasses of rum and apple cider, smiling at Vieve. Thomas Paine had disrupted Mal's intent to belittle. Henry Laurens, ever the statesman and diplomat, raised his glass as well.

"To the Patriot cause, then. May it flourish and grow, as well as a peaceful resolution to the conflict we now face. Thomas, I believe Elias has that brandy close at hand now."

Elias motioned for Dumplin to pour the post-meal libation, while Vieve began removing plates and utensils from the table. He turned to Henry Laurens, who was seated on his right, opposite Thomas Paine, who was seated on his left side.

"Henry, you are no doubt pleased with the results of the latest efforts in Charlestown, I feel certain." Elias took a hardy sip of the proffered brandy.

"Indeed I am. While I am still hopeful of a peaceful solution, however slim that hope might be, I am pleased with the resolutions of this committee. It is imperative that we have a strong militia prepared for whatever harm might manifest itself."

"And what of the general feeling of our backcountry brethren, then?" Elias turned toward Thomas Paine. "Were they so moved by your pleas for reason amid the tyranny of Great Britain, seeing as how you, yourself, are from the motherland?"

"I am honored that you give me credit, Sir. However, I must say that there were many learned men present, and all had a voice in bringing about direction for this and all of the colonies, with regard to any loyalty to the Crown or no. The notion of self-governance by the people, with God-given rights, has grown stronger due to the recent actions of the King in his attempts to quell such." Thomas Paine looked around the table. "No one should be happy about the possibility of battle – of what might be a long and difficult war. But these colonies here sit at the brink of true greatness. Nowhere in history has the right to create such a magnificent country been pursued in a manner that would give humanity a whole new direction. A very risky endeavor which will require unwavering dedication and loyalty to the concept of real freedom and responsibility."

"Mr. Paine, if I may – how did you come to believe in our Patriot cause?" Oliver crossed his arms, resting his elbows on the table.

"Young Oliver, is it?" Thomas Paine delighted in the question posed to him. "It is quite clear that British rule has created almost all – if not all – of the problems in the colonies. Great Britain, a mere island, is now ruling a continent. There is no representation in Parliament for colonists being so taxed. It is past time for colonial independence, as the colonies are no longer in the stage of infancy. I do not believe that such will occur unless there is greatly unified action of some sort. No one wants war. But real freedom bears a heavy price in the wake of blatant tyranny. The Crown is acting only in the interests of Great Britain, with no sign of concern for the people here."

"But how are we any different from other colonies or countries?" Oliver asked.

"Each colony or state now has its own constitution, but all are quite different in a variety of ways. The only way to face this down and ward off any potential threat to freedom is to band together to form a union the likes of which has never before been imagined or conceived."

"Other countries have faced tyranny, is that not so?" Lucy asked, "and they have sought peace and freedom?"

"Very much so, young lady. However, none have embraced fully the notions of such unprecedented freedoms that are being discussed in these colonies. Liberty for all, egalitarianism—that is, the rights of the individual to be treated the same under the law, regardless of social stature and circumstances, the ability to express and even print ideas freely, and to worship as one pleases without government interference or sanction, are all the talk now. The idea of republican democracy—that is, a government by the people that is rooted in elections rather than being ruled by a monarchy, has become the central focus. In Philadelphia there is much talk of developing a system of judicial law that will allow for the means of keeping these concepts in balance and therefore the potential nation free from the type of tyranny the colonies are under now."

Thomas Paine grew more animated as he spoke, the libations of the late afternoon meal also taking effect on his delivery. Vieve watched the faces of those seated at the table. Even Elizabeth Montague and Mal were enraptured by his charisma; the fervor about what could lie ahead in such a possible nation as he described. He made the likelihood of war seem less horrific and more necessary with each spoken word.

"Dumplin, you may take the leftover mincemeat pie to share downstairs now."

"Yes, Mistress, we sho' thanks you . Anything you be needin' before I go?"

Elizabeth Montague shook her head, motioning the older woman toward the cellar to join the remainder of the house slaves. She had sounded almost contrite until she spoke again. "Vieve, you will assist Lucy to her chamber now."

"But I wish very much to remain here, please," Lucy pleaded, "to talk about this more."

"Lucy, your mother is right. You need your rest and Vieve will assist you in getting ready." Elias raised his eyes to those of his daughter. "Goodnight, my love."

Vieve gave Lucy her arm. Lucy frowned, her expression just short of a full-blown pout, as they made their way to the staircase.

"Stop," she breathed, when they reached the top of the stairs, grasping both of Vieve's arms. "I want to hear what they are saying. I must hear it! They can blame me if anyone catches us."

"Then let us both be as quiet as we can be, for your mother will surely be unhappy if she finds us. I think we can hear them if we are careful. But we must stay here at the top so that we can reach your bedchamber if the need arises. I have a feeling this could be a most engaging discussion."

From the room below, the words and voices drifted up the staircase.

"Now I must ask you, Sir." Elias Montague placed both hands on the table, facing Thomas Paine. "Before one of my sons is so inclined to ask this question, I wish to inquire. You have likely already been made aware of the utmost importance of slavery in the Southern colonies. Our land is not plentiful with cities such as those found in the North. Our very livelihood depends on the production of what can be grown, produced, and sold for profit. And that is not possible to achieve without the institution of slavery."

No sound was heard, no movement. Vieve felt light beads of sweat on her forehead as she strained to listen. Elias reached for the bottle of brandy to refill his cup before continuing to address Thomas Paine.

"I am told that you abhor this so-called peculiar institution, although you have written very little about it. It is said that you would have all slaves freed if it were in your purview to do so. Is that your opinion on the matter?"

Thomas Paine leaned back in his chair, savoring the remains of brandy, and waiting to respond until Elias Montague had also refilled Mal's cup.

"I am grateful for the hospitality shown to me by all of the Montague family, and of course by Henry, who also has slaves, though he has attested to the abhorrence of such. Indeed, I also do not openly rail against the institution, though I have expressed my thoughts at times. It is a most delicate and complicated thing here in the South. Many slaves are brutally treated. Many are treated with a degree of dignity. And yet, should any man be owned by another? I appeal to your reason and your intellect." Thomas Paine folded his fingers together on the table in front of him before continuing.

"You are a most gracious people in all of these Southern colonies. Southern plantation masters have accomplished much success in the endeavors to create thriving businesses to supply the needs of many. In that regard, I admire you and each one of the Southern colonies. And while I wish to see all continue to thrive, and I believe that the South can indeed flourish, I am not a proponent of the institution of slavery."

"You speak in contradictions, Sir." Mal's eyes narrowed, the ever-present smirk on his face revealed the disagreement he no longer tried to hide. Thomas Paine was not deterred.

"I believe that all human beings—all of us!—deserve to live as free men. Throughout history, many civilizations, many religions, nationalities, the White man, the Negro, even the Indians in this land, and yes, my own Great Britain, have all fought others, enslaved others, and been enslaved, also. Throughout history, such is true. To what avail? Slavery has never ended in peaceful, mutually beneficial, rewards or resolutions, but has always pitted one against the other, with fear and resentment being the distasteful fruits of such. I believe – and have stated more than once – that the world is my country, all mankind are my brethren, and to do good is my religion."

"But you are not a Christian, so we have heard?" Elizabeth Montague was more than happy to interject herself into the discussion. "You do not believe in God? How can you profess any religion, then? And my husband says that you have given mention of what the Bible says in your oratory. It seems a contradiction, as well." Vieve could feel the dagger hidden in Elizabeth Montague's triumphant smile. The Mistress of Montague Hall reveled in the attempt to reinforce the position of power in the Montague family.

"Ah, but I do believe in a god. A very benevolent and powerful god. But I do not believe that God Almighty is Jesus Christ. There are indeed those who profess to calling themselves Christians who have desecrated the Bible by removing the parts contained therein that would appear to promote freedom. All in an attempt to keep the Negro both complacent and compliant."

Vieve stared at Lucy, whose fingers tightened around her arms. Could it be true that parts of the Bible allowed for use by the slaves had been removed? Did Lucy or Oliver know? Or had Elias and Elizabeth managed to keep that atrocity from them also? The expressions on Lucy's face told her that she had been oblivious to that knowledge until now.

"There are many instances of slavery in the Bible," Elias retorted.

"There are many instances of good, evil, polygamy, contradictory statements and more in the Bible," Thomas Paine responded in kind. "Turn the other cheek, or an eye for an eye? Your Bible is confusing at times, is it not? Simply because there is an account of something in the Bible does not mean that it is specifically condoned by God. In fact, that may not be God's intent at all, even if your Bible is authentic in every word. The Bible also says to forgive, to love one another. There are many excellent ideas contained within. However, upon my studious efforts, it is not my belief that Christ is God." Thomas Paine paused, hearing Elizabeth's sharp intake of breath.

"I make no apology for my beliefs. I also do not fault anyone for believing such if they so choose. Christian beliefs are ideals adhered to by many who value independence, so I do not turn them away in the quest for what is right. Slavery, in my humble opinion, should cease to exist in a land of true freedom. With all due respect, I believe that a successful endeavor such as Montague Hall can be maintained by means other than one man owning another."

"With all due respect, Mr. Paine, that is not for you to decide for us. You speak of independence, of a democratic republic, of government by the people. While I share your thought that slavery is indeed a complicated issue at times, it has been everywhere in these colonies. In every colony. Nowhere more than in our Southern colonies. Perhaps you should keep your focus on independence from your homeland and leave Southern welfare and decisions to those who must provide and make do here." Elias Montague was firm in the reproachment of his guest.

Thomas Paine uncrossed his fingers, tapping them in a gentle rhythm on the table.

"I fear I have deeply offended my gracious hosts, which was not my intent. Forgive me. I sincerely beg your pardon. It is only my intent to support your Patriot cause. Please excuse my absence while I visit your privies."

In the quiet of the stairwell, Lucy leaned close to whisper. Her body trembled as she gripped Vieve's shoulders. Vieve could feel the dampness of her tears.

"Go to him! Go talk with him. Find out more! I will get to my room."

"Lucy, what are you saying? Talk with him about what?"

But Lucy had already placed her hands against the wall, making her own way to bed.

CHAPTER TWENTY-THREE

Maybelle made her way through the now still courtyard, carrying an extra blanket and leftover bread to Ashwiyaa in the barn area. This night would prove to bring more of a chill than was usual along the Ashley River this time of year.

"Vieve! Why are you out here?" Maybelle hugged the blanket close.

"Have you seen him? The guest who came out here. He was headed to the privies. Lucy has this wild idea that I must speak with Mr. Thomas Paine."

"You must talk with me? How very amusing. And why is that, Miss Genevieve?"

Thomas Paine appeared from behind the privies, struggling to fasten his pants and straighten to his full height. The brandy had imparted a mild diminishment to his capacity.

"He know yo' name!" Maybelle said, reverting to the dialect she used when unknown White people were present. Vieve frowned at her before facing their guest.

"Yes, I have met Miss Genevieve, the lass from my homeland. Though I believe you are called 'Vieve' isn't that so?" Thomas Paine made a deep bow, brushing disheveled hair out of his eyes, now somewhat glazed with the help of the liquors. "Let me apologize also to you lovely ladies. Perhaps I have imbibed a bit more than I should. My views were not all well-received, it seems. And what must you speak with me about, Miss Vieve?"

Vieve made a quick perusal of the courtyard area. Ashwiyaa had emerged upon hearing the voices.

"An Indian?" Thomas Paine stared at the young girl standing proud as the bravest of men. "What manner of dream is this? Who are you?"

Vieve smiled, suppressing laughter at the mumbled words of the most distinguished guest.

"This is Ashwiyaa. We call her 'Ash' as I am called "Vieve.' She was traded by the Cherokee to Master Montague. We have become good friends, Mr. Paine. Almost like sisters. Ash has taught us all how to use a bow and arrow and even a bit about the land around us.

"And you?" Thomas Paine faced Maybelle. "Are you a friend as well? What is your name?"

"I's Maybelle, Sir," Maybelle replied, glancing sideways at Vieve.

"Tell him, Maybelle. The way you talk with us. Tell him. He will not betray you."

Maybelle stared at Vieve, then Ash, unable to face the White man she did not know.

"Mr. Paine, Mistress Lucy, who is also our friend, sent me to find you, but I am not at all sure why." Vieve faced Maybelle once more. "Tell him, Maybelle!"

"Tell me what?" Thomas Paine was amused at the young girls before him.

"Mr. Paine, my name is Maybelle," the Negro slave girl began in a whisper. "I was born here, born into slavery for life. I can speak as you, but I dare not in front of those I cannot trust. I learned to speak this way by listening to Master and Mistress Montague and their family, or when they had guests. Listening has been most of my schooling."

Thomas Paine once again made a low, exaggerated bow, observing the diminutive slave before him.

"I am pleased to make your acquaintance, Miss Maybelle. Listening well would help us all, I dare say. I am delighted to meet you as well, Miss Ashwiyaa. Miss Ash."

"He called us "Miss," Maybelle grinned, her white teeth gleaming even more against the ebony skin.

"Mr. Paine, we heard all that was said before you left for the privy, Lucy and I. We were standing at the top of the stairs. She sent me to talk with you. I'm not sure what about. It seems that those here at Montague Hall are divided about many things. Lucy and Oliver are our friends. They have the unpleasant task of disagreeing with their parents about all of us." Vieve gestured toward her friends. "You appear to believe as we do, at least about enslaving people, even though you do not share the belief in Jesus Christ."

"May I ask why you do not believe that Jesus Christ is God, that He is divine?" Maybelle asked. "I believe that He is God. But I am most interested to hear why you think as you do."

"Well said, Miss Maybelle. I appreciate the respect with which you ask. Yes, I find that the Bible has confusing, and I believe erroneous, stories. It was written by men. Man's reason – his intellect – should be above all. I believe that the true God is all powerful, the wisest. The Old Testament is filled with horrific stories of murder, brutality, debauchery, and revenge. It could not possibly be the word of a loving god of any kind. Jesus may have been a good man, perhaps. But not God."

Vieve let her eyes wander to Maybelle, who loved to speak about Jesus, even as a person who had been enslaved all of her life. She wished Lucy were present to hear it all.

"Mr. Paine, I know you are very smart. Vieve told me what you think. I believe that Jesus is truly God, but I do not have all the answers. My mother says that He gave us all knowledge and that we are free to choose to believe or no. That is a real gift." She smiled at Thomas Paine. "I believe that the whole Bible tells the story, not only about God, but about all of mankind. About our evil ways, our good ways, and our choice to believe or no. Most of all, God has come to us – in a way everybody can understand, and He has given us a way to do and be better, to have life forever, even when we fall and fall again. And that is the most loving God I know. If Jesus is not who He says He is, then He could not even be a good man, do you think?"

Thomas Paine stared at the young Negro girl, a slave in appearance, but in spirit and in soul, she was something much more.

"What would you be if you were not a slave?" He waited for the girl's answer.

Maybelle looked at the ground, then back at Thomas Paine. Tears rose in her ebony eyes.

"A teacher. I would be a teacher of all children. I would teach them to think for themselves. To ask questions just like you do, and to listen. And to understand the cost of freedom, also as you do."

"Miss Maybelle," He spoke in a slow, almost reverent, tone of voice. "I sincerely hope that one day, your dream will be realized. I believe that these colonies have the potential to be the greatest example of freedom – real freedom – in the world. But – not unlike childbirth – that process may be slow, painful, difficult. And not without great sacrifice. I don't know how long that will take. You and I may not ever see it. None of us. Many people – of all kinds – have and will die in the process. But one day – the joy – oh, the joy! – will come. I believe that. The good will rise. The good must win."

"But this fight is not for my people, is it? Or Ash's people?" Maybelle asked.

"In truth – though hard to see for now – yes, it is about all of mankind. History can give testimony that all peoples have fought against others, with each other, enslaved and been slaves. Although the White man here is largely responsible for enslaving others, no race or religion, or peoples can claim innocence here. Before the times we live in now, many thousands and more of White European Christians were enslaved in Great Britain and shipped here or enslaved by Muslims of the Barbary Coast. Brothels were raided in hopes of providing breeders for the colonies above us. Even now our men on the seas are also captured and enslaved. Before Negro slaves began to be so utilized here, indentured servants, such as Vieve, here, were the primary slaves and could be sold and traded as Negroes are now. Young street urchins were grabbed off the streets as well."

"But what about the Negro people here now?" Vieve asked. "They are not involved in this fight for this country, I don't think. But I've heard that the British will offer them freedom if they fight for them."

"It is true, Miss Vieve, that the Negro in these Southern colonies are more enslaved than in the Northern colonies, but they do exist there, just as some free Negro men and slaveowners exist here. And Negroes have indeed fought for the Independence of these colonies. I heard tell of a Mr. Crispus Attucks in Boston in 1770, when the Redcoats were sent there to put down the protests of the Patriots there. A man of both Negro and Indian descent who was born a slave in Massachusetts but escaped. He became a leader in Boston and was killed when British soldiers fired two musket balls into his chest. He was one of five men killed that day in Boston. A most brave man who fought for freedom. His death was the very first in this fight for independence. A most honorable man, Mr. Attucks was. I imagine that eventually the Negroes, the Indians, too, will be divided as to their allegiances in this war. But I am convinced that one day, freedom will be for us all."

Vieve looked at the faces of all. Even Ash, who was the most stoic and strong, regarded Thomas Paine with a measure of unspoken admiration.

"I believe that could be so, too." Maybelle smiled. "That is what faith is about. We disagree, Mr. Paine, about some things, but not everything. But I believe with all my heart that Jesus – God Almighty – will work for the good for all who truly believe. If you do not mind, I will keep you in my prayers. And I will pray so hard for the freedom of all."

Thomas Paine smiled at the young Negro slave.

"Miss Maybelle, if anyone could convince me, teach me, or make me believe in your Jesus, I do believe it would be you. I must go now, before my gracious host becomes offended at my lengthy absence." Thomas Paine gave an embarrassed smile. "I do believe I have shaken off the worst of the brandy. Keep us in your fervent prayers for peace, then, if you wish, Miss Maybelle. Tonight, and beyond. I bid you all a good night. And a most happy future."

On her way to the slave stairwell, Vieve stopped to listen as best she could to the ongoing talk. The discussion in the dining hall had become more amiable, with talk of Mal going to Great Britain, of which Thomas Paine had much knowledge. Lucy had been right in her insistence that she talk further with the charismatic guest. Although she was not sure that any problem had been solved, she knew one thing for sure. Opening the window in her sparse room, Vieve gazed up into the now dark winter sky at the sliver of pale moon. Mal would leave soon. Thomas Paine had ignited the passions and dreams of the Patriot cause in all of them. Closing her eyes, she felt the soft tears trickle down. Hope had been restored amidst the threat of looming war.

CHAPTER TWENTY-FOUR

Christmas Day 1776

The feast had been magnificent, with sumptuous fowl, fish, wine, and pie. Montague Hall appeared festive, for now, with much merriment. The scent of fresh greenery and cinnamon permeated the great hall. Slaves had been granted the day to celebrate with their own, share a roasted pig, and engage in rollicking games and relays. Vieve smiled, thinking of what it might be like to have such a day when so many were filled with back-breaking woe. Elias Montague had provided new clothing, shoes, and rum to insure as much enjoyment and compliance as possible. He and Elizabeth had also gathered the slaves and read the Biblical story of the birth of Christ to them. Vieve had been required to both attend to, and celebrate with, the Montagues, joining in their singing and partaking of their leftover feast when they were done.

Now she stared at her reflection in the small wall-mounted mirror in Lucy's room. A budding young woman, almost thirteen, returned her gaze. Lucy had gifted her with one of her dresses, beige with soft lace that trimmed the neckline, the likes of which Vieve had never owned before. During the feasting, she had felt the perusal of all, especially Oliver, now almost fifteen, a young man in his own right, who had paid her tender regard whenever she filled his cup or brought him bread. How loving his eyes had been when she sang carols with Lucy, who now smiled at Vieve from beneath the covers of her bedding.

"Father has agreed to my request to allow Oliver to help you deliver a basket of goods from me and him to Maybelle and her family, and to Ash as well, now that the day is done. He will wait for you in the courtyard with the basket that I helped him prepare. He said to wait until all had settled, as Mother was not so willing to allow it. It is odd, is it not, that a woman can hold such feelings of ill-will, instead of nurturing, toward others. But then, again," she gave a sad smile to Vieve, "I, too, once felt such sentiment."

Vieve paused before responding. What was even more troublesome, to her own mind, was how a family with so much, with wealth and power, could harbor such feelings of fear, unhappiness, and regret. The Montagues were fractured from one another, though they each cared for one another. Lucy and Oliver, were more vocal in the choice to cast their lot on the side of freedom for all. Elias, though kinder and more diplomatic, remained staunch in the position of mastership, as did Elizabeth and Mal, who was still in Great Britain, doing well at the latest news they had been given.

"Lucy, you made your choice, you made your stand. You and Oliver both have chosen the more admirable way. Perhaps Mr. Thomas Paine was right, not only about the birth of a truly free country, but about truly courageous and strong people, all of which takes much painstaking time to build. You know that you and Oliver have chosen to live those qualities, at great risk to yourselves. You could have stayed safe in the same views as many plantation masters, but you did not. And the issues are many and complicated, and they run very deep, I know." Vieve patted her hand. "But you need to know how thankful I am – always – that you are my good friend. In all honesty, you, Oliver, Maybelle, and Ash, have become my family. My much-loved and dear family."

Lucy squeezed Vieve's hand, smiling and handing her own woolen shawl to the indentured servant girl.

"Take this and go now. Oliver will be waiting. Give them all my regards. I would go myself, but these legs just will not allow that to happen. I fear I am getting worse."

"Get some rest. It has been a long but good day." Vieve stood, wrapping the shawl around her shoulders, and tucking her friend into the added thick blanket before blowing out the bedside candle and closing Lucy's door.

Oliver was waiting for her in the courtyard, his tricorn hat pulled down on his head. The large basket, covered with a cloth, was filled with knitted scarves, warm bread, candles, and small wrought iron bars that had been layered in powdered charcoal and heated, no doubt by Big Zeb and Oliver, to produce the tools used with flint to build fires.

"There you are. I was beginning to wonder if my sister had forgotten to tell you." Oliver smiled as she lifted a corner of the cloth that covered the Christmas gifts.

"Oliver, they will love these. How thoughtful of you and Lucy both. The blocks for fire must have taken some time to craft." Vieve walked beside him, helping to carry the basket.

"Yes, they did," he smiled back. "I hope they will be helpful."

"What have you heard from Mal, of late?" Vieve ventured.

"He is well, at last report from both letters and Henry Lauren's acquaintances. Why do you ask? Are you not glad he is gone?" Oliver stopped walking.

"Of course," Vieve whispered. "Yes, you know I am glad. I do wish him well, and I hope he will learn in many ways and return to Montague Hall as a more benevolent man. I wish those things because he is your brother and because he will be more in charge upon his return."

"Vieve." Oliver was firm in addressing her now. "You have no reason to fear my brother. I will always protect you. I promise. I, too, hope he returns to Montague Hall as a man of good character. I'm glad that both of my parents saw fit to send him abroad. Of course, his return will depend on all that is going on now, as war is indeed approaching this lowcountry."

"What is happening, Oliver? With regard to war?"

"You know that back in June, Washington appointed Colonel William Moultrie to thwart land and sea attacks on Sullivan's Island, though General Charles Lee wanted to abandon the fort. Charlestown is the fourth largest port in the colonies, so it is important to us and also to the British. The Patriot forces were able to prevent British ships from entering our waters. All of the training for our militia was quite successful. Patriot support has finally increased, and further battle was put down. Who knows for how long that will be, though. For now, the British have retreated back to New York and South Carolina is safe. But that is only temporary. They will try again."

"Why is that? Are you sure?"

"On July 4, the Continental Congress officially adopted a Declaration of Independence, making all of the colonies now The United States of America." Oliver grinned. "You know that your Mr. Thomas Paine's writings, entitled, *"Common Sense"* made a critical difference in this fight for freedom from the tyranny of the Crown. He was right, Vieve. At least about that."

Vieve saw the candlelight coming from Maybelle's small cabin. She was happy to be able to see them all again on Christmas Day. She had made small, scented sachets of lavender and mint as gifts for Lucy, Maybelle, and Ash, and a dried clay pot for Oliver, which Ashwiyaa had taught her how to do, much as her Catawba people did. Upon entering the meager abode, she was even more elated to see Ash and Big Zeb sharing in the cheer of the sacred day. Oliver bent low to whisper in her ear.

"I have a surprise momentarily for you. It is a gift for Maybelle. But mostly, for you. I hope you will like it." He smiled at Vieve as the door to the cabin creaked open.

"Master Oliver! Vieve!" Evaline rose from the rustic table where all were gathered around, the flames of their fire adding needed light and warmth.

"Evaline, I know who and what I am to you. To all of you. But on this night, again, I ask you. Please call me 'Oliver' when not in the presence of my parents."

"You know that hard fo' us all to do," Evaline responded, as Jude came to stand beside her. "You is the master's son."

"I am that." Oliver winced, then smiled. "I cannot, or will not, force you to do so. Call me what you wish. But tonight, please call me 'Friend.'"

"Come and sit, come sit, please. What brings you here?" Jude wrapped an arm around Evaline and the other around Maybelle. We can offer you some rum that your father gave us. Oliver held up a hand, shaking his head, and remained standing.

"Thank you, no. We wanted to be sure you know, my sister and me, that you are dear people to us. Please forgive the scantest of manner, I know, for returning all that you do for us every day here, though not by your own choosing. I wish I could give you that choice. I cannot. But please accept this very small token from me and Lucy." Oliver set the basket on the table. "Maybelle, perhaps you would do the honors of handing out the contents now. Vieve and I cannot stay here long."

Maybelle came forward, gesturing to Vieve to help her. Vieve grasped her hand and that of Ash, nodding her head and smiling at Oliver as the contents were doled out to the appreciative gathering.

"What is this?" Maybelle's eyes widened in surprise. She lifted the last item, a black Bible, soiled with dried bits of mud and dirt, out of the basket, and opened the cover. "This is yours." She looked at Oliver. "This is your Bible."

"And now it is yours, Maybelle. I know that you and Ashwiyaa have been taught to read. It is my hope that you read the contents with those you choose, with particular attention to the pages with folded corners. And that, one day, the truth of God may be known to all of mankind."

Vieve had never seen Maybelle so overcome with emotion, not even when she had first seen Jude at Drayton Hall. Her hands trembled. She thumbed through the pages, finally resting on one of the pages Oliver had referenced. Tears clouded her eyes as she read aloud, wiping her eyes as she read:

"Exodus 21:16. 'And he that stealeth a man, and selleth him, or if he be found in his hand, he shall surely be put to death.'

Evaline made an audible gasp, clinging to Jude and wiping tears from her cheek, and whispering aloud.

"Ephesians 6:5. 'Servants, be obedient to them that are your masters, according to the flesh, with fear and trembling, with singleness of your heart, as unto Christ.' The Bible does have some conflicting words, too, like Mr. Paine said?" She turned inquisitive eyes to Oliver.

"It does. Yes, that is true. And there were slaves in the time of Christ as well, I know. Mr. Paine has said that all peoples, throughout time, have enslaved one another at some point. Man's inhumanity to man, I suppose. But I, myself, believe the words 'according to the flesh' mean that slavery is not of God, but of mankind. I do not claim to fully understand. But I believe that God takes us all where we are and changes us by means of Jesus Christ, whom we are all to serve with joy." Oliver looked at Maybelle while motioning for Vieve to prepare to follow him outside.

"Maybelle, I need you to remember that I lost my treasured Bible near the Ashley River, should anyone ever discover that it is in your possession. At which time, I am certain that you would then say you had just discovered it among the cattails on the shoreline when you were fishing with Jude. Hopefully that will not occur. But should it happen, your memory and mine will be the same. Good Christmastide to you all."

The short walk back to the big house was made in silence. Vieve reached for Oliver's hand when they stood at the entrance to the slave stairwell. Her feelings for the son of Montague Hall's master were undeniable, stronger than they had ever been.

"Thank you, Oliver. I can't thank you enough. You are the best friend I have ever had." She felt strong arms about her as she hugged him close. "I will never forget what you did tonight. You are so special to me." She kissed his cheek before disappearing up the dark stairwell.

Merry Christmas, Vieve. Oliver watched until she had disappeared from sight. *I wish you knew how much I care for you. I hope I show you as much as I can. One day, maybe I will tell you.*

CHAPTER TWENTY—FIVE

1778

"Vieve? Vieve, are you awake?" Oliver rapped on the door to the attic.

"May I come in, please? It is important."

"Oliver?" Vieve rubbed her eyes, trying to see in the dark. She felt rested, though dawn had not yet arrived. "What is it, what's wrong?"

Oliver made a gentle push against the attic door. His breath caught somewhere deep within his chest at the sight of Vieve, now almost fifteen, in her sleeping gown, the soft hair falling about her delicate shoulders.

"I have to talk with you. May I sit?"

"Yes, yes, sit." She drew her knees to her chest underneath the blankets on her pallet. "It must be very serious."

"My father has told me that Mr. Benjamin Franklin has negotiated an alliance with France against Great Britain and for future trade relations. The British have tried to make peace, but the efforts have been too little, too late. The British will most certainly be more aggressive, both in the northern and southern states."

"And you had to wake me now to tell me this?"

"No," Oliver looked toward the window, then let his eyes meet hers." But this has made a necessity of what I must tell you. I had to wake you to tell you that Mal is on his way home."

Vieve wrapped her arms around her knees, frowning. This was not the news she wanted to hear. Life had been more pleasant in Mal's absence.

"The decision was made to get him out of Great Britain. Henry Laurens and Irish sympathizers paid heed to our cause, the latest events, and are assisting in getting him to safety, just in case. If he had remained there, he might have been labeled a traitor, and hung. In truth, I don't know Mal's heart now, or even where his allegiances lie. But he is coming home. I thought you should know."

"Thank you for telling me, Oliver. Lucy knows this, as well?"

"Yes. She knows. She wanted to come down with me, but you know her legs no longer work most of the time, and we might have awakened my parents. She knows I was going to tell you." Oliver reached for her hand. "Vieve, Lucy and I will watch all we can. So will Ashwiyaa and Maybelle. Let us all hope that Mal has had a change of heart and perhaps, now, even a woman he loves."

"Oliver, Ashwiyaa said she's had some kind of vision or dream about me. That I was attacked by a snake-like creature. Do you suppose she meant Mal?" Vieve asked.

"I would not pretend to understand all of Ashwiyaa's Indian ways," he smiled. "But we will all take care and be watchful. Do not worry."

Vieve rose to shut the window. The chill of the morning air was more biting than usual. In all of his imagination, Oliver had never seen her more beautiful. Her bare feet made soft pattering sounds against the floor in the early morning stillness.

"I had better go now," he followed her to the window, standing close beside her, feeling the warmth of her nearness. "Vieve," he murmured, reaching for her, and cupping the angelic face in his hands. The surprise rose in her eyes. He kissed the softest of lips, holding her as close as he dared, almost afraid of crushing the girl in his embrace.

"I love you, Vieve Whittier. God help me, I love you more than you could ever know." He released her, moving toward the door.

"Oliver," she whispered, the emotion rising in her voice. "I love you, too, Oliver Montague. God help us both."

From where she stood, she could feel the warmth of his smile. What would Claire Whittier think, if she knew? Vieve crept back to her pallet, savoring the soft, sweet kiss and the unwavering strength of the man that Oliver Montague was becoming.

CHAPTER TWENTY—SIX

Late 1778

"Hello, Vieve."

She heard the resonating, now older voice of Malachi Montague before she saw him approaching the well. She clutched an empty bucket close, unsure of how to greet him. Apprehension clouded the welcome she knew was expected. There was no more boyishness left in the man standing two hands taller before her now. She surmised him to be at least eighteen, perhaps nineteen. He removed the tricorn hat, making a quick bow of his head before her. Deep brown hair groomed the chiseled face and equally dark eyes that took in every inch of her servant-girl appearance. He was handsome, like his father and brother, and though his smile seemed genuine, she could not ascertain the maturity or depth of character. Was he indeed the snake-like creature Ashwiyaa had envisioned?

"Welcome home, Master Montigue."

"Let me help you with that bucket. You are drawing water for Evaline in the washhouse?" He came to stand beside her, his hands brushing hers as he lifted the bucket to the edge of the well and drew the water with deft strokes.

"The cookhouse, actually. They are preparing a meal for your return and need to set the water to boil."

"Then I will assist you in carrying it to them. I trust everything here has been well. I have greatly missed the comfort of being home, although my stay in your London was all I had hoped it would be."

Vieve watched as he filled the pail with water. The silence was awkward and unsettling.

"You are how old now, Vieve."

"Almost fifteen," she bristled, her intuition once again piqued.

"You have become a most lovely woman in my absence. One day you will be a free woman."

Vieve grasped her side of the filled bucket of water and remained silent. *Please do not speak to me so,* she wanted to say aloud but did not dare. This was the Mal who made her feel small and insignificant. *Like the indentured servant that I am.*

"And how is my dear brother, Oliver," Mal's voice was tinged with a measure of sarcasm. "He is almost seventeen now, I believe. Hopefully, he has done well in my absence. Become a man, perhaps?"

"Hello, Malachi," Oliver appeared before them, having made his way to the front of the great house. He stood as tall as Mal, holding the reins to his horse, Remiel. "Welcome home, Brother. Father just asked me to see if your boat was in sight yet or if I could see you approaching by land. I see you have already arrived safely and are making yourself most useful for a change. How encouraging that they added an inkling of courtesy to your tutelage." He smiled at his brother, then Vieve, who returned his smile with appreciation and relief.

"Ah, finally, my little brother has grown a sense of humor while trying to emulate my example as the older, wiser brother. You look well." Mal took the bucket of water from Vieve and set it on the ground. He opened his arms to shake Oliver's outstretched hand before giving him a warm embrace. "It is good to be back in my own homeland, even despite the burgeoning war."

"How was it that you attempted to leave Great Britain for home without being labeled a traitor?" Oliver asked.

"Quite simply, in fact. With increased French aid to the Patriot cause, the British were forced to alter their strategy. Rather than persist in mounting a full-scale attack on the Continental Army, they made the decision to keep their focus on the Loyalists, who they falsely believe are still in the strong majority here in the South. They hope to secure South Carolina by enlisting the support of slaves in the fight. Poor ignorant souls, being used by all, even the British, who would rule them as they do us." Mal stretched his fingers before once again reaching for the filled bucket and giving a broad smile. "The British believe that I am a staunch Loyalist, come home to assist in that cause. Of course, they are sadly mistaken."

"You are aware that the British have secured Savannah now? It is a matter of time before they set their sights on Charlestown once again."

"You are not sent to fight yet, then, Brother?" Mal questioned. "I'm sure some are very glad of that." He stared at Vieve, who returned his gaze with confidence now that Oliver was present.

"No, not yet. But I fear that day is coming for all of us. Father and I both have been training as part of the militia. When war reaches here yet again, then fight we will."

"Please pardon the interruption. I would respectfully request to take my leave now. Mistress Lucy is not feeling well and needs attending before supper, now that the water has been retrieved."

"Of course, Vieve. Go to her. Mal and I will get the water to Evaline before we find Father."

"Thank you, Master Oliver." Vieve replied, noting the pained expression on his face. "Again, Master Mal, welcome home. Good day to you both." Vieve turned her back to the brothers, who watched her make her way back to the big house.

"She has become quite a beautiful woman, Vieve has. You've no doubt had your way with the servant girl, Brother?" Mal raised amused eyes to Oliver, who took the bucket of water from his brother to carry himself.

"I would never hurt Vieve. Never." Oliver took a step toward Mal, glaring into the amused eyes. "And neither should you. Welcome home, Brother."

CHAPTER TWENTY—SEVEN

"Tell me, truly. Are you sorry that Mal has returned to Montague Hall?" Lucy patted the covers on her bed for Vieve to sit beside her. She was still beautiful, Vieve thought, with her blonde hair now swept about the slumped shoulders, though her blue eyes no longer shone as clear, due to the illness that had ravaged her body.

"Sometimes, yes, I wish he was still in London," Vieve admitted. "I so wish that I felt differently. If I could be sure that he was as much of a friend to me as you and Oliver have been, I could feel more amiable toward him." She smiled before adding, "But right now you are my main concern, Lucy. Have you any idea what your friendship has meant to Maybelle, Ash, and me? Without you, my life here —and theirs—would not have become such that it is, even though we are all but servants and slaves. You and Oliver have made it so much more bearable. I could never thank you enough."

Lucy coughed, covering her mouth, motioning for Vieve to wait on her response.

"Then, it might surprise you to know that I envy you, all of you," She gave a wistful smile. "Ash is so strong, so knowledgeable about the very heart of the land. She knows how to take care of herself. Maybelle—may God bless her—is not aware of how smart she really is. Her undying faith in Jesus Christ, despite her life-long enslavement, is a magnificent and sobering thing to behold. Though she has the most to resent in this life, thus far, with all of it caused by my family and others like us, she rises still."

Lucy paused, holding Vieve's hand, then rubbing her legs to ease the discomfort.

"And you, Vieve, you are so grounded in your own sense of who you are, and so caring. You overcame the loss of your mother and brother, your country, your home, even your dignity and honor when you first were brought to us by my father. But you didn't wither away or give up. Even as a child, you were faced with unspeakable loss, alone in this world, and yet you found the strength to be true to yourself. You are the strongest person I've ever known, man or woman. Sometimes, I feel so ashamed of myself, my selfishness and vanity, that I can scarcely stand to see my own reflection."

"Lucy! Dear amazing Lucy, do you still not understand?" Vieve smiled, shaking her head. "You are so much stronger than you know, as well! You, who had power over all of us, and still chose to lay it aside for what you knew in your heart was right! We all, in some way, have our own inequities to overcome. But don't you see? You could have chosen to remain on the path you were on, but you humbled yourself in the most difficult and loving way possible. You chose to reject cruelty and evil. And you have given so many the hope of a better life because of your change of heart! Don't think for a minute that all of us here don't appreciate what you wrestled with to do so."

"Oh, Vieve! Because of my friendship with you, I can see more clearly. All of you have gifted me with a better way in your examples to follow. Because of you and my chosen sisters, my faith is stronger, my happiness is greater, and my fear of rejection by my family is not as frightening as it was." She smiled, coughing once more, and stopping to catch her breath. "Though you know how hard my mother can be."

Lucy motioned for Vieve to help her sit more erect, coughing once again.

"You might find this amusing. I was so jealous of your beauty and the way my brothers looked at you. If I could dress you as the finest in Charlestown, what a sight you would be, with many suitors, Vieve. Oliver loves you, you know that. He has loved you since you first arrived, and never saw you as anything but his valued friend."

"I love Oliver, too, " Vieve whispered. "Though it took me longer to know his heart. And now this war threatens to undo us all. But I believe that Mr. Thomas Paine is right about the independence of the colonies, now declared states. Just as surely as our pale moon rises, these states, these free United States, will be bought with terrible blood sacrifice, no matter how long it takes. The painful mistakes that have surely been made along the way may very well continue, as Mr. Paine also said."

Vieve held Lucy's hand.

"But freedom! It must be bought, especially for the descendants of the poor souls whose blood has been and will be shed. Perhaps even ours. And Lucy, we can never turn back. We have to do all we can to bring about that freedom for all. Teaching the slaves to read and providing them with Oliver's Bible is a good start, dangerous as it is. The war may change what happens next, however."

"You know that I am not getting better," Lucy said with quiet affirmation. "I am in fact getting worse. I don't want to live having to be carried everywhere or spend my life here in bed. I want you, Ash, and Maybelle to pull me in the wagon back to the Ashley River, to that spot where we first became real friends and splashed in the cool water there. Sunday, perhaps. Remember how that corn and watermelon tasted? It was the best, was it not? Please promise me."

"We will go, Lucy, I promise, as long as your parents will allow it. I need to let you rest now. Sleep, and I will speak with Oliver and your mother to make the arrangements. Ask her also when you are able. You know that she will listen to you. She does want to see you happy."

Elias and Elizabeth Montague had exchanged worried glances when Vieve reported Lucy's intended absence from the supper meal, which was less conversational than usual. Elizabeth wiped her mouth with meticulous care before excusing herself to check on her daughter. Vieve handed her the warm bread and honey she had wrapped in a cloth napkin for her friend before helping Dumplin to clear the table of the light sandwich repast. Elias and his sons continued to discuss the war.

"The time is approaching when we will have to make our stand here. Either by fighting or devising some potential plan to keep Montague Hall from being burned or destroyed by the British."

"You are sure it will come to that?" Oliver asked.

"I am certain of it. I just don't know when. Your mother and Lucy will have to be cared for as well. I don't know how to best handle that at the moment. There is much to consider." Elias tapped his fingers on the tabletop. He looked worn beyond his years and tired.

"What about the slaves? What will we do with them? We will have to do something." Mal insisted.

"We should discuss this in the sitting room now. If your mother returns from attending to Lucy, her thoughts will be noted as well. Vieve, you are excused until the morning."

"Thank you, Master Montague. Good evening to you all."

"Good night, Vieve." Mal followed her with his eyes as she moved toward the doorway. Oliver frowned, then spoke.

"Thank you, Vieve. Good night."

Vieve dipped her head in deference to them all, not speaking but hurrying to make her way first to the privy before heading up the slave stairwell. This would be a conversation she did not want to miss. She knew also that Oliver would come to talk when they were done. She wanted to talk with him, more now than ever.

CHAPTER TWENTY—EIGHT

From her hiding place in the attic, Vieve could feel the tension permeating the sitting room and beyond. Elizabeth had joined them and was speaking, her voice fraught with concern.

"We must think about what is best for everyone, especially Lucy. She is ill and getting weaker every day. I want to take her to Charlestown."

"For the love of the Almighty, Elizabeth, I have told you this before! Nowhere will be truly safe. Charlestown will be the least safe of all in these parts!"

"When do you think they will attack, Father?" Oliver's calm voice was soothing.

"That I do not know," Elias stated. "But I believe it will be within the year. The British have turned their efforts toward securing the South. We know they have taken Savannah. Charlestown will be next. They are a behemoth force now. They intend to do what they could not do the last time."

"And the slaves, what about them? How will we manage them all?" Mal asked.

Elias Montague leaned against the wing-backed chair, his elbows resting on the arms, his fingers tapping together, then folding into a single tight fist in front of him.

"The Crown will offer freedom to slaves in exchange for fighting for the Loyalist cause. Many will accept that offer, though the British will have most serving in a non-military capacity, and they will again be subject to monarchy rule when this is over, if they succeed in defeating us. There will be some plantation owners who will attempt to stop them, even kill them, if they attempt to leave and fight with the Redcoats. To what useful purpose that would truly serve, I do not know."

"So that's it, then?" Elizabeth was incredulous. "Montague Hall is ruined? We are done?"

"War will destroy everything for now." Elias lamented. "If we lose, the Crown determines who and what we will become, including Montague Hall. If we are victorious, we gain our independence and can run this place as we see fit once more. If we all survive. But it will be an extreme rebuilding process. It will take years to recover."

"What do you intend to do with our slaves?" Mal demanded. "You have not said."

" I have given this a great deal of thought, as unpleasant as it is." Elias took a deep breath. "I will offer them all a choice if they can discern it. Remain with us, help us, and I will gift each family a small parcel of their own land to own and wages to work for us."

"Pay them?" Elizabeth gasped. "They would no longer be our slaves? You are not serious, Elias?"

"Yes, Elizabeth, that is what I said. Those are my intentions." Elias's voice had an edge of angry frustration. That, or they may leave to make it on their own as they choose, as Loyalists or Patriots. Those are our options, as best as I can foresee them. If Montague Hall is to survive at all, we must be willing to move forward in the best way we can."

Vieve covered her mouth with the palm of her hand. Could that be true? Would the slaves be free before this war was over, and where would they go? What would happen to the likes of her, or Ashwiyaa?

"What will we do, Father?" Oliver asked. "Our family, what will we do?"

"Most likely, Mal and I will go to fight. It could be that you might not have to do so yet. Your mother and Lucy would remain here, and you with them, perhaps to care for the wounded here on both sides, if it will keep Montague Hall secure. Or we will find the best place to send you all when that time arrives."

"What about the slaves who have no family?" Oliver asked, a hint of desperation in his voice.

"You mean our indentured servant girl. The lovely but lowly Vieve." Mal smiled. "Admit it, little brother, you have always been smitten with her. I cannot blame you. She has become a rare beauty, despite her station. You need to see this more clearly. Her beauty will serve her well. Now she can choose her freedom on the streets of anywhere, make her way the best she can, as her prostitute mother did. Who knows, someone might marry her." Mal gave a sly smirk to his brother. "Plenty will pay for her services in the meanwhile. You certainly can."

Vieve heard a loud thudding sound, along with Oliver's exploding anger. She could hear the thrown cup smash against the wall, as Oliver unleashed his rage.

"Shut your mouth, Mal, or I will shut it for you! Do not speak of Vieve in that manner!"

"Enough!" Elias's voice boomed above the rest.

"Stop it, stop this now!" Elizabeth demanded.

Elias stood between his sons, hands raised.

"You will not do this here, not now," he thundered, "The girl is the least of our worries. Do not speak of this again! Do you both understand me? Do you?"

From her place in the attic, the silence was deafening. Oliver finally spoke.

"I'm going to my room," he stated with firm determination. "Forgive my outburst."

Vieve could hear weary footsteps climbing the great stairwell. *The girl is the least of our worries.* The words resonated in the most visceral of places. How small she felt, yet again. But somewhere inside, another voice screamed.

No! No, it isn't true! Oliver loves me. Lucy loves me. I am so much stronger than the girl who first arrived in this place. If Thomas Paine is right, I will determine my future one day, no matter my beginnings. I will be Claire Whittier's legacy and make her proud!

Vieve brushed the hot tears out of her eyes. Oliver would come to her soon, she knew, and there would be much to discuss. She unbraided her dark hair, using her fingers to fluff out the woven tresses. Hanging the work dress on a hook that Oliver had given her and smoothing the simple beige night garment to her bare feet, she listened for the last of the Montagues to retire to their bedchambers.

An hour or so, she surmised, had passed before the gentle knock on the attic door. Even in the dark, Oliver's eyes were beset with a penitence and sadness.

"How much did you hear?" He whispered, hugging her close.

"All, I believe," she breathed, "yes, everything, Oliver. I'm so sorry."

"I hardly know what to say." He released her and went to stand beside the now open window. "No, that's not the truth at all. If I could, I would saddle Remiel and take you away from here. Take us both away from this place." He smiled. "You know, this has been my home since I was born. I love the beauty, the grandeur of it all. I never really saw the other part of it. At least not until you."

"Again, I am so very sorry," she whispered. "I think you are the bravest, most honorable, and most loving person I have ever known. I would be lost without you, Oliver Montague. And I am thankful beyond words for having you in my life, no matter what happens."

Oliver cupped her face in both his hands, searching her green eyes and placing the softest of kisses on her lips and cheeks.

"Vieve," he murmured, his breath quickening, "you have no idea how much I do not want to stop." He held her at arm's length, gripping her shoulders. "But I don't dare, not here, not now. You know I want to give you the best that I can, the perfect setting for you."

"I love you all the more for it, Oliver." She reached for his hands. "I only want the very best for you also, whatever that may be."

"I promise you this," he held her close again and whispered. "Whatever happens now, whatever this war brings, I never want to be without you, Vieve. If we get separated somehow, I will find you, I swear I will."

"I hope that does not come to pass, Oliver," she whispered back, "but, if it does, what shall we do?"

"We make a firm plan," he responded. "There is a fort and fur trading post north of here on the west bank of the Congaree River. Fort Granby. It is currently under control of the Crown. A ferry is there that connects the fort with the settlements on the higher ground on the east bank side. Should we get separated somehow, go there, or send word there, however you are able, as to your whereabouts. Also send word to Charlestown, to where the seat of government lies there when this is over. Perhaps to the family of Henry Laurens. I will do the same, and I will come find you, no matter where you may be." Oliver smiled, holding her close and breathing in the scent of her soft hair. "I can't lose you, Vieve. Whatever happens, I can't lose you."

"I pray for your presence in my life, Oliver. And for the safety of us all amid these horrible times."

"Get some sleep," he brushed strands of dark hair out of her eyes. "There will be much happening, and we must be ready. As soon as I know more of my father's intentions, we will make our plan stronger. I am going to talk with Lucy as well. I fear she is getting much worse and I do not know how much more her body can take of whatever it is that has crippled her. Our plan will include her, Vieve." Oliver whispered in her ear. "And they will include Maybelle and Ashwiyaa if you wish. Not as slaves. As our friends. If they will allow us to do so and we can find a way to make our paths known for all of us."

Vieve smiled, the tears returning. "Oliver, I want that more than you can imagine. I know we must all be safe first. You have my pledge that I will honor that plan and you, always."

CHAPTER TWENTY-NINE

Late 1779

Vieve looked across the landscape as far as she could see from her favorite secluded spot by the Ashley River. She was almost sixteen, though the meager celebration of birthdays had long been relegated to childhood memory. The wild beauty of this land and the rare quiet time alone were great sources of peace for her, despite what she had come to know of the evil that one human being could do to another. Sundays had always been her favorite at Montague Hall, especially this time of year. These cool fall Sundays proved to be more relaxed, as most of the slaves were allowed respite enough to attend to their own needs and chores. Even the house Negroes were granted a measure of unencumbered time, though not as much as the field hands.

Sundays had been the days that she, Maybelle, Ash, and Lucy had pursued their educational endeavors together in the secrecy of the woods, but Lucy's condition had dampened those recent efforts. On this day, Maybelle was with her family and Ash was attending to the needs of the barn and helping Mal and Oliver with their horses and shooting with bows and arrows. Vieve reveled in the crisp freshness of the day, the light brush of seasonal colors and the brisk seasonal air. Today, she did not want to think about the war that would come to them soon.

Elias Montague found great delight in leisurely horse or carriage rides through the grounds of Montague Hall with his wife and family, though those times were often laid aside of late, with the machinations of war closer at hand. Today was a rarity. All was quiet. Elias had spirited Elizabeth away from the great hall for a wagon ride to the garden area and beyond, while Lucy had her now requisite daily long naps, and Oliver and Mal were otherwise occupied with their chosen tasks.

The Ashley River, laden on each side with thick vegetation, was swollen from the rains and the high tidal flow. The sun cast warming rays on the cool waters, the crystal reflections dancing and sparkling their way across the rippling waves. The air was rife with the intoxicating scents of the woods. The day was perfect. Vieve removed her work dress and brogan shoes, hanging the dress on a nearby branch and tossing her shoes on the grassy riverbank. Raising the white woven undergarment gown above her knees, she gathered the hem and tied it into a secure knot before wading knee-deep into the bracing waters, now too chilly for a swim, but invigorating, nonetheless. She untied the front of her gown, baring one shoulder, and tilted her face upward into the warmth of the sun. Scooping a cupped handful of water into the air, she let the light spray fall about her, dampening her braided hair that was woven about her head. She stretched her arms, and with open palms skyward, smiled up at the heavens. How Claire and little Simon would have loved her secret place and this land teeming with natural beauty.

"Vieve."

She heard the deep, masculine voice of Malachi Montague before she turned to see him easing back in the saddle atop his horse, the lascivious stare causing her body to shiver and her pulse to quicken. She pulled the shoulder of her gown back in place.

"Master Mal," she said with all the firmness she could muster, "I was enjoying a brief moment alone before returning to attend to Lucy."

"So I see," his lazy smirk remained as he dismounted from the horse and tied the reins to a nearby branch. "It is a beautiful spot, to be sure. Is this where you hide when you are not working?"

"It is never my intention to hide, only to enjoy a moment of peace and solitude," she bristled, "and others are always close by and all around." Vieve crossed her arms about her, grasping each arm beneath her shoulders.

"You are more alone than you think." Mal moved to the edge of the water, noting her discomfort. "That is good, if it is what you desired. All are on the other side of the plantation, quite involved in their pleasures or duties at hand. I saw the direction in which you were going." He took note of the gentle breeze that molded the hand-woven undergarment against her femininity. She felt the intensity of his gaze, the desire in his eyes.

"Come here, Vieve." His voice was sensual, deep, and insistent.

She froze, her lips parting as understanding began to dawn. *Please, no. Please don't do this to me.*

"Come here, Vieve. I don't care about sharing you with Oliver. It doesn't matter to me. But I want what I want. Now."

She took small steps toward him, her mind racing to find a way to divert his intentions.

"I really must go now. Lucy is expecting me."

Mal took a step into the water, grasping her by the wrist and pulling her close to face him. He placed his hands on her trembling arms, then stroked a cheek with the back of his fingers before lifting his hand to remove the bindings of her braided hair. The dark hair swirled and fell in wild abandon below her shoulders. Her head throbbed with the fear she tried to hide.

"You are even more beautiful standing here close to me. Bewitching, you are. You are indeed a witch, and I cannot resist. It matters not to me that you are infatuated with my brother. But I can give you so much more if you come to me willingly."

Mal seized both arms and pulled her against him, wrapping her close. She could feel his warm breath against her; feel the strength she could not match in the arms that would not relinquish her until his intentions had been carried out.

"Please, Master Mal," she pleaded in desperation, "I must go to Lucy."

He searched her frightened eyes.

"You don't have to be afraid of me, Vieve. I told you I can do so much for you if you will cooperate. I can make your life easier. What I can't do is stop thinking about you."

He forced a kiss as she struggled against him, which only heightened his desire.

"Don't fight me, Vieve. I hold your fate in my hands." He kissed her once more. She tried to pull away, turning her head.

"Please, no," she whispered, "please don't do this to me."

"Why do you resist me?" She could hear the anger rising in his voice. "Do you resist Oliver in this way? He can't give you nearly what I can! You forget that you are but a servant, witch or no."

Vieve fought with all the strength she could muster, pressing his chest hard with her hands.

"No! No! Please don't."

Grabbing her shoulders, Mal thrust her against the live oak tree beside them.

"Come to me, Vieve. Come to me. I want you. Do not force me to go elsewhere. Ashwiyaa, perhaps?"

From an unknown deepest recess of her soul, Vieve felt the years of underlying resentment and anger, even from her childhood back in Great Britain, overflowing, exploding into this real time and place.

"You leave Ashwiyaa alone!" She tried to scream." She's done nothing to you! She would never tolerate your taking her in this manner. She could kill you! You know she could."

Mal smiled, eyes burning with desire, while his voice stung with amusement.

"You surprise me, Vieve. You are more spirited than I had you figured for, talking to your master as you are. You forget," he leaned close to whisper, the anger at her refusal returning, "there's always Maybelle. And I could easily take her, but I won't, unless you choose not to cooperate with my offer. Neither she nor her sister are who I want, but my choices can change."

Vieve could no longer fight the tears that hung in the corners of her eyes.

"You leave Maybelle alone. Leave her be! You've already hurt her family enough."

Mal relaxed his hold, pressing her body into the oak tree with his chest. He stroked her hair, whispering once more.

"The slaves do not count. But I can make you count. I'm going to have you. And you will like it if you stop fighting me. I'm giving you more chances than any slave or servant. You should appreciate that."

He kissed her neck, her cheek, her lips. Vieve closed her eyes, trying to suppress the sob rising in her throat, praying that this horror would end soon.

The sound, strong and swift, was that of a sudden rush of wind that ended with a sickening thud in Mal's back. He tried to reach for his chest, as if to push back the arrow that had plunged through the sinewy tissue. Surprise lept from the eyes that widened with shock and pain. His body shook, rocking with a gentle motion as he leaned into Vieve. She felt the burst of blood, oozing in spurts from his torn body, where her hands had grasped his back, then saw the crimson red spread across her hands and arms. Nausea rose in her throat. Mal grasped for her shoulders once more, eyes wide, pleading, into hers. Vieve was paralyzed with fear. She held her captor, watching the life drain from his body. Mal's eyes, that had only moments ago held hers with power and desire, now faded, the fixed gaze staring into oblivion. His grip loosened as he slid down the length of her body, coming to rest in an unceremonious and lifeless heap onto the ground below. Vieve's hands were blood-drenched as she raised them to her face, then wiped them down the sides of the woven undergarment. Throwing her head back against the oak tree, she screamed, the guttural fright overtaking her.

"Vieve! Vieve, it's me, it's Oliver!"

Oliver raced to her side, his quiver of arrows across his back and his bow thrown to the ground. He grasped her arm with one hand and felt for Mal's breathing with the other. Out of the corner of her eye, Vieve caught a glimpse of Ashwiyaa running toward them, her own bow in her hand, and arrows in tow. Shaken from what had just happened, Vieve collapsed in Oliver's arms, tears erupting with the force of unbridled shock and grief. Oliver held her close, his own tears warm on her face.

"What happened here?" He whispered, examining every inch of her to be sure she was not hurt, then knelt beside his fallen brother. "Mal, why? Why?"

He placed shaking hands on his brother's arms. Vieve leaned against the strength of the oak tree, closing her eyes, and crying in uncontrolled sobs. Oliver bowed his head, using his thumb and forefinger to close the now lifeless eyes of his brother. Reaching for Vieve once more, he held her to him, letting her cry, his body rocking with hers.

"I'm here. I'm here now, Vieve. I've got you. I'm so sorry I was not here to stop this."

"Your brother," she breathed, unable to get the words out. "Oliver, I…"

"Shhhh, don't speak. It's going to be alright. I promise."

From the worn path nearby, the wagon carrying Elias and Elizabeth Montague rounded the corner. Elias rushed from the wagon with his wife, seeing the body of his oldest son on the ground, an arrow plunged deep into his back. Big Zeb jumped down from the front of the wagon.

"Mal! Malachi!" Elias flew to his son's side, Elizabeth screaming and running behind him. Placing a hand on Mal's neck, he felt for any sign of life. There was none. The arrow, still buried in his son's body, bloody and macabre, was a terrifying scene. There was no sign of movement, no rise and fall of breathing. Mal was now an empty, soulless vessel. Elias felt lightheaded, consumed by the horror of this moment. Only Elizabeth's screams, mournful and desperate, reached the void now left inside him.

"Who did this?" he demanded, holding his hands over Mal's body. "Who killed him? In the name of God Almighty, Oliver, why? Tell me why!"

"I killed him." Ashwiyaa stood before them, quiet but unafraid, one end of her bow resting on the ground beside her, the other, against her side. "Vieve tried to push him away and the arrow must have hit him. I only wanted to stop him."

"No!" Oliver turned to face his father, one arm still holding onto Vieve. "No, Ashwiyaa did not do this. Her arrow did not hit him. I killed him, but like Ashwiyaa, I did not mean to do it. He was going to harm Vieve before I could reach him. I took aim only to distract him, to prevent him from hurting her. He must have turned into my aim. This is my doing. I'm so sorry, Father. I'm so sorry about all of this!"

"That savage killed my boy!" Elizabeth screamed, now beside Mal's body. She pointed at Ashwiyaa, unable to hold back the hysteria. "She has already admitted her guilt. and over a mere servant girl, a slave who belongs to us to do with as we see fit!" Elizabeth dropped to her knees, overwhelmed with grief. "I will see you hanged!" She raged at Ashwiyaa. "I will see the red skin stripped from every piece of your worthless body-and you!" She turned her wrath to Vieve, "I will see you punished alongside her! You have caused us nothing but trouble since you came here!"

"Stop it, Mother!" Oliver released his hold on Vieve, moving to kneel beside his mother, hugging her to his chest. "Mal is the one who acted wrongly here. Vieve has done nothing but serve us honorably. She loves Lucy as a sister. You know that." He hesitated, his voice softening. "And I love her very much. I love her."

"No!" Elizabeth wept, her voice shaking. "What are you saying? No! I have lost one son. I will not lose another to a servant. I forbid it!"

"You cannot stop this, Mother," Oliver whispered. "I love her. And that is my heart, my choice. We have lost our Mal, and it is a most unfortunate consequence that could happen. But this is his fault, alone. Let us tend to him for now. Too much else remains at stake. Let Father and me put him in the wagon." Oliver's voice softened. "Come now, tend to Malachi and our family."

Elizabeth Montague was inconsolable, clinging to both Oliver and now Elias, then wailing once more at the sight of her oldest child, now devoid of life, being wrapped in a blanket and placed in the wagon by Big Zeb, before they boarded once again.

"Son," Elias, whose face was covered in misery, leaned down from the carriage wagon to address Oliver. "We must talk about this once more after Mal is attended to and your mother is able. We must also tell Lucy."

"Allow me to tell her. I want her to hear it from me." Oliver made the request in the most firm, resolute voice he could manage. Elias nodded his head.

"Very well. Your mother and I should be there for her also. You must see to it that Ashwiyaa and Vieve return to the barn and the house where they will stay until we decide what must be done. They will have to be dealt with in some way. You know that."

"I will be sure they return. They will, Father, I know. I agree that more discussion must happen when all are not aggrieved as we are in this moment. Clear heads must prevail. I'm so very sorry about Mal. I could not let him do what he intended. Not to her."

Elias nodded once again, his large shoulders sagging and weary, no doubt from the collective loss of his oldest son, the weight of approaching war, his daughter's deadly malady, and the lingering unhappiness of his wife. No one knew more than Elias Montague how much more change was coming to Montague Hall, sooner than anyone would know.

CHAPTER THIRTY

From the imposed sequestration in the confines of her attic dwelling, Vieve could still hear the anguished screams from Lucy when she was given the news of Mal's death. Her utter grief had been more than Vieve could withstand. The thought of Lucy knowing that she and Ashwiyaa had been involved in the cause of her brother's demise had brought her to tears once more. Sitting on the bare floor of her room, now in the darkness, Vieve had revisited the horrific moments many times, searching for anything she might have done differently.

Mr. Bennett, the Overseer, had been given authority to manage the plantation in the absence of both Elias and Oliver. A palpable veil of sorrow now draped across the entirety of the grand plantation. Even the slaves must be whispering among themselves, since their more jovial and animated Sunday banter had ceased hours ago. However, in truth, Vieve was certain that none were sad that Malachi Montague was no more.

The grim quiet was interrupted by something hitting the floor of her small room. Whatever it was had entered through the open window. Vieve jumped to her feet as another object landed beside her. It was an unshelled pecan, no doubt from one of the trees in the courtyard. Looking out the window, she saw Maybelle peering up at her.

"You alright?" The slave girl stepped closer to the house. "Everybody so worried about you and Ashwiyaa."

"You shouldn't be here, Maybelle. You could get in trouble."

"I can run faster than them," Maybelle smiled. "Besides, I'm not staying here long.

"Mama and Jude are so worried. They love you. Because of you, they are together now. But they know how bad this is. He was her favorite. We all know that.

"No one ate the supper meal. They had to tell Lucy."

Vieve winced. "I could hear her screaming. I think Oliver will come soon and I will know more. Have you heard anything about Ash?"

"I just left the barn. She knows Mistress Elizabeth holds her responsible, even though Oliver took the blame. Do you know who really did the killing? Which one killed Mal?"

"I am almost glad that I did not see which one of them might have done it. It was awful, Maybelle. I still see all that blood. I still feel it. My gown will never be free of the stains, nor will my thoughts."

A soft knock at her door made Vieve know that Oliver was there.

"Vieve? It's me, Oliver. Who are you talking to?"

"Go!" She motioned to Maybelle. "Oliver is here."

"Come in," she tried to force a smile that would not come. "How is Lucy? I feel so terrible. Maybelle was just checking to be sure I was alright."

Oliver appeared distraught, though calm. He reached for Vieve, wrapping her in his arms and feeling her tears yet again.

"Lucy is quite overwhelmed, as are my parents. I was able to speak with her privately after we gave her the sad news. She knows what Mal was going to do and who killed him. She holds no ill will toward you. She loves you. She loved Mal, too. He was good to her."

"Oliver," Vieve leaned back to look into his eyes. "Who killed him? Tell me the truth."

Oliver stroked her arms, saying nothing, then pulled her close and whispered.

"Maybelle came to Ashwiyaa in the barn. She saw Mal riding in the direction you had gone when she was by the washhouse. Ashwiyaa found me and I came as soon as I was told. We had been practicing with our bows and arrows, so we each had those weapons. Ashwiyaa must have come behind me." Oliver's voice shook. "I truly had no intention of killing him, I meant to just stop him from hurting you. But Vieve," his voice broke, "I'd have killed my brother if I had to."

"You didn't kill him? Then, Ashwiyaa did? There was only one arrow that I saw."

"Hear me, Vieve." He held her face in his hands. "Ashwiyaa did not kill him, although I suspect she wanted to do so."

"I don't understand. I saw you and Ash there. There were no others."

Oliver pulled her close enough to whisper next to her ear.

"Maybelle killed him."

"Maybelle! How, how could she have? I never saw her!"

"No, you did not. The truth is, neither did we. After Maybelle told Ashwiyaa that she saw Mal following you, Ash then came to find me so that I could stop him. But Maybelle ran to retrieve her own bow and arrows and rushed to where you were before we got there. She hid among the trees and she left as soon as she had made her shot. She saw that Mal had no intention of stopping. Maybelle also knew that no one besides perhaps Evaline had seen her leave. She thought only of protecting you. Nothing else."

"Maybelle killed Mal?" Vieve whispered. "Maybelle?"

"Yes. It seems that reading and schooling are not the only endeavors you girls all have learned in your secret times together." Oliver gave a soft smile. "And I imagine that Maybelle had the most reasons to be so inclined to act on your behalf."

"But Ashwiyaa admitted that she killed him! Oliver, you did so as well. Why would you both do that?"

"It's very simple. Ash and I both knew that it had to be Maybelle, since no one else knew where Vieve had gone. Maybelle would be beaten and then possibly hanged if anyone knew what she had done. Ash took the blame because she knows that my parents would easily believe she was the one who did it, even though she also said she had not intended to kill him, but only to stop him.

She also knows that, even though she is but a slave, she is somewhat feared because of her knowledge and her Indian ways. Ash is well aware of how much she has helped us at Montague Hall, and that we would not be predisposed to ridding ourselves of her. She also is your friend. She was willing to act for you. And everyone would believe that she made the shot."

"And you, why did you claim responsibility for killing your brother?"

"That is even more simple. My parents would not kill me, you know that. If I claim responsibility, they will have a much more difficult choice to punish anyone else with such terrible consequences, even if they wanted to do so."

"What will happen now?" Vieve searched his eyes for answers. "I know your parents want to blame Ashwiyaa, and even me, for Mal's death. It is why they have kept us away from everyone for now."

"My father is truly not only filled with grief, but quite conflicted. He suspects that someone else killed Mal. He cannot believe that my actions caused Mal's death, and yet he knows that is the best way for it to be for Montague Hall. He wants to appease my mother, as well. He knows that something must be done to keep the slaves from rebelling also, should they come to believe that Ashwiyaa was brave enough to kill Mal, even if by accident. They also know how well she shoots, and that an accident for her is rather unlikely, unless of course you pushed him into her aim more."

Oliver held both her hands in his, taking more than one deep breath.

"Vieve," he held her eyes with his, "yes, my mother also blames you for all of this. To her, you have caused Mal's death and disrupted every aspect of life here. You have become Lucy's friend—changed her heart even—and made the slaves your allies. And of course, she knows now that I love you very much." He smiled. "She would have me married to someone in Charlestown, or another master's daughter, if she had her way. She had been plotting to match me with the girl you saw at Drayton Hall, remember? Right now, my mother holds equal anger toward you and Ashwiyaa."

"Oh, Oliver," Vieve stared out her window. "I'm so sorry. Maybe I have truly disrupted your family and caused ill will between you and your parents."

"Listen to me, Vieve. Listen well. Their views and their beliefs have caused the problems they have with you. You know that. I love my parents very much. I am in the unique position of seeing their goodness. It breaks my heart to see the underbelly of that goodness, to see with all clarity the light and dark in them. But I have searched my own heart and have no room to judge them. Of all people, you have made me see that we are all capable of benevolence and malevolence, depending on what we allow ourselves to believe and by the choices we make. I accept the responsibility of my choices. I choose you. I hope you freely choose me."

"Oliver, I love you. That is my choice. And I, too, will do whatever I can to bring about the best for everyone, but especially for you."

"Then we will find a way, somehow," he smiled down at her, stroking her soft cheeks and dark hair. "Try to get some rest, Vieve. "Tomorrow will bring new challenges and decisions. I will know more after Mal's funeral. Lucy wants to see you also. So much is happening now. Nothing is safe anymore."

CHAPTER THIRTY-ONE

With war looming in an ever-present vigil, Mal's funeral had been conducted with immediacy and was kept succinct and simple. Big Zeb and Jude had crafted the wooden coffin for him and assisted in the creation of a headstone. Elizabeth Montague and Dumplin had overseen the intimate preparations and final dressing. The service, if it could even be called that, was brief, conducted in the early twilight hours, so that the house slaves, and any other, could attend after most of the chores were done. The somber ritual was held in the cemetery plot on the grounds of Montague Hall where the parents of Elias Montague were buried. Both Elias and Oliver Montague read from the Bible and offered prayers on behalf of Malachi. Lucy remained in her wagon, visibly shaken by the events of the past two days.

Neither Vieve nor Ashwiyaa had been asked to attend and remained sequestered in their respective dwellings. No one but Oliver had spoken with her since Mal's death. In the dim light of late afternoon, Vieve could see the flickering torch lights approaching the main house from the distant burial ground. The family would have leftover food remaining from the already-meager earlier dinner, then a libation in the sitting room before retiring for the night. She anticipated listening to as much of the discussion as she could before Oliver would come to her once again.

Waiting in the dark from her place underneath the firing hole, Vieve stretched her legs and tried to ease the hunger pangs, as she had not eaten much since Mal's untimely death. She had been escorted to the privy by Dumplin, when the need arose, which had been her only contact with anything outside her room. She wondered how Ashwiyaa was managing the imposed isolation, and what would be done with them both. Finally, the muffled voices wafted up to her room. She stood and peeked through the hole, straining to see and hear as much as possible.

"My oldest child has been buried now. We must talk about what is to be done with those two slaves." Elizabeth Montague wasted no time in addressing the yet unspoken task, sipping on her rum, and leaning back in her chair.

"Why would anything need to be done now with Vieve or Ashwiyaa? Oliver has said that Mal's horrific death was an accident by his own hand. And he is already suffering greatly for that. Isn't it enough?" Lucy spoke, an edge of frustration in her voice.

"Ashwiyaa had no business even being where Mal was!" Elizabeth's tone was more angry than sad. "As for Vieve, we've given her everything when she had nothing and no one. Mal was a Montague, as we all are. He was her master, too. She enticed him with her feminine wiles, and he but responded. She had no say in the matter at all. Her place was to submit to him."

"I disagree! Oliver interjected; his voice also tinged with irritation. "I loved Mal. But his actions were wrong, even toward a servant."

"A servant girl who you have also declared your love for, I might add," Elizabeth sneered. "Your actions are understandable, no matter how inappropriate your choice of affection. But you will change your mind, Oliver. She is beneath your station in every possible way. The law and society expectations would support your brother here, as well you know. Once war has dissipated, you will find a woman deserving of your affection."

"There is no other woman more deserving than Vieve. In fact, Mother, it is I who does not deserve her! She is the most caring, intelligent, and bravest person I know, man or woman. She might have come from unfortunate circumstances, but she has shown fortitude and character of unmatched integrity and honor. If that is not noble and worthy, then nothing is. I value those qualities far more than any pedigree! I will not see her disrespected, even by you!" Oliver thundered, then quelled his anger.

"I'm sorry. You know I love you. Do not make me have to choose between my family and the woman I love. Do not force me there."

"You are naïve," Elizabeth shot back. "That servant girl only cares for you because you are a Montague. She knows what you can give her. Don't be a fool, Oliver."

"If that is all she cared about, she would have willingly given herself to Mal's advances. She did not. She refused them at even greater risk to herself. I love her, and that is the end of it!" Oliver was firm in his stance with his mother.

"Mother, I know you want the best for Oliver, for us all," Lucy pleaded, "He loves Vieve, and she, him. Look at her heart, that is who she is! Is that not who any of us truly are – that which we carry inside ourselves, that no one can take from us?" Lucy was adamant in her support of Oliver.

"Elias," Elizabeth implored her husband for assistance, "you must talk some sense into your remaining children."

For a brief moment silence ensued, with all waiting for a response from Montague Hall's master. Elias Montague rubbed his forehead, then pressed his fingertips together, mired in deep thought.

"While these are trying times, to be sure, with the wretched, terrible loss of our Malachi, I fear that much greater loss is coming. Loss that will be more than any of us are prepared for. Loss far greater than the station of anyone, or even more important than who one might choose to marry." The voice of Elias Montague was weary, plagued with worry, yet solid in resolution. "I will not worry now about who anyone might hold affection for, or no. I am grieving the immense loss of my oldest child. We are facing war, the likes of which we have never seen before. We are facing the destruction of all that we have worked for and hold dear." He paused, making eye contact with each one. "And in the balance hangs the making of a country, the likes of which has never been seen before by any civilization. These are unprecedented times. They demand our attention, even our very souls."

"But the slaves must be managed, Elias. Order must be maintained here, if we are to keep control over all that we have achieved."

"For God's sake, Elizabeth! You refuse to understand!" Elias thundered at his wife, his patience all but gone. "It is no longer about if war should occur. War is coming here and far more destructive than you can possibly imagine! I must decide what to do about the Crown's enticing of all slaves in the South to fight for Great Britain! I must not only try to protect Montague Hall from total ruination, but also to keep all of us alive at any cost I can bear. And I believe that every man and woman here will have to decide which side they will ultimately support and thus, be willing to lay their very lives down to do so!"

Elias rested his forehead in one of his hands, holding onto the arm of his chair with the other. No one dared speak. All were contemplating the words of the plantation master.

"I have made my decision regarding this most unfortunate event. Malachi is gone forever. My only happiness here is that he will be spared the damnation of war. My biggest regret is that all of us will face what may be insurmountable obstacles in the near future. Tomorrow morning, very early, the Overseer will address all of the slaves before their duties and our workday begin again. He will announce that Oliver Montague tragically and accidentally killed his brother while out in the woods. He will insist that all rules and protocol at Montague Hall still stand, and that there will be no punishment meted out for anyone. He will say that Oliver is punished enough in the loss of his brother at his own hands. He will say that I very much appreciate the hard work of everyone here and that we will weather whatever comes our way and that, when war does indeed arrive here, we will talk again about what it means for everyone. That is my decision, and it is beyond contestation for now.

Elias stood, running fingers through his dark hair. "I am going to bed now. Oliver, please carry Lucy upstairs. Your mother will come to assist you, Lucy, once she is also prepared to sleep. Come, Elizabeth. Goodnight to all."

Vieve let herself sink down to her seat on the cold wooden floor. The words of Elias Montague played in her head yet again. No further punishment for her or Ashwiyaa, and certainly none for Oliver. There were far more threatening issues at hand, though his decision must have angered Elizabeth. She rested her head on the wall behind her. All of this seemed so unreal. She closed her eyes to think more clearly about what was happening. Sleep came, needed as it was, before she could move from her place under the firing hole.

"Vieve! I'm coming in now!"

Oliver's voice woke her from the temporary reverie. The door to her attic space had swung open. Peering through the dark, she saw Lucy, arms around the neck of her brother, smiling, as he carried her to the pallet on the floor.

"Lucy! Lucy, is that really you?" Vieve clapped her hands together. "I can't believe you are here. I've missed you so!"

"I've missed you, Vieve." Tears rose in Lucy's blue eyes. "I'm so sorry about what my brother did." She reached to hug her friend. "And that your room is such as this. It is my first time here, you know." She gave a regretful smile to Vieve.

"Do not apologize for anything, Lucy. It is done and was none of your doing. I have no ill will here. Only thanks that Ashwiyaa and I will be spared. I am truly sorry for your loss of Mal. I know that he was good to you, and he was your brother." She looked up at Oliver. "I heard most of what Elias said, and he is right, you know. I fear we will all be in grave danger, and perhaps sooner than we know. We must all think together about what to do."

"Lucy and I will not stay here longer. Lucy was insistent that she see you. I wanted to, as well, of course. Tomorrow, things will return to as normal as we can make them for now. As soon as we know more about this war and what is happening, we will be better able to make more sound plans. You will be able to return to normal duties tomorrow, as will Ashwiyaa." Oliver hesitated before adding, "Vieve, I think it best that you refrain from any mention of Mal to our mother. She is in a difficult place for now, and I hope she will manage to work through her confusion and anger. Perhaps just attend to Lucy for now and allow some time and space for our mother, if you can do so."

"Of course, yes, I can do that. I agree that focusing on that which is yet to come, that surely will be, is the soundest plan of all. I hope that I can find a way to speak with both Ashwiyaa and with Maybelle soon. I just want everything to be as good as it can be. I hope you both know that I will do whatever I can to make things better for everyone, but especially for you."

Oliver held her hand and reached for that of his sister, who leaned against him for solace from her growing weakness.

"Then it is settled. We will all wait for things to play out in whatever manner they might and make our plans accordingly. There is too much at stake to make any kind of reasonable decisions for now. Life will go on as usual here, and we will all have to be as vigilant as we can be. I want you both to know that I will do my best to see you safely shielded from any destruction this war might bring to us. We might all have to make the most difficult decisions very soon. And the actions we will be forced to choose might be even harder. Together, we will face them."

Vieve stood by the open window once Oliver and Lucy had gone. Staring up at the sky, she searched for the moon, to no avail, as she offered her nighttime prayers.

"I know you're there," she whispered. "Looking over all the changes we might face. Another season. Another journey. Another mighty challenge. Send us your light from the heavens. Forgive us all for our human frailties. Help us. For we will surely need the help of God Almighty in the days to come."

CHAPTER THIRTY-TWO

Late January 1780

"And you are certain of this?"

Elias Montague peered out over the pristine Ashley River from the banks on the Montague Hall side.

"Yes, Sir, quite certain." The messenger in the boat wiped his brow before continuing. "You know our forces and the French failed to retake Savannah back in October in that bloody battle. General Clinton himself, Commander of the British Army in America, and General Cornwallis both have sailed southward in another attempt, after that loss three years ago. They are on the Savannah River, at last look. Many troopships and warships. They will surely not have much trouble defeating us. Won't take them long to cross the Stono on into Charlestown. They could be here in these parts by mid-March, most probably. You'd best be prepared, Sir, and any help spreading this word would be much appreciated."

"Thank you kindly, much obliged to you. I will send a rider to warn as many small farmers as possible inland from Montague Hall." Elias took a last look at the peaceful waters before turning to Oliver and motioning toward the courtyard and the main house.

"Go find your mother. Get Lucy, as well, if she is awake. I will come to the dining room. First, I will have a brief word with the Overseer before I join you there."

Oliver burst through the door from the courtyard into the house. Vieve and Dumplin had just returned from helping Evaline and

Maybelle in the wash and cookhouses and were preparing for the light supper meal.

"Where is Lucy?" he demanded.

"She's sleeping but should be waking up. Mistress Elizabeth just went to check on her."

"Lawd, somethin' wrong, Master Oliver, ain't it?" Dumplin placed her hands on her full hips. "You look mighty worried, sho' nuf."

"Vieve, come with me to get Lucy downstairs, my mother as well. Dumplin, leave the meat and bread on the table, the cider, too. You may go downstairs with the others. Vieve will call you when we are done. Thank you."

"Yes, Sir." Dumplin glanced at Vieve, then proceeded with setting out the light supper meal as instructed, before making her way to the cellar.

Mounting the stairs in the great hall, Vieve knew even before she asked Oliver about the urgency in his behavior.

"The war is here, isn't it? Or it will be soon? That's it, isn't it?"

"Yes," came the curt reply. "War will be upon us faster than we thought, and we must all be prepared." Oliver stopped on the stairwell. Vieve, whatever happens, you know our plan. Do you remember?"

"Yes, of course I do, Oliver."

"Stay in the room by the courtyard while we are having supper. Stay there, out of sight, and remain quiet. You will hear everything there. When supper is done, call Dumplin back up to help clean, then go to your room. We will talk later, I promise."

"Of course, Oliver. I will wait for you."

Lucy was awake, sitting on the edge of her bedding with Elizabeth by her side when Oliver and Vieve arrived.

"Father wants us all in the dining room now. Vieve and I will get Lucy downstairs, Mother, if you'd like a moment with him before we join you there." Oliver's words were more of an instruction than a request. Elizabeth patted Lucy's hands before rising.

"Of course. I will find him now." She glanced at Vieve in a disapproving stare. "See that Lucy's night gown is ready for her when she returns."

"Yes, Mistress Montague."

Elizabeth Montague rose from her place, making a slow and deliberate exit down the steps.

After the light nourishment of the supper meal, a grim Elias Montague faced his family in the sitting room, where he sat in his designated chair. The talk of war was the focus of discussion. Vieve had remained quiet, as Oliver had asked, even cleared most of the table alone, so that Dumplin would not have to be called from the cellar.

"I have given much thought to the best possible options for this place and for our family," he began, "and I have made some difficult decisions about how to proceed, in hopes of sparing Montague Hall from complete ruin."

He looked into the eyes of each, struggling to continue.

"Mr. Bennett, the Overseer, will explain to the slaves what their choices are. They may choose to join the British to fight against the Patriots. That is one choice, and one I hope they do not make. They may also choose to remain here at Montague Hall for the duration of the war. If they do, they will be given a small parcel of land to own as they see fit, then paid for their continued work once the war is over. Of course, if the Crown is victorious, their choices may change somewhat. If the Patriots are victorious and slavery abides, I will still honor my promise to award them their own land, in hopes that they will remain and help us. We will not be as prosperous and it will take years to rebuild in some form, but, to my mind, this appears to be the most prudent path to take."

"Father, what about the fighting? You and I have trained to do so, as did Mal." Oliver asked.

Elias rose and stood by the fireplace, staring into the dancing flames.

"Your mother and I have decided on a plan that will divide the family for now. These actions may very well save Montague Hall and give us a bit more time before we are forced to fight, Oliver. This will also be the best for Lucy, as her illness is worsening." Elias smiled at his frail daughter, who now could no longer walk, but also had difficulty hearing or seeing on occasion, with slow speech and shortness of breath, and pains in her chest, at times. "I will take Lucy northward to the upper part of South Carolina to stay with my cousin John Geiger and his daughter, Emily in the Saxe Gotha area. A fine young physician friend, trained with the esteemed Dr. Benjamin Rush, will also be visiting John, who is an invalid himself, of course. The physician will attempt to treat both John and Lucy during the remainder of his stay. Your mother will remain as Mistress here, and Oliver, you are Master in my absence. The gardens and our rice and indigo will only be able to be maintained as the war allows, and dependent upon the number of slaves choosing to remain here. Also, the house will be designated a place of medical quarantine for all, again, in hopes that Montague Hall will be spared. There is no guarantee, of course. Jude and Evaline, also Dumplin and Big Zeb have already agreed to remain, as they are a bit older than some, and they will have first choice of available land to hold as their own."

Vieve held her breath waiting to hear what the fate of Maybelle, Ashwiyaa, and herself would be. *Lucy will surely share my thoughts.* She smiled as Lucy Montague now spoke, as if on cue.

"If I must go, I want Vieve, Maybelle, and Ashwiyaa to go with me." She paused to catch her breath. "I need them. They all know how to help me best and can also help Father on the trip. Besides, Ashwiyaa can scout the land better than anyone."

"You may take Vieve and Ashwiyaa. I think Maybelle should remain here and help." Elizabeth stated, turning to Elias for support.

She did not hesitate to get rid of me or Ash, Vieve noted. *Maybelle is no threat to her.*

"Mother, they each know how to care for me. Father will be busy tending to other things. With all of them, they can tend to me, lift me, pull me; but this way will also be of great help to Father. Evaline, Dumplin, and Merrilee are more than capable of handling the cook and washhouses and other domestic needs now."

"I have a notion to consider," Oliver spoke up. "Why not let Maybelle choose to remain here or to go, as she chooses? After all, her mother and Jude are remaining here. In the spirit of necessary change with this war, why not give her the choice as well?"

"I agree." Elias added. "Giving her a say will most certainly reinforce the idea of choices for them all and certainly look more amiable for us. Oliver and I must go immediately to Charlestown to attend to my legal affairs. We will return after spending a night there and assist Mr. Bennett in handling slave and plantation affairs. Elizabeth will manage while we are gone."

Vieve covered her mouth with her hands, a small grin spreading across her face. She had no doubt that Maybelle would choose to go with her friends. But a part of her felt the deep hole left by the knowledge that Oliver would remain at Montague Hall. She felt the emotion rise in her throat, trying with all her might to suppress it. There would be no way to know how long their separation would last. Or if they would all survive what was surely on the horizon.

CHAPTER THIRTY-THREE

"Wake up, Vieve!"

The voice of Elizabeth Montague was both firm and laced with pent up anger. Peering into the dim light of the candle that had been set on the open window ledge, she could see the aggressive expression on the face of the older woman. A cold hardness had set into the usual detachment that almost always emanated from her when dealing with those deemed beneath her station. Vieve felt the fear, ever-present, but up until this moment, somewhat elusive, now seeping unabated into her body. With Oliver and Elias in Charlestown and Lucy unable to make it up to the attic on her own, and the remaining house slaves in the cellar, she knew that the Mistress of Montague Hall had planned this visit. Vieve raised the back of her hand to her brow, squinting at her mistress and trying to see more clearly in the dead of night.

"Mistress Montague, is everything alright?"

Then she saw it, the whip in Elizabeth's right hand, coiled like a snake prepared to strike. Was this the snake-like creature in Ashwiyaa's vision? Without warning or hesitation, Elizabeth drew the black monstrosity back and brought it down, in one forceful motion, across the middle of the helpless girl lying on her pallet. The blistering sting of a thousand blades sliced into her back and side as she tried to maneuver her way from the attack. She cried out in agony. Elizabeth struck once more, then again, the blows piercing Vieve's back, side, and shoulder. Blood oozed through her night garment, as did the unbearable pain. Vieve struggled to breathe

"You were caught stealing food," Elizabeth smiled through the hazy light, pointing to the crumbled remains of Dumplin's fresh bread that had been placed on the attic floor near Vieve's pallet. "And you also stole one of my necklaces, which I have now recovered." She gave an evil grin to Vieve while fingering the silver necklace around her neck. "There is no one here for you to bewitch or cajole into helping you now."

"No. I would never steal from anyone." Vieve moaned, unable to quell the pain or emotion, as she tried to sit up on her pallet. "I would never do that."

"You have stolen and destroyed my family with your conniving ways! You have turned my daughter against my judgment, cast a spell on my youngest son, and caused the death of my oldest because you did not know your place. You never have known your place, which is why you were sent to the colonies to begin with. Now I have made sure that you know. I will never let a simpleton servant girl come between me and my family."

Vieve let the tears fall, overcome with fright and the intensity of the pain that Elizabeth had inflicted. She dared not respond at all, for fear of angering her mistress further.

"You will not speak of this to anyone. But even if you did, Elias will always support my authority, whether he disagrees with me, or whether he believes you or no. Because, as the Master here, he knows his place is to support my decisions, as well, to keep things running smoothly. Should you steal again, he would have no choice but to rid us of you entirely. I, alone, have the power to see that you do not do such again. I can ruin your life if I so choose. Make no mistake about that. Do not cross me, or you will not live to tell the tale. You are lucky I only struck you thrice. You deserved much more. Next time, you will surely know the full measure of my capability."

Elizabeth Montague coiled the whip and stuffed it into a cloth sack she had placed beside the door. Lifting the candle from the windowsill, she left without another word.

Vieve could feel her body trembling, both from the pain and the seasonal winter chill. The sadness was overwhelming, along with the knowledge that such as what she had just endured was only a mere taste of what had been routinely done to the slaves. She lifted her night garment over her head, then pulled the blankets up to her waist. Lying on her stomach, she rested her forehead on her arms and cried until exhaustion calmed her body. Her back and side, now exposed to the night air, hurt more than she thought possible, but she knew the chill would help to alleviate a measure of the physical pain. The emotional pain would take much more effort to heal.

"I miss you, Mama," she whispered into the darkness. "I wish you were here with me now."

Closing her eyes, she imagined Claire Whittier sitting beside her, talking in soft motherly tones.

"Remember how I used to run my fingers over your back when you were a little girl and could not sleep? Be still now. I will help you, my sweet girl."

"I remember, Mama," Vieve breathed, whispering. "I used to say that you were tickling my back. It was always so relaxing, so calming when you did that, and I felt so safe. You really loved me, didn't you?"

"I will always love you, Vieve. And I am here with you. Always… always…"

CHAPTER THIRTY-FOUR

"Best be quick about takin' care o' Vieve with that Sampson root and sage," Evaline murmured, watching for passersby at the door to the cookhouse. "Ain't no tellin' who out and about keepin' an eye on us all. She an evil one, Mistress, sho' nuf' is."

"I'm 'bout done, Mama," Maybelle made one more cursory rotation across the cuts and burns on Vieve's back and side with the pasty concoction. Used at face value for treating cooking injuries, the herbal medicine made with coneflower and sage was never discussed anywhere near any of the Montagues, for fear that they might discover what it was most used to treat. "There, that should help keep the pus from rising up too much."

"I apologize, Evaline, for telling you and Maybelle and Ash about what she did. But it hurt so much, and I was afraid it might get worse." Vieve looked down at the ground. "I knew that you would know what to do. It still pains me more than I can say when I think about the hobbling that Henny took, or the beatings given to others since I've been here." Vieve smoothed the front of her work dress, smiling at her friends.

"You think Mr. Thomas Paine is right about all that he says? Maybelle asked. You know if anyone ever knew that any of us had been allowed to read and hear that *Common Sense* writing that he did, we would all be whipped and more." Her eyes grew wide. "I believe him! He has stirred up people all over with his words. More folks around here are ready to fight."

"They are, yes," Vieve shook her head. "This war will have great consequences for us all. Perhaps none more important than for slaves.

I pray all the time that this country will one day be the great one that Mr. Paine thinks it can be. For all of us."

"Mama, I know you are sad that I'm leaving soon," Maybelle offered. "One day, we will all be together again. I can feel it. Jonsie, too. One day all this hope will bring good things."

"Sweet baby, I's happy you going to go," Evaline smiled. "You know Jude and me, we will miss you all, but this is better. You gots a real chance, all my girls here, at freedom. I happy you gonna go." She turned to Vieve. "Master Oliver, though, he mighty sweet on you. He don't want you to go, do he?"

"No, he does not want that," Vieve said, "but he knows that it is for the best and that we will find each other when this is all settled."

"You still ain't told him 'bout what his momma done to you?" Evaline asked. "That she the one that is the snake-like creature that Ashwiyaa saw?"

"No," Vieve responded, "I have not told him. I want him to know, but it will also hurt him that it was his own mother who did this. When he attempts to put his arms around me, I have tried very hard to conceal the pain. The physical scars will heal one day. The other ones, not so much. Maybe later I can tell him. But for now, he and Lucy have so much to deal with, you know, with Mal being gone, the war, and deciding about what to do with Montague Hall. I can tell him after time heals things up more. You know he is thinking hard about what to do so that one day all of us could live here. Live here in peace and not have to worry about being beaten or owned by another."

"We still a long way off from that, I fear." Maybelle responded. "The snake creature Mistress Montague wants none of that. But I trust Master Oliver and believe he means what he says. What he does is the same as what he says and that means a lot, to my mind."

"He still has to live with his family for now. So, there is much for him to be thinkin' on." Evaline said. "What about Mistress Lucy? Any hope she 'gon get better?"

"I don't honestly know, Evaline. She's pretty sick and I fear getting worse with time. I hope that this upcoming journey won't be too hard on her and that the doctor who will see her can actually help. We must all keep praying for her, for sure."

"We will do that, sho' 'nuf, we will pray for everyone," Evaline smiled. "Well, maybe not Mistress Montague, unless it's 'fo a change of heart. But she ain't got no heart, so that may be hard indeed."

"Mama," Maybelle grinned, "you'd best not be saying such too loud. You know other people might hear you."

"Then lemme go on back outside to do the pot stirrin' and such, so we all has some dinner." Evaline laughed. "I's tryin' to keep myself out of the troubles." She gave a wink to Vieve as she exited the cookhouse, mumbling a song under her breath.

"Maybelle, I have to ask you something. You've never told me this, but I know."

"What do you think you know?" Maybelle smiled again.

Vieve looked all around the cookhouse. No one else was close at hand. She lowered her voice, barely audible to anyone.

"I know you did the killing," she whispered. "And that you did it at great risk to yourself. And that you did it for me." Vieve smiled through tears. "You are the best friend I've ever had, Maybelle, and I love you so much."

Maybelle placed both hands on her hips, staring at Vieve, then out the doorway at Evaline tending the cooking pots.

"You right, I did it for you. You the best friend I ever had, too. I did it for my sister, also. And for all the sisters that bastard might have ever hurt. I've never wanted to be glad that anyone is dead." Maybelle pursed her lips. "But I'm glad he's gone. And I'd do it again if I had to. You'd best be getting on back to the big house. They will be calling for you soon, you know. Mistress Montague will be keeping an eye out for you until you're gone. Until we are all gone." Maybelle wiped her hands on the front of her apron and made her way outside toward Evaline.

Vieve stared at the cookhouse surroundings. Some of the best times in her life thus far had been spent here with Maybelle, Evaline, and Dumplin, with Ashwiyaa and Merrilee too. Cooking, washing, sharing work and time with one another in the midst of the wretched life of being owned by another. When Mistress and Master Montague, or the Overseer, Mr. Bennett, were not around, they had reveled in the moments of the briefest glimpse of what freedom might be like, being happy with trusted friends Vieve closed her eyes, picturing the scene of an imaginary Christmas dinner table, perhaps outside in the courtyard or under the Spanish moss, or *itla okla,* that she had come to love, with greenery and candles all around. The air would be laden with seasonal scents of a blazing fire, warm meats, sweet potatoes and nuts with cinnamon, mincemeat pie, and cups full of cider and rum for all. Singing, handholding, and a heartfelt blessing before the big meal would be lively and loving. Most of all, she imagined the laughter, and saw the faces of all the people she loved, void of any man owning another, together in one place, delighting in the festive celebration. How Claire Whittier and little Simon would have loved them all, as well.

Whether the British won or the Patriots were victorious in this terrible war, Vieve wondered what her fate would be, and those of the slaves, as well. Would it be possible to be free, as citizens of a new county, or would they find themselves still naught but possessions of whomever would be the ultimate victor? If the colonists were successful in staving off British rule, how long would it take for all in this brave new endeavor to realize the full measure of freedom for every man, woman, and child? She shared the beliefs of Mr. Thomas Paine, that this land was on the verge of being the most promising place in the known world. But she had taken heed of his warning that real changes of the heart and minds of people often took years beyond what anyone could see. Either way, the risk of joining the fight for freedom challenged and excited her more than anything ever had. What if, in years yet to be, her own children and those of Maybelle and Ash, could live in conditions far better than what any of them had ever known? This alone was worth that fight.

CHAPTER THIRTY-FIVE

Late February 1780

Ashwiyaa had gathered all of her meager belongings, along with her bow and arrows, and cleaned out her space in the barn except for her pallet bedding. The twilight hours had brought a strange but welcome sense of peace to an otherwise active day in preparation for the changes coming to all at Montague Hall.

"You say the British are approaching the Stono River?" She turned an inquisitive expression to Vieve. "They won't be long getting to mainland Charlestown, then up this way by late March, maybe."

"Yes, that's what Oliver said. We will leave at first light on the morrow. I think we are all prepared for the journey, as difficult as it will be. Lucy says that we will make extended stops along the way, seeking shelter with both Loyalists and Patriots alike, to give her and the horses rest, so the journey will be easier but a lengthier one, to be sure."

"The Cherokee have all but gone from around here and are now in the upper westernmost part of the province of South Carolina. Between the battles of war and the smallpox, many Indian tribes, Catawba too, are no more. My people fight for the Patriots, as you know. We have land in the northern part of South Carolina, though. I hope to get there one day, perhaps never to return to Montague Hall. But knowing that we will not see many Cherokees out there should make our travels safer. I will pray to *Wakan Tanka* for protection also." Ashwiyaa smiled.

"I will pray also," Vieve promised. "And pray for strength for Lucy to make the journey without too much difficulty. She just keeps getting weaker."

"Will you see Oliver tonight before we leave?"

Vieve smiled, fighting back the feeling of loss that rose inside her at the mention of Oliver Montague. She would miss him more than she was willing to admit.

"Yes, I will see him. We have much to talk about before I leave. I wish he were coming with us." Vieve hesitated, then added, "I fear I may never see him again."

"Do not let your heart and spirit hold those thoughts," Ashwiyaa said. "Whatever is going to happen, will happen. Have courage. *Wakan Tanka* has already smiled upon our courage. Perhaps your god will smile also."

"I do believe that God Almighty smiles when people are brave and courageous. Let's pray hard for our journey and for the journey of this land that we all live in. I'd best go now. I will see you in the morning."

The hours until she was alone with Oliver Montague had passed in a slow and painful creep into the darkest of night. Vieve had never been so glad to hear his soft knock on her attic door.

"Come in, Oliver." She struggled to hold her emotions in check, even as he approached her with his warm smile.

"Why do you still have on your work dress?" His smile grew bigger. "I'd have thought you would be quite prepared for the needed sleep tonight."

Vieve smiled back, knowing the blood-stained night garment she wore underneath her work dress was hidden, as were the wounds Elizabeth Montague had inflicted.

"I have just not yet managed to change into it," Vieve said. "There has been so much to do to prepare for this journey, Oliver …" her voice trailed off into silence, the tears rising in her eyes.

Oliver was by her side before she could act to keep him from holding her. His arms wrapped about her body in a way that made Vieve know he never wanted to be without her in his life. She flinched, struggling to recover from the wave of pain his hold had created.

"What is this?" He frowned, pushing her at arm's length. "What is wrong, Vieve?"

"It's nothing, you just surprised me, Oliver, that's all." She held his hands in hers.

"I am so sad at the thought of being away from you, of course."

Oliver let his arms envelope her once more, the firmness of his hold more intense than before. Her sharp and immediate intake of breath was not lost on him. He pushed back yet again.

"What is it, Vieve? Am I making you uncomfortable?" Frustration mounted in his voice.

"No. No, not at all, I just…I…" Vieve grasped for recovery, but to no avail. Tears clouded her vision. "I hurt myself, is all."

Oliver stared in silence, searching the green eyes for the meaning of her hesitation. He scowled, the recognition beginning to dawn.

"Turn around!" His voice was insistent, the hint of anger unmistakable.

"Oliver, it's alright, I just –"

"Now, Vieve. Turn around." His eyes burned into hers. She knew he would not be convinced otherwise. Shaking her head and biting her lower lip, she turned from him. She could feel his hands on her shoulders – gentle, soft, searching. He moved closer, pulling the work dress from her body and letting it fall to the floor. He stood in silence taking in the reddish streaks across the back of the night garment before he lifted the gown to reveal the partially healed cuts and burns across her back and side.

"Who did this?" He demanded, the rage simmering beneath the angry whisper. "When was this done to you? And why did you not tell me?" Oliver could see the delicate shoulders trembling. Soft sobs shook her body. "Vieve," he said her name with a gentler maneuver of turning her body to face him. "What happened?"

"It does not matter now, Oliver. It is done. We must let it be."

"You know that I will not let this be! I cannot. Who did this to you and why?"

"I cannot tell you. Others will be hurt if I do."

"Then I will tear Montague Hall down, piece by piece, until I find who is responsible. Tell me, Vieve! Now."

"Oliver," she whispered through tears, "do you not understand that what was done to me is only the tiniest part of what has been done to the slaves here – men and women most undeserving of such – and that is the real tragedy here."

"You are trying to deter me from finding out the truth!" He frowned eyes blazing. "The Overseer did not do this. The marks are not deep enough to be his. But they are red and deep, nonetheless. Who, then?" His tone was demanding.

"Please, Oliver," Vieve murmured under her breath, "don't make me tell you. You will only be sadder and angrier."

Oliver's darkened eyes clouded with both tears of revelation and anger at the abominable act.

"My mother did this, didn't she?" His voice resonated with quiet rage. His fists clenched in attempts to control the building emotion. "My god, Vieve, why? Why?" He grabbed her shoulders, then released her. "I can't even hold you to give you comfort! Damn her. Damn her!" He turned toward the door, running fingers through his dark hair.

"Oliver, no!" Vieve stepped in front of him, placing her hands on his chest. "We are leaving in the morning. What's done is done! Leave this be, for me. For Lucy. Please, come and sit."

"Tell me what happened," he asked after taking his place beside her on the floor pallet.

"She came here the night you and your father were in Charlestown. She blames me for turning you and Lucy against her. She blames me for Mal's death."

"I should have known. I should have seen this coming, with her deep sadness at Mal's death, Lucy's illness, the war, her wanting to return to Charlestown to live . Vieve, I'm so sorry. She has blamed you for her inability to face what she herself has done."

"Oliver, you must promise me two things," Vieve stroked his arm before holding his hands again in hers. "Promise me that you will let me handle this in my own way. After all, she wronged me and not you, even though I know you do not like what has been done. You must promise me that."

"Very well, then. I give you my word, Vieve. But only because I love you more than you could ever know. So, what is the second thing?"

"I want you to stay here with me tonight. Just be close to me. Because I love you more than you will ever know and the thought of being away from you is almost more than I can bear."

Oliver brushed the locks of long hair from her eyes and stroked her face with his fingers.

"Vieve Whittier, nothing would make me happier than to stay here with you. You remember the plans we talked about for when this war is done? You must because I do not want to live this life without you. Stay beside me this night, as close as you can. There are one or two things we must discuss further before the morning is here."

CHAPTER THIRTY-SIX

Vieve woke first, anxious about what the day would bring, as only the dimmest fingers of pinkish light had begun to stretch across the still dark sky. Oliver bestowed the gentlest of morning kisses before he made his way back to his bedchamber. She braided her hair and slipped on the dress that Lucy had given her for the long journey inland. Carrying her cloth bag that had held her few belongings when she arrived here, Vieve placed her straw hat on her head and gazed out the attic window one last time at the courtyard of Montague Hall. She had said her goodbyes to all but the land she had grown to love. London had been crowded and dirty, though filled with magnificence. But this place, this South Carolina, had intrigued her with its pristine beauty from the first moment she had witnessed the undulating waves of *itla okla* in the massive live oak trees. The fields of rice and indigo, the abundant harvests of fresh fruits and vegetables were sights to behold. If not for the terrible plight of the slaves, she would have loved them that much more. But the slaves had also become her best friends, beloved family, when her own had been torn apart in a most cruel fate. She would miss them all.

"Goodbye," she whispered. "Maybe when I return much will be better after this terrible war, this price for freedom that we must all pay. I pray that it is so."

Washing down the morsels of fresh bread with several sips of cider, she helped Maybelle and Ashwiyaa load Lucy into the back of the wagon, along with supplies for the journey, before climbing aboard. Elias had seated himself into the front carriage seat and was adjusting the reins for the ride after bidding farewell to Elizabeth and Oliver, who waved them onward from the top of the stairs before making their way back inside the big house. As the traveling party started down the worn path from the front of Montague Hall, Oliver appeared in the doorway, shouting.

"Father, stop! Could you send Vieve back, there's one thing she needs to retrieve."

Vieve jumped from the wagon, moving before Elias could respond.

"I will make haste, Master Montague, for whatever it is that has been forgotten."

"Be quick about it, then," Elias Montague admonished her.

From the back of the wagon, Maybelle, Ashwiyaa, and Lucy all exchanged wondering glances. Maybelle smiled, shrugging her shoulders. Once inside, Vieve faced Elizabeth standing in the drawing room with Oliver.

"What has she forgotten?" Elizabeth turned to her son. The questioning disdain was evident in her voice. Vieve glanced toward the dining room where Dumplin and Evaline were cleaning the table, and able to hear every word.

"I forgot to tell you what must be said before I leave this place." Vieve spoke in a confident and calm voice, surprising even herself at her resolve to see this act of defiance through.

"I do not need to hear anything from you. Leave us now."

"No," Vieve took a step closer to the Mistress of Montague Hall. "I must say this to you. I am seventeen now. My time as your indentured servant is almost over or will be very soon."

Elizabeth raised a hand to silence the girl, but Oliver intervened.

"Listen to her, Mother. I insist upon it."

Elizabeth Montague's eyes narrowed. Her brows knit together in an angry frown.

"I regret the death of your son, though it was by his own doing and none of mine. You loved him. I regret his loss for you, as I know all too well about losing beloved family. I regret that you have witnessed the decline of your daughter's health. I regret that you do not know the measure of the man that your son Oliver has become, and cannot accept that I love him more than I ever thought possible. You raised two children who have searched their hearts and minds and chosen the way of true freedom and integrity."

"Stop talking to me!" Elizabeth spat the words between gritted teeth.

"I will not, Elizabeth," Vieve stated with all the calmness she could muster. "I could hate you not only for what you have done to me, but mostly for the indignity and cruelty inflicted upon those who have only served you despite your wretched treatment of them. You are an unhappy woman and you've acted accordingly. So, I pity you instead. I choose happiness. I choose life, my faith, and freedom. And from this moment on, I choose to be better than what you have chosen. I forgive you. And pray that God will one day change your heart and forgive you too, when you are brave enough to seek His forgiveness. Goodbye, Elizabeth."

Vieve turned to face the man she had grown to cherish.

"I love you, Oliver Montague. And I will wait for you."

"I love you, Vieve Whittier. Now and always."

She did not wait to see the tears in Elizabeth's eyes before bounding down the front stairs of the great hall. The plan she had made with Oliver had been successful.

"What did you forget that took so long to retrieve?" Elias Montague asked, as she climbed back into the wagon, nodding at the curious glances from her friends.

"My soul," she breathed in the softest of whispers, "but I found it at last. Thank you for waiting for me, Sir."

Elias Montague shook his head and the reins, urging the horses and wagon forward. He wondered what the young woman meant. Regardless, he admitted to himself that she had done more to help his daughter than anyone. Servant or no, she was becoming a fetching, polished, and bright young woman. No wonder that both his sons had been taken with her.

CHAPTER THIRTY-SEVEN

Somewhere near the Broad River, Cedar Creek in the Saxe Gotha area of the Fairfield District of South Carolina, 1781

The journey to the South Carolina area in the upper part of the province near the Broad River had been an arduous one, even with more overnight stops than needed for the benefit of Lucy, who often struggled with the discomforts of the wooded paths. Though Vieve knew her physical condition was worsening, she delighted in seeing Lucy happier than ever before, laughing, and trying to sing with her friends, with less of the burdensome trappings of social class at Montague Hall. Even Elias Montague appeared more unencumbered with the demands and expectations of plantation mastership, singing with the traveling party on occasion, and smiling more than Vieve had ever witnessed.

Why can't he be this man all the time? Like Lord Carrington, back in London, who behaved more like a father to me when Lady Carrington was not present. Vieve had known, in an instinctive sort of way, even as a child, that Lord Carrington had loved her mother, and that his marriage to Lady Carrington had been one also born of societal demands, though she had not understood precisely where she and Simon, along with Claire, had stood in the hierarchy of individual prominence. Over time, she had come to understand her place, as both Lady Carrington and Mistress Montague had reiterated it in excruciating detail. For a brief moment, she pondered it all, how she had come to see herself in a different way more in keeping with the visions of Mr. Thomas Paine.

She knew that Claire Whittier would be more than proud of the young woman she had become here in this country, though she could never forget the poverty or station from which she had come, nor her status as an indentured servant in this place.

During these travels through the forests, Vieve had spent many a quiet moment, perhaps most often at night whenever the light of the moon was in sight, giving thought to the machinations of this war for independence. In some ways it mirrored the behaviors of humans, with certain expectations of class and allegiances. Ardent Loyalists and Patriots alike were often vocal about their beliefs and yet the barbarity of war was also being carried out with a measure of ordered rules of engagement. Though she had heard tell of physical altercations between groups of local people, she was aware that both the British and the Patriots were more interested in convincing colonists to adhere to their side without the threat of violence, as both desired the acquisition of support. Though plenty of Loyalists were prevalent in South Carolina, she could sense that there was a strong and growing spirit of patriotism in the making, no doubt fueled by the fiery rhetoric of Thomas Paine and others. While Elias Montague favored a patriotic bend himself, his behavior and words often carried a more neutral and diplomatic tone, perhaps in the interest of safety, or the prevention of destruction of his Montague Hall. Regardless of his intention, his diplomacy had also added a layer of safety in their travels to their final destination.

"Cousin, it is so good to see you once again! Welcome, all!"

The voice of John Geiger rang out from the top of the steps of his affluent home situated on a sprawling farm. The area here possessed a gentle rolling terrain, not as flat as their lowcountry, and no *itla okla* was in sight. Thick woods, green and sweet, graced the richly soiled ground, and the nearby rivers were clear and fresh, with wildlife in abundance. The air in this upper part of the province was somewhat cooler at times, less humid, but not much. Towering pine trees abounded, appearing to touch the sky.

John Geiger had been a Grand Juror in these parts, but was now quite invalid, his right arm and leg having been hampered by apoplexy. He required the assisting strong arms of his daughter, Emily Geiger, a statuesque, dark-haired young woman, who appeared close in age to Lucy. Vieve felt a kindred spirit with her personable nature, despite her obvious place as the mistress of the farm, since her mother had been gone for some time. Two of the house slaves carried the belongings of Lucy and Elias and helped to carry a tired but happy Lucy into the house, where the visitors were given refreshment and the opportunity to rest. Lucy was placed in the bedchamber with Emily, while Elias was given a room close at hand. Vieve, Maybelle, and Ashwiyaa were given bedding pallets in the nearby livery stable, which pleased Ashwiyaa. Lucy had made Emily Geiger aware of her unique relationship with the servants, and the young woman had been obliged to entertain the wishes of her guest by welcoming the servants into the shared bedchamber to help and visit with Lucy.

"You are friends with these servants and slaves?" Emily was curious. "How very odd indeed. "I don't know what to make of this. Our slaves are a necessity, and they are treated well, unless of course they are negligent in their duties. Then their punishment is done by an overseer, of course."

Vieve made an uncomfortable shift toward Maybelle and Ashwiyaa, who stood in awkward silence before Lucy and Emily. The conversation reminded her of childhood days in London, followed by the days when she had first been introduced to Lucy. How inferior she had felt.

"Emily," Lucy began, "I implore you to hear me about my friends." The ever-present halting breaths and coughing interrupted her words. "I was cruel. I thought it acceptable, that it was my place to be such to those who served us. I was wrong. Terribly so. I implore you now to permit our interaction in private, not around your father or mine, as we have come to be more than slave or mistress in our exchanges with one another. Please, even if you disagree, allow us this temporary courtesy during our time here, I beg you."

Emily Geiger stared at the young women, her eyes darting back and forth between them all. Such a strangeness she had never heard. She knew of Lucy's weakening condition and decided to honor this most odd of requests.

"Very well." She turned to the servants. "You may all speak freely in my presence, and I shall do so in yours."

Lucy gave a triumphant smile to her friends. Maybelle decided to be the first to speak.

"Miss Emily, might I request some water and soap, perhaps a soothing spirit for Lucy, so that we might help her prepare for sleeping?"

"Good heavens!" Emily exclaimed, turning to Lucy. "She speaks as we do. How is this so? Did you teach her even though it is forbidden?"

"You will find that we have all taught each other many things," Vieve spoke up, "but Maybelle taught herself to speak in a formal way, as we learned to do, before we knew one another. She is one of the smartest people I know. Of course, she has to keep that a secret from those who would not condone it."

"And you?" Emily turned her attention to Ashwiyaa. "Can you speak, as well?"

"Yes," Ashwiyaa responded, a hint of irritation in her voice. "I speak."

"Ashwiyaa taught us how to use a bow and arrow, and information about the land around us. She has a tomahawk as well. I know how to use a bow and arrow also, but I can no longer do so." Lucy rubbed her legs as she sat on the bedding, with pillows propped behind her.

"I must say, I am astounded and bewildered by this," Emily shook her head. "I find it all most curious and daring, especially for women" she smiled, "so I will keep your secret."

"Please tell us about yourself, Miss Emily." Vieve asked.

"Very well," the young woman close to their age agreed, weaving a lock of wayward brown hair around her finger. "However, if I am to hold your secret in confidence, then you must not call me by any title, as well, when we are alone. And you must keep my secret as well when

I have one to keep. I will be simply 'Emily." She gave a quick nod of her head and flashed a bright smile to the delight of them all.

"I can ride as good, or even better, than many men around here, even side-saddle. My father has taught me a lot about farming, and I can shoot a flintlock rifle. Of course, I can attend to all of the womanly duties, as required, and help in the matters of business. We are Patriots, my father and me. I would fight if such were permissible for women. There are many Tories who live in this area, but we are liked by most. Lucy, I know you and your father are Patriots. What of the rest of you?"

"I am a Patriot," Vieve declared, "though I am from London, and still speak with my British voice of sorts. I believe that slavery or any form of forced servitude should be abolished and is wrong. I have come to learn that these unfortunate conditions have been a part of most every country in history, and that all of our peoples have been both enslaved and enslaver. Therefore, it seems truly strange to me that such an atrocity is still embraced, or that any so-called civilized country could condone it. No disrespect intended to you, Emily. But you asked where our allegiances lie, and that is where my heart is. I want freedom and independence for all, a reconciling if you will."

"I believe as Vieve does," Ashwiyaa spoke up. "My people have fought with the Patriots against the British and the Cherokee. We have been treated with cruelty and deception many times. We have also been treated with honor and friendship by some, and we have engaged in slavery as well. I, too, want to see a free land, especially for my people, who have suffered much."

"How did you become as you are now, not a savage?"

Ashwiyaa bristled, crossing her arms and planting her feet apart in a wider stance of defiance. Vieve held her breath.

"What do you mean by 'savage'? We are the same as your people in many ways. We have been made slaves and we have enslaved, as Vieve said. We are fierce warriors when called to protect our own." She took a step toward Emily, a smile crossing her face as Emily retreated with a backward step. "Indians are peace-seeking, able to care for ourselves and the land, as the Great Spirit commands. If that is 'savage,' then we are that."

"I have offended you. I am sorry. It is what I have been taught for a long time. I have not known an Indian or anyone such as you." Emily wrung her hands together. "And you, Maybelle?" She raised her eyes to the Negro slave. "I have never spoken with a Negro like you. I imagine you would side with the Crown?"

"I want to see freedom for all people, especially mine," Maybelle's eyes blazed. "But, unlike you and your people, I do not know what will be done with my people when this war is finished. Will we be free, as you are? Or made slaves again, perhaps even more cruelly than now, if that is possible. If the British win, will we also have those hard-won liberties taken from us in some way? Patriots are fighting for the same self-rule, are they not? There are no good answers as yet. For now, I am a Patriot, as you are. But much is still unknown for me. I would like to believe that one day Negroes would be free men also. I would fight for that. I do fight for that."

Emily studied them, these young women like herself in some ways, and yet a vast sea of difference remained between them. They had become the most loyal of friends despite everything. She wondered at the pangs of envy pulling at her heart.

"I must say again that I do not know what to make of all of this, of the lot of you. I feel as though I will be awake for a long spell this night, thinking about all that we have discussed." She paused in deep thought. "I am most interested in talking with you more if you will oblige me. Perhaps this will be a great and unusual and daring and forbidden adventure, will it not?"

CHAPTER THIRTY-EIGHT

July 1, 1781

"Lucy?" Emily Geiger dropped the handle to the wagon and rushed to her second cousin. "Are you alright? Perhaps this morning's walk was ill-advised."

Maybelle knelt by one side of the wagon and Vieve, the other. Ashwiyaa stopped walking, a fair distance in front of the rest. Lucy lifted a hand, with noted difficulty, from her seat in the wagon, leaning forward and coughing in violent spasms. She could no longer walk, despite the best efforts of the young physician who had also attempted to treat John Geiger. Though he had been trained by the renowned Dr. Benjamin Rush, no treatment had been successful for Lucy, including the small administrations of calomel, emetics, and even bloodletting, The teas that Ashwiyaa created from mint and black cohosh seemed to provide more relief to her wracked body than any other treatment. With gentle care, Elias Montague and Lucy had been told of the severity of her condition, and that the deterioration would continue. She struggled to breath at times, and often feared her heart would stop beating, the pain would never cease, and that she would lose complete control of her body and limbs.

Vieve placed a hand on Lucy's back, stroking with gentle motions and retrieving a cloth to wipe the damp brow and mouth. She had dreaded the conversation with Elias Montague about his daughter. Closing her eyes, she tried to remember all that he had said when he had summoned her outside for a private conversation. His face had been worn, his shoulders slumped, as if he had carried the weight of all of South Carolina.

"I need you to tell the others that her condition will not improve. All has been done for her that can be done. Her body is overcome with illness. She would not survive an attempt to journey back home. I ask that you give her your best attention and care until her days are done."

Vieve had felt the tears threatening to rise, looking up at the sky to avert them, and avoiding exchanging glances with the others until she had to tell them. While Lucy had slept, she had apprised them of the news delivered by the doctor and Elias. Though none had been surprised, all had been overcome with intense emotion at the thought of losing their friend. Vieve wondered what Elias Montague intended to do with them all, upon Lucy's death, whenever that might be. There was no way that she could leave these friends who had become family. As Mr. Thomas Paine had once told her, she wanted to be sure that she had given adequate thought to all of her choices, whatever they would ultimately be.

"I'm so tired," Lucy breathed hard. "I need to sleep."

"Let's get you down in this wagon. You can sleep while we walk back to the big house." Maybelle and Vieve held her hands and supported Lucy's back while stretching her out on her side in the wagon Oliver had made. Emily fluffed the blanket together into a soft pillow for her head.

"Thank you," Lucy tried to smile. "Vieve," her eyes fluttered open. "Oliver sends his love." The weak and weary eyes closed once more. Vieve held a hand over her own eyes, struggling to suppress the tears at Lucy's repetition of news from a recent letter and at the sadness she felt from missing Oliver more than she thought possible. Her correspondence had to come by way of Lucy, as letters to any slave or servant would be read, if permitted at all.

Emily Geiger knelt beside Vieve, placing a hand on her shoulder, and smiling.

"Oliver must love you so much. How wonderful to have each other in that special way. I envy you sometimes, Vieve. I'm so glad that you all are here with us."

"We should get her back to the house now. Emily, if you wish, we can work some more on teaching you how to use a bow and arrow and a tomahawk." Ashwiyaa offered.

"I would very much like to learn how to use your rifle also, if you could teach me," Vieve added.

Emily pulled the wagon, letting Ashwiyaa lead the way back to the farmhouse. The light dinnertime repast would give them each time to absorb the emotions and any of the war news that might come their way. Rounding the path to the farm entrance, the walking party saw a visiting wagon tethered in front of the Geiger home.

"That is a neighbor from down the road aways," Emily explained. "Mr. Herman Kinsler is a good friend of my father's and also a Patriot who hears word of the battles and keeps my father apprised as much as he is able. He visits when time allows and almost always has news to share. Perhaps today will be good news for us."

"Ash will take the wagon to the livery stable," Maybelle said. "Vieve, you and Emily and I can get Lucy upstairs to her bedchamber."

"I will visit with Father and Mr. Kinsler after we take care of Lucy," Emily responded. "I will let you know of any news."

When Lucy was resting in Emily's room, Vieve offered to stay with her while Emily visited with their company.

"Come for me, if she takes a bad turn," Emily insisted, waving to Vieve as she made her way to the door and down the stairs to the drawing room to join her father and his guest.

"Good morning, Mr. Kinsler," Emily smiled at the pleasant man before her. "Father always loves it when you are able to visit with him." She accepted a cup of cider from one of the house slaves and settled into a chair for the conversation.

"Good day to you, Miss Emily," Herman Kinsler gave her a broad smile. "I do bring some news, both good and less so," he offered.

"So, after the terrible Southern defeats of General Gates in Camden, back in August of '70, then in Charlestown in May of '80, and Camden in August of '80, where we lost a majority of our army, there is good news?" John Geiger clasped his hands together.

"Indeed, there is," Herman Kinsler responded, smiling "We are fighters here in the Carolinas. Cornwallis has discovered that our Patriot militia here in the backcountry, under the auspices of Francis Marion, Andrew Pickens, and Thomas Sumter, have been diligent in preventing more British successes in battle. To be sure, they were defeated at Kings Mountain, in October of '80 by Ferguson and the Overmountain men, and also at Cowpens, near Thicketty Creek, under Daniel Morgan, who defeated that odious Colonel Banastre Tarleton, back a few months in January."

"Ah, that is most excellent news!" John Geiger exclaimed, raising his cup of cider with his left hand, and tapping the arm of his chair with the less-functional right hand. "And what is this news of General Nathanael Greene that you bear today?"

"As you already know, there are inadequate supplies all around, for us and the British," Herman Kinsler explained. "General Nathanael Greene was given command of the Southern Department of the Continental Army, after the defeats we suffered. He knew that our forces, dedicated as they are, were inexperienced and poorly supplied in contrast to the British forces."

"How has he achieved his victories then?" Emily Geiger questioned him.

"General Greene was aware that the British were slow-moving and predictable in their endeavors," Herman Kinsler stated. "He knew that he could make successful sudden and brief attacks and perhaps conquer them by attrition. He also divided and weakened his own army, which was quite a risky and daring move, as it forced Cornwallis to do the same. He then decided to have his men retreat, which forced Cornwallis to follow them far from their base of supplies in Charlestown. As a result, General Greene outwitted his enemy."

"And now?" Emily leaned forward in her chair. "Where is General Greene now?"

"His encampment is about two miles from here," Herman Kinsler said, near the Enoree and Broad Rivers. His forces have taken the interior British garrisons one at a time. The last British stronghold is the fortified town of Ninety-Six, where Greene's siege began. Lord Rawdon was bringing two thousand troops from Charlestown to relieve the weakened British, who were awaiting his arrival. With Rawdon only thirty miles away, General Greene was forced to raise the siege and retreat north across the Broad River."

Herman Kinsler shifted in his seat, accepting more cider before continuing.

"Rawdon, however, knew that his forces were too far from Charlestown to receive the necessary support, so he has burned the fort and the town, and has relocated the garrison near Orangeburg. General Greene wishes to enlist the help of General Thomas Sumter and General Francis Marion in defeating Lord Rawdon once and for all."

"That is good news, is it not?" John Geiger asked.

"There is a problem, however," Herman Kinsler paused, looking at both Geigers. "The Patriot forces are severely weakened by battle and lack of supplies. General Greene is in dire need of a courier to deliver a message to General Sumter. The journey is past Fort Granby through some swampy land to General Sumter, who is encamped on the Wateree River. At best, it is a full two-or-more day ride, I'm afraid."

"Father, that is past Uncle Jacob's house, not very far from there, I don't think?"

Emily studied her father's face, the intense frown evident.

"It is, yes," he responded. "I would give anything if I could fulfill that mission for him." He patted his legs with his left hand. "Sadly, that is not possible, I regret to say."

"Knowing General Greene, I feel certain he will not rest until someone is found who can make such an important and dangerous journey," Herman Kinsler noted, "or he will be forced to wait until one of his men is recovered enough to do so."

"Mr. Kinsler, Father, please excuse me, I think I should go check on Lucy. Thank you so much, Mr. Kinsler, for your visit, and for informing us of the latest news about our Patriot cause. Good day to you, Sir, and safe travels back to your home."

Making her way to the livery stable, Emily found one of the slaves.

"Saddle my horse," she demanded, "I will be back momentarily. And tell no one that I have left for the day."

Ashwiyaa stood in silence behind one of the stalls, listening as Emily gave further instructions. The young woman was up to something important. Leaving the livery, Ashwiyaa found Vieve and Maybelle and relayed all that she had heard.

"Follow her, Ash. Can you do that? Take one of the horses. Maybelle and I will take care of all here."

"I can follow her, and she will never know I'm there," Ashwiyaa smiled. "What do you think she is doing?"

"I have no idea," Vieve said, "but it's safe to say that she thinks it necessary. It is concerning that she wants it kept a secret. We will say nothing to anyone here. But she should be followed, even if it is just for her safety, as dangerous as it is out there now."

"I can go ask one of the slaves for some provisions for you, while you are preparing," Maybelle offered. "I agree with Vieve. Lucy is on the verge of death and yet she leaves. Something is amiss.

CHAPTER THIRTY-NINE

Ashwiyaa had no trouble trailing her prey through thick woods and weaving around worn paths. The ability to scout, read the land, and remain hidden from enemies had been taught to her when she was young by her father, a respected Catawba chieftain, the knowledge of which had served her well. Emily Geiger knew where she was going and could identify the route she would take to reach her destination. But her skills were no match for the Indian girl who tracked her from a safe distance. Ashwiyaa rode in silence behind the girl, making careful note of all that was around them.

Judging from the position of the sun and the resulting shadows, it was mid-day when Emily came upon a military encampment in the vicinity of the Enoree and Broad Rivers. These soldiers were Patriots, without the trappings of the well-trained British. Ashwiyaa secured her horse nearby and crept closer to the entrance. Emily Geiger had been halted by guards and was being questioned about her intentions there.

"It is imperative that I speak with General Nathanael Greene." Emily tilted her hat back on her head, wiping her brow "It is my understanding that he seeks a courier. I should like to speak with him about his request."

Ashwiyaa could not see where the girl was being taken, but her horse was given water and rest while one of the guards escorted her, no doubt to General Greene's headquarters. Ashwiyaa headed back to her own horse, where she decided to wait for Emily Geiger to begin her return home.

Inside the makeshift headquarters, General Greene, sturdy in stature, was flanked by two officers and standing beside a sizable rectangular table. He wore the standard tan breeches and blue military coat with gold trim and epaulets. Personable in demeanor, he was a self-taught man who valued a strong work ethic and the notion of independence. General Greene pointed at a map laid out on the table and was engaged in discussing pertinent information about a location therein. All discussion halted when Emily Geiger was announced. Each of the men smiled when the young woman appeared before them, her farm dress and hair disheveled by the ride through the woods in the June South Carolina heat.

"Good day to you, Miss Geiger. What a most pleasant oddity it is to receive the company of a woman such as yourself in the middle of war. How might I help you?" General Greene inquired.

"Thank you for seeing me, General Greene, but it is I who can be of great assistance to you, I hope," Emily retorted, not smiling. "I understand you are seeking a courier to deliver a message to General Sumter near the Wateree."

Nathanael Greene stepped from behind the table, smiling alongside his men, and regarding Emily with mild interest. He crossed his arms, studying the young woman before him.

"You have a courier for me?" His smile was more exaggerated.

"Yes, Sir, I do. I can deliver the message for you."

The officers smiled, not hiding their collective amusement. A few whispered to one another. One whispered something to Nathanael Greene, who was diplomatic in his response, but unreceptive to her intentions.

"Miss Geiger, I have just been told that you are the daughter of John Geiger, a most ardent Patriot in this area, is that true?"

"Yes, that is correct. My father is invalid, or he would have been most insistent on carrying your message himself. I am as ardent a Patriot as he, so I am prepared to act in his stead."

General Greene relaxed his stance, resting against the table, arms still crossed, now extending his legs, and crossing them at the ankles in front of him.

"Miss Geiger, I appreciate your dedication to the independence of this fledgling country, and your most courageous offer to assist with our war efforts. I do seek a courier to deliver a message to General Sumter. I deeply admire your willingness to place yourself in such danger. However, for many reasons, I could not expect – much less, ask – a woman to place herself in such a tenuous position."

"May I speak in earnest with you?" Emily maintained her steady gaze on the general.

"Please do so," General Greene responded.

"Your men, though capable, are battle-weary, I have been told. You lack supplies and fresh horses, and need someone who is a strong rider, who knows the land and the route needed to make this journey, do you not?"

"That is correct." General Greene still held his smile.

"If I may be more direct, Sir," Emily continued, "you have failed, to date, at taking Ninety-Six. You seek the help of General Sumter and possibly Francis Marion to defeat Lord Rawdon, so it is imperative that a message reach General Sumter."

General Greene's eyebrows raised in surprise at the knowledge the young woman possessed. He nodded his head to affirm her comment and motioned for her to continue.

"Ninety-Six has been burned, destroyed, and Lord Rawdon has moved the garrison to Orangeburg, if I have been told accurately by my father and his friend, Mr. Herman Kinsler, also a Patriot. I live two miles from this encampment. My uncle Jacob Geiger and cousin John Conrad Geiger reside past Fort Granby, not terribly far from where General Sumter is said to be encamped at the Wateree." Emily paused, making eye contact with each of the officers and resting her gaze on General Greene. "While you might question my capability, I am as accomplished a rider as any man in this area. I am intimately familiar with the most dangerous part of the route, as my uncle's house is roughly five miles past the British-controlled Fort Granby. I know how to circumvent the worst of the journey."

General Nathanael Greene was listening with great intent to every word she said, Emily was certain. The smile disappeared from his countenance. He raised a hand to rub his chin before the smile returned once again.

"You have my attention, Miss Geiger. Tell me, precisely, how would you proceed with this endeavor, what route would you take?"

"I would cross the Saluda at Kennerly's ferry, just above it's junction with the Broad River, then cross the Congaree at Friday's ferry, just below the river junctures, then as directly as possible onto General Sumter, taking circuitous routes as needed in the event the enemy is near." Emily paused, noting the attention she now commanded.

"General Greene, if I might plead my case, a woman is a sound choice for a currier. I can ride side-saddle during the day, to further disguise my intentions, and the British would be much less suspicious of a woman going to see her uncle and cousin."

She studied the faces of each of the men. Their expressions had softened from disbelief to reserved admiration for her knowledge and willingness to serve in such a dangerous mission. General Greene exchanged glances with each of them.

"Sir," Emily pressed him further, "I know that you are reluctant to send a woman to do as you need. With all due respect, if the men here can dedicate years of their very lives and souls to the Patriot cause, why would it not be permissible for me to eagerly volunteer to assist in any way that I might? If I am able to do so for you when you and our soldier most need help from a countryman – or woman – and deeply desire to help, why should I not be allowed to serve my country as well?"

Emily gave a broad smile to all. "I implore you to let me do this. I fully understand the dangers, accept the risk involved, and I know I can deliver your message. I want to help our cause in some truly meaningful way."

"Miss Geiger, I must say you have presented a well-thought-out plan and display an admirable knowledge of the terrain and route needed to accomplish this task. While I do not enjoy the notion of placing a woman in harm's way, as women are the bearers of our children and the keepers of all that make us successful in this life, I am inclined to accept your most unusual and brave offer. How soon could you depart?"

"In the morning, Sir. Just before first light."

Emily listened to his repeated instructions, then stated them aloud for General Greene to be sure she had noted every detail. While he penned a letter to General Sumter, she reviewed the instructions in her head as he had requested her to memorize them. Once, twice, thrice, she repeated the message to commit the entirety to memory. Mounting her horse to make the return journey home, she waved to the appreciative soldiers. All but two had given her the most gracious of smiles.

"We need to get word to Lowry, somehow," one of the British spies embedded in the Patriot camp whispered to the other. "He will be able to find a way to stop her, or anyone giving her aid."

CHAPTER FORTY

"Wait," Vieve demanded of Ashwiyaa as the girls huddled with Lucy after supper behind the closed door of the bedchamber, "Emily went to the Patriot camp of General Greene, and they applauded her when she left the encampment? What is she up to, what is she going to do?

"I do not know. I could not get anywhere close enough to hear what was going on, and I could not see or hear her conversation with General Greene."

"Why did she not tell anyone where she was going?" Maybelle wondered aloud.

"I know," Lucy offered, breathing harder and allowing her friends to help her sit up to face them. "She swore me to secrecy, but it seems you now know most of it, so I will tell you."

The girls listened to Lucy, as slow and difficult as her telling of the mission was, and stared at her in disbelief.

"For certain, she intends to attempt this most dangerous journey alone. If they capture her, they will imprison her, or much worse!" Vieve exclaimed. "We can't let her do this."

Lucy rubbed her legs with the hand that now functioned the best and took a deep breath, coughing and leaning against Vieve.

"There is something you all need to know," she breathed. "And I have been trying to think about how to help. Vieve has not shared this, I don't think, but it must be shared." Lucy's voice wavered as the tears gathered and found their way down her cheeks. "My mother has convinced my father to get rid of Vieve."

She coughed again, noting the horror on the faces of Ashwiyaa and Maybelle.

"She would get rid of Ashwiyaa also, if she could, but she knows that my father and Oliver need her skills. She wants Maybelle to come back, as any slave would be needed, but the war is changing everything, of course." Lucy turned to Vieve. "I'm sorry. I know you were not going to share it, so no one would worry. But Emily received a letter from Oliver, as any correspondence with you would be read. He sends his love, along with his assurance that he intends to honor the plans you made to find one another, and that he will not rest until that is done. Emily has sent him a response as well, though of course she has taken care in case it is read by my mother."

Vieve embraced the sickly girl and looked to the others. What a dilemma they now faced, each with an uncertain future.

"I don't know what to do," she brushed back her own tears, "I miss Oliver so. I must think about what I can do."

"I will not go back to Montague Hall without you!" Ashwiyaa was defiant. "Even though there are more Cherokee in these parts and westward, I will not leave you all."

"Nor I, "Maybelle added. "Mama and Jude have each other and they will be free to leave if they choose to do so. Even Jonsie can join them if freedom is still given to Negroes by the British. They might not even be at Montague Hall if I were to return."

"I have a solution," Lucy struggled to speak. "It is the best one."

"What about you, Lucy?" Vieve reached for her hand. "We can't leave you either."

"Yes, you can," Lucy breathed hard once more. "You must. You all know that I will not live much longer. I would never make it back home. My life is almost finished, and I have fully embraced that fate. I will be with My Lord in heaven, and I rejoice in that, truly, I do not despair."

Vieve tried to respond through her tears, but Lucy intervened.

"Let me finish this." She gave the best smile she could manage. "I have already figured this out and you must do it, all of you. For me."

"What do you mean?" Ashwiyaa asked.

"You must go with Emily."

"What? Go with Emily? How, what would we do? Even if we were to do so, we would likely be sent back to Montague Hall, or severely punished, if caught." Vieve said, "Then a worse fate might await us all."

"No," Lucy explained, "with this war as it is, you could go as Emily's slaves or servants, all of you. And upon reaching the camp of General Sumter, I know he could get you all at least to the Catawba Reservation. They are allies, as you know. With Ashwiyaa there, the Catawba would not be inclined to send you back."

"What about Emily, will she even allow us to accompany her? What if we slow her down? And Elias, what of him?" Maybelle asked.

"Leave my father to me," Lucy smiled, "and as for Emily, I have already secured her agreement. With you alongside her, the secret intentions are more hidden, as your being her servants would be most believable. You are all strong and can handle the difficulty of such a journey, especially with Ash there."

"We must think this through," Vieve insisted. "If we return to Montague Hall, we could be forced into the same as before. Or, the British have given Negroes and those forced into servitude the choice of fighting for them or remaining there. We are not men, so our choices are further limited. And Elizabeth Montague would look for a way to get rid of me. She has already tried to encourage my silence."

"If we do this with Emily Geiger, we could also be captured and returned anyway," Ashwiyaa reminded them all, "but we just might make it."

"If we do make it, would we not be helping South Carolina?" Maybelle asked. "We don't know how this war is going to end, but either way, slavery might still be my fate. Making it to the reservation sounds like it is worth a try to me. I say we should try."

"Lucy," Vieve held her dying friend, "I don't want to leave you."

"And I would love to go with you, and I would," Lucy whispered, "but I cannot. You must do me honor by granting what I now ask. It gives me great pleasure to think that I might have a small part in securing your safety. All of you have been the best friends I have ever had. In fact, you are sisters to me. I love you so much. Promise me that you will do this. And Vieve," she paused, coughing once more, "I can get word to Oliver. You will see him again."

The girls held hands, sitting in silence, feeling the enormity of their decisions and of the coming days, the massive weight of it all.

"There is one more thing that I would ask, "Lucy said, "and I implore you to consider it, even while I know I have no right to ask it of you all. My parents did not treat you well, none of you. You have every right to hate them or hate what they have embraced. Please do not seek revenge on them. For me and Oliver, please try to find it in your hearts to let their consequences be left to God Almighty, or to a new government, should we have one," Lucy's voice grew weaker. "They are my parents, and they are flawed, as we all are. But they are all I have, and they were good parents to me. I hope that one day, they will choose atonement for their erroneous choices."

It was Maybelle who reached again for the hand of the mistress's daughter. She smiled at Lucy, eyes shining, and her voice soft and tender.

"Lucy, you are my friend. That was a long time coming," she smiled. "But we did it, you, and I, against all odds, a poor Negro slave girl and a once- spoiled plantation daughter." Maybelle paused before continuing, looking at each.

"I would be less than honest if I said I did not hate what has been done—what is being done—to my people and my family. Strangely, I pity them, your folks. They are so consumed with trying to hang on to their power that they have lost all happiness and godly purpose, even with all of their wealth. So, yes, I do pity them. And I don't ever want to be as they are. I want to be able to rise to forgive them. Perhaps one day I can. For now, I can only pray for them, and I will do so because my faith demands it." She paused again, "But, my prayers of thanksgiving will always be for you—all of you—in my life."

"Then you will all be prepared to depart with Emily in the early hours of the morning. You must speak with her about provisions, what to bring, and take one of our horses. Ashwiyaa will ride with Emily while Vieve and Maybelle will ride our horse. That way, Emily and Ash can guide, and you will all move as swiftly as possible." Lucy stopped talking while her friends helped her to lie on her side, so that she might rest and breathe easier.

"I have one more request," she whispered, "please fetch Emily to see me alone, so that I might have a few private words with her, while my father is not about. Come say your last goodbyes before you go to sleep this night. You will need lots of rest for your journey. Don't forget, when you look up at our pale moon shining in the sky—think of me with fondness as your friend and know that I love you all more than you could ever know. Pray that we win this war, as costly as it will be, and that our country and all in it, will be free."

CHAPTER FORTY – ONE

Montague Hall, July 1781

Oliver Montague faced his mother from the chair that his father most often used when he was in the sitting room. Oliver had seated himself there in a deliberate move to assert his own authority at a time when he knew his mother would disagree with his decisions. Before he began, he motioned for Evaline, Jude, Big Zeb, Dumplin, and the few Negroes who had chosen to remain on the plantation to come into the sitting room. They stood together in silence, each feeling the awkward tension.

Elizabeth Montague made an uncomfortable shift in her chair and crossed her arms. The slaves seemed to be watching her, all but Evaline, who clung to Jude's arm and kept her eyes anywhere besides Elizabeth, who seemed to take pleasure in her discomfort.

"Thank you, all of you, for being here with my mother and me," Oliver began. As you know, the British have allowed us to feed and tend to the sick and injured here from both sides, and thus, to keep us from total destruction. I have made the necessary provisions for you to each retain the parcels of land that you now own forever, and to do with as you see fit."

Oliver stood, running a hand through his dark hair, and glanced out the front windows where men in various stages of sickness and injury continued to arrive at Montague Hall for care. He turned to face the gathering once more.

"Perhaps you will one day provide me with the good measure of care that you have given to these men here," he sighed nodding his head.

"What is this all about, Oliver, what are you saying? Elizabeth asked. "I believe that everyone has done an admirable level of work here, what more can be done?"

Oliver smiled at his mother, then at those gathered together.

"I am leaving Montague Hall, Mother. I am joining our militia to fight for independence."

"Leaving?" Elizabeth could not hide the stunned and surprised response. "For the love of God, why? You cannot leave us, Oliver!"

"For the love of country, Mother," he replied. "In the hope that one day we will all have a free country that will be a beacon of example for the world as to how humanity can overcome our tendency throughout history to rule over one another." He turned to the slaves. "You all have worked hard, very hard, both before this war, and now in times of greater conflict. Together we have managed to overcome many obstacles, the least of which has been the British. All of you know what must be done to keep this place alive and ready for anyone who might come to us. I am no longer needed here. I have asked Big Zeb, who has been like a grandfather to me when he did not have to treat me thus, to act in my place and work alongside my mother to run what remains of Montague Hall. Mr. Bennett has been relieved of his duties here."

Oliver paused to allow for the incredulous reaction of both his mother and the remaining slaves. to all that he had shared, and to rein in his emotions before continuing. "You are all free to come and go, as you know, even to leave this place," he said. "I value each of you, will pray every day for you, and ask for your prayers, and hope that I might be most fortunate to see you here when this war is over. I have some thoughts as to what we could do together to create a sound means of a living and a good life here for our families for many years. I will do my best to convince my father, upon his return, of the beneficial nature of such a plan. It is my intention to return here with Vieve as my wife, if she will have me, to begin our own family."

Oliver made a quick perusal of his mother's face, noting her stoic despair. Was there also a minutia of acceptance or repentance in her expression? Or would she remain the snake-like creature Ashwiyaa had seen in her vision?

"I would be most pleased and honored to count you all as friends. But there will be no harsh feelings, should you decide not to remain at Montague Hall. Please consider these possibilities. I leave in the morning at first light."

He faced the slaves, these people who had been kind to him, despite the grueling work they had done, the suffering they had been forced to endure, and the indignities with which they had been subjected.

"If you would indulge me," he smiled at them, "Vieve always wanted to do this, and I want her to know that we did. Before I am off to fight, I wish to share the supper meal with you this evening, after we tend to our injured. Perhaps we can bring some blankets, perhaps sit beneath one of the oak trees for a moment or two."

Big Zeb spoke first.

"I be there, fo' sure."

"Sounds mighty fine," Jude added, wrapping an arm around Evaline.

Dumplin and Merrilee offered to arrange the outdoor grounds for those attending. Evaline, who had said nothing thus far, remained emotionless, but took a timid step toward Elizabeth Montague.

"Mistress Montague," she began, then stopped. Reaching for Jude's hand, she whispered. "Elizabeth. I hope that you will consider joining us with your son."

No one spoke, not even Oliver. The silence spoke for them all.

Elizabeth rose from her seat, looking first toward her son, then at those to whom she had meted out years of indifference and at times, cruelty. She could not swallow the lump in her throat.

"Please excuse me."

All eyes watched Elizabeth Montague ascend the staircase making heavy, slow steps toward her bedchamber. Her trembling shoulders and heaving chest had not gone unnoticed. Oliver wondered if the regret he knew she felt was because Montague Hall and her life would be forever changed, or if miracles and answered prayer were indeed possible, and that his mother might one day allow wounded pride, massive guilt, and years of blind ambition to be laid aside for better angels.

CHAPTER FORTY-TWO

The Geiger Home, July 2, 1781

Vieve leaned against the outside wall of her friend's bedchamber. She had waited behind Maybelle and Ashwiyaa to be the last to say a final goodbye to Lucy Montague. She had dreaded the wait, the act of letting her friend go. The prospect had resurrected the same overwhelming intensity of grief, loneliness, and loss that she had experienced at the death of her mother. She had come full circle in her relationship with the young mistress of Montague Hall, from dreaded foe to dearest of friends. In their private time together, they had shared their frailties, fears, and dreams of the future, only now to have to relinquish all, as the harbingers of death grew more prominent. Lucy's breathing had become shallow and slow, while she could no longer speak loud enough for her words to be audible, unless one sat close in proximity to her, and waited for the labored breathing to settle.

"Lucy," Vieve sat on a small stool that had been pushed next to the bed and held the hand of her dying friend. "You don't have to say anything. I'm here."

Lucy's eyes opened, closed, then opened once more. She tried to smile, her lips parting to allow as much air as possible to fill her chest.

"Vieve," she whispered. "I'll miss you most of all."

Vieve's eyes clouded with tears. There was no use in trying to stop them now.

"I love you, Lucy Montague. I will never forget you, never."

"It won't be long now. I'm not scared." Lucy tried to smile again, coughing, and putting a hand on her chest. "You keep my wagon."

"The wagon?" Vieve asked. "Your wagon that Oliver made you?"

"Keep it. Pull my nieces and nephews in it. That will make me happy."

Vieve let her head rest against Lucy's shoulder, putting an arm across her friend to hold her, and wiping her tears with her other hand.

"My children—Oliver's children—will know all about you, Lucy. I hope one will share your name and your courage." Vieve rubbed Lucy's arm, watching her struggle to breathe and smile at the same time.

"Find Emily and my father, please. Tell them to come."

"Yes, of course. I'll get them now before I go back to the livery."

"Vieve."

"Yes?"

"Never give up hope. Think of me when you look at the moon."

"Always, Lucy. You will be in my heart and in my prayers every day, you know that. Every day."

Vieve rose from her seat, drying her eyes and looking at her friend one last time.

"You think about all of us, how much we love you, Lucy Montague. Go with God. I'm going to find your father and Emily now."

When she opened the bedchamber door, Vieve found Emily waiting in the hallway. The girl hugged Vieve and whispered words of condolence.

"Best fetch Elias now," she said. "I will stay with Lucy."

"Yes, she wants to see you both."

Vieve made her way to the front of the farmhouse. Elias and John Geiger were in the sitting room engaged in serious discussion.

"If you go fight, Elias, when Lucy is gone, what will you do with the slaves you brought?"

Vieve felt the breath catch in the back of her throat. She placed a hand against the wall in the hallway, unable to move.

"Sell them, of course. Elizabeth wanted Vieve and Ashwiyaa gone. She begged me to not bring them back. Do you have a need for extra help here? If you wish to keep one or two, they do work well, although I doubt you have a need for the Indian."

"I have no need for them here. But there are a few families who might. Herman Kinsler will have a better idea of that sort of thing, who needs what, you know. He should be coming this way again soon."

Vieve smoothed her dress and rounded the hallway to the sitting room.

"My apologies, Master Montague. Lucy has asked for you."

"Thank you, Vieve. I will see her now."

"Yes, Sir. Good evening."

Vieve hurried to reach the livery as fast as her feet would take her. Maybelle and Ashwiyaa were seated on a bedding of hay in a vacant stall.

"Are you alright?" Maybelle demanded.

"No," Vieve responded. "I'm not. Not at all." She relayed all that she had overheard in the sitting room.

"He is going to fight, and sell us all?" Maybelle asked.

"That's what he said. And not necessarily together. Elizabeth Montague wants nothing more to do with us.

"Then we are doing the best thing in leaving here. Perhaps Lucy can talk with him."

"I don't think she is going to make it through the night," Vieve said. "She knows she is dying, and she has embraced that fate. Leaving is the best choice we have."

In the wee dark hours of early morning, Emily Geiger, wearing a simple dress and boots, her hair tied in a meticulous bundle at her neck, arrived in the livery. She loaded the saddle bags already stuffed with dried food and a change of clothes. She had General Greene's letter hidden and secure in the bodice of her dress, with a canteen slung across one shoulder. Motioning to the girls to follow, she led them around the back of the barn and livery, away from the main house. They walked in complete silence until they were far enough away for no sound to reach the ears of those who remained.

Mounting the horses, they rode with haste to the end of the Geiger farm, then made their way down the path toward the junction of the Broad and Saluda Rivers, where it became the Congaree.

"What of Lucy?" Vieve asked. "Did she make it through the night?"

"She was sleeping when I left her. But I fear she may not last through tomorrow." Emily replied. "This is for the best. We all know that."

The first leg of the ride through the dense forested surroundings was uneventful, though the traveling party remained vigilant of every nocturnal sound. Emily and Ashwiyaa set an admirable pace, pushing the horses forward without overburdening them at a full gallop. The daylight hours passed with light and amiable, but sparsely paced, conversation before they arrived just short of the designated crossing of the Saluda, close to the juncture with the Broad.

"There's the Elwood place," Emily pointed ahead of her at a white farmhouse nestled near the river. "We will stop there, spend the night, refresh the horses, and be prepared to cross the Saluda at the best spot first thing tomorrow morning."

Remember, for now, you are my slaves, and I will treat you in that manner. I know these people, and though they are friends of my father's, they may be Tory. We must not divulge our mission to them under any circumstances. If anyone asks, we are going to visit and help my uncle, Jacob Geiger."

Back in the area of Emily and John Geiger's family farmhouse, Mr. Lowry, the self-proclaimed noncombatant, who was in truth a Tory, reassessed the situation out loud with Billy Mink, another Tory neighbor. Considering the information provided to him from the Patriot encampment under General Nathanael Greene, he mapped out a plan with his henchman.

"That girl most likely left here after the night passed," he surmised. "She couldn't have gone too far, and she has no knowledge that anyone is on to her plan. Take the best horse you have. Think you can overtake her? She does know the terrain, but we know where she's headed. I have no doubt that we will be rewarded in a most handsome manner if we can stop her from reaching General Sumter."

"Yeah, I think I can take her," Billy Mink gave a notorious smile. "She might know her way around, but it's a hard ride to go all that distance without being seen at all. Especially for a woman. I know the route as well. She'll have to make stops for the horses, too. We'll get her."

"Why, Emily Geiger, what a surprise to see you!" Mrs. Elwood, a kind and generous woman, called to her husband. "Look who has come to see us! It is young Emily Geiger, here with a friend." She reached for Vieve's hand, unaware that she was a servant. "I don't know you, my dear."

"Oh, Emily," she continued with hardly a breath, "your slaves can take your horses out back to the barn and care for them. We will send some refreshment momentarily. Come inside, girls, you must be exhausted. Emily, you are such an adventurous girl, to be out these days with this turmoil of war. And is this a friend? Aren't you a pretty thing!"

"Yes," Emily turned to the girls, eyes wide, not having planned for anyone mistaking Vieve for a girl of acceptable stature. She spoke louder than usual. "This is Genevieve, 'Vieve' for short. She is a cousin on my mother's side." Emily winked at the girls. "I did not want to make this journey alone. And I am quite tired. We are on the way to Uncle Jacob. He's been feeling poorly of late, and Father has good help with Vieve's folks at our place, so I am going to spend some time with him and Cousin John while I can."

"You must spend the night here and let your horses rest. We don't have as much these days, like everyone else. But our boys have gone off to fight, so we welcome some company, and any news, if you have it."

Emily turned her back to Mrs. Elwood and Vieve so that neither could see her face. She spoke with curt authority.

"Take the horses out back and water and brush them down. Miss Vieve and I will come out there in a few moments to check them and to retrieve an item or two from our bags. We will bring some cider or such to you."

"Yas'm, Mistress Emily, we sho' nuf will." Maybelle adopted the odious slave verbiage, cutting her eyes at Vieve. Ashwiyaa gave an audible grunt but said nothing and complied by taking the reins of both animals.

"You come to the back door, now, and I'll have someone bring something to you," Mrs. Elwood added, nodding her head.

"Yas'm, we do that," Maybelle responded, frowning at the forced but necessary return to slave ways. "C'mon then, horses, we get you all rested up too."

"Emily," Mrs. Elwood smiled again, "I can put you both in one of the bedrooms. The two on the left side of the house might be the coolest to sleep in during these summer months, but you can choose what you wish. I'll have a wash bowl brought to you both to freshen up a bit, and the privy is out to the right, as you know. Then we can visit some before supper time. You girls will need lots of sleep for your journey to Uncle Jacob's. I'm so sorry to hear he's down a bit with his health."

Vieve wanted to wave to Ashwiyaa and Maybelle but dared not to do so. How awkward it was to be in this position, somewhere between servitude and one who was served. This, she had never known before. The discomfort was most unsettling.

CHAPTER FORTY – THREE

July 3, 1781

From the comfort of the bedroom with a window closest to the barn, Vieve was awakened by voices in the middle of the night. The girls had left the bedroom door ajar so that they could hear any interloping noise. Placing a hand over Emily's mouth, Vieve shook the sleeping girl until she opened her eyes.

"Who, again, are you seeking?" Mr. Elwood asked, leaning against the front door to the farmhouse.

"Who is it?" Mrs. Elwood called out, wrapping her arms around her shoulders as she pattered down the short hallway to join her husband at the door.

"Billy Mink, Ma'am," the visitor said, "I do apologize for waking you. I've been sent to find a girl who might be carrying a message to the Patriot General Sumter. She was seen at General Nathanael Greene's camp a day or so ago. Her father is a Patriot, so we have reason to believe she is involved in that cause. Might she be here?"

Emily and Vieve tiptoed to the bedroom door, listening to every word, and clinging to one another. Emily knew that the Elwoods were fond of both her and her father, despite their Tory leanings. She held her breath, squeezing VIeve's hand.

"We do have a guest here, yes, but of course all are asleep." Mr. Elwood began. "I don't recall the young woman's name, but she is looking forward to a meal with us in the morning before traveling to see relatives, she said. Why don't you come in, Mr. Mink, and get some rest. You've had a long journey also. If it's her, you can take her in the morning just as easily with a fresh horse and some rest."

"Thank you kindly, Sir," Billy Mink replied, "I appreciate the hospitality and could use the rest for sure."

Behind their bedroom door, Vieve and Emily breathed a collective sigh, still gripping the arms of the other. Billy Mink would tend to his horse, where Ashwiyaa and Maybelle would see him and know that something was amiss. They would have the horses prepared for the ride, Vieve was certain, since all had agreed on the decision to sleep in travel clothes for the duration of the secret mission if the need to act with immediacy arose. Shutting the door and pushing the open window as wide as they could, the girls prepared for their departure. Emily raised a finger to her lips, securing her boots while Vieve did the same. She pressed the bodice of her dress, making sure that General Greene's letter was once again secure. She had read it several times again by candlelight before sleeping, having committed the entirety to memory. Once ready, they waited for Billy Mink and all in the house to sleep. Only then would a safe escape be possible.

Vieve surmised that at least an hour had passed before Emily motioned toward the window. The snoring noise coming from Billy Mink's room gave the girls a brief moment of humorous reprieve. Emily eased herself out of the window, landing on the ground with a soft thud. After a moment of waiting, she stood ready to assist Vieve. When they reached the livery, they found Ashwiyaa checking the saddlebags already on the horses, and Maybelle holding the reins. No one spoke. Emily motioned toward the back of the livery where they would not be seen by anyone in the house. Vieve stared at the tomahawk lashed to Ashwiyaa's waist. No one needed to remind her that Ashwiyaa would use it if she must.

When they had put enough distance between themselves and the Elwood farmhouse, Emily slowed the ride just long enough to whisper to rest.

"We will have to cross the Saluda as quickly as possible and will have only the light of the stars to do so. We need to put as much distance between us and Mink as possible. Stay right behind us. I know where to cross. We will not stop again until daylight, and only then for me to ride side-saddle, as a proper lady should, " she smiled, "but for now, use your legs, too, for support and keep moving. Once we cross here and head to Friday's ferry, we will have made most of the journey."

Vieve held on to Emily, squeezing her knees into the horse's side and leaning forward as the gentle waters swirled around their knees, soaking everything. Water sprayed in her face and hair, and she felt the chill of the night air permeate her body. *Thank you for this South Carolina summer, or this could be much worse. Please guide us safely to the other side,* she prayed with fervent earnestness. When the party had crossed the Saluda and was once again surrounded by woods, Emily urged the horses on, taking care to ride as fast as they dared. The group rode in silence for miles, each hypervigilant in their perusal of the forest around them, and in the sounds of the pre-dawn morning. Vieve found herself delighting in the aftermath of the river crossing and the impromptu bath that all had needed. Their clothes had almost dried out when Emily stopped riding.

"It's beginning to get lighter now. I need to switch to side-saddle; in case we are spotted. Stretch if you need to do so, but we must keep going." She dismounted long enough to stretch her legs then to have Vieve assist in her making the appropriate mount.

"Emily, look." Ashwiyaa's voice was low, but the serious tone told them that danger was ahead. In the dim gray morning light, there was no mistaking that the three red-uniformed men on horseback were British soldiers. The Redcoats had seen them, as well, as one pointed in their direction.

"Oh, God," Emily muttered. "We can't run. Remember, you are my slaves once again. Say nothing."

"Halt there!" The soldier closest to them commanded, holding up a hand. "Who are you and why are you here at this hour?"

"Good morning to you all, Sir. I am Elizabeth Gray, and these are my servants. I am journeying to my uncle who has taken ill and needs care."

"Good morning, Miss Gray. And why, pray tell, are you out at this hour of the day?"

"I'm surprised you have not come to an understanding about the weather here in South Carolina," Emily tried to appear confident. "The days of summer are sometimes quite unbearably hot. As I've made this journey more than once, I know the advantages of traveling in the coolness of the morning. We are most anxious to complete our journey and would appreciate being on our way."

The soldier who had spoken leaned forward on his horse, regarding each of them with caution. Vieve could sense that he was not convinced of the story Emily had tried to weave.

"You crossed the river at night, did you not? Your clothes are dirty and still damp." He did not wait for a reply. "Empty your saddle bags."

"Sir, I beg you to reconsider. Time is of the utmost importance for us. Search the bags, if you feel you must, but please allow us safe passage."

The soldier motioned for another to attend to the saddlebags on Vieve and Ashwiyaa's horse, while he moved his horse next to Emily.

"You are aware that a war is all around us, Miss Gray, and yet you travel? We will examine the bags, to be sure."

The soldiers next to Vieve and Ashwiyaa took notice of the uncomfortable displeasure they had caused, rifling through the bags for any suspicious item.

"This is a rather odd group of women," the man next to Vieve and Maybelle smiled. "A Negro, an Indian, and who are you?" He demanded of Vieve.

"She is my indentured servant, and you need not address her. She answers to me alone," Emily shot back. "They all do. You address me only with your questions. Leave them be."

"Very well, Miss Gray," the speaking soldier's eyes narrowed. "I find it quite unsettling that you and this rather unusual group of females are out at this hour, in this place, and that you found it necessary to cross the river at night. You will come with us." He reached for the reins to Emily's horse.

"I most certainly will not!" Emily feigned exasperation when fear was the underlying culprit. "I have done nothing wrong and must be about my business!"

"Not to be alarmed, Miss Gray, we will take good care of you all at Fort Granby. You will each be rested, fed—and then searched, once a woman is secured to do so. If you are not in possession of anything that would amount to treason, then you will be released."

"Treason?" Emily retorted, "I have done no such thing!"

"Perhaps you have not," the soldier smiled, "but we must be sure. Lord Rawdon will want to speak with you, I am certain." The smile left his face. "So you will be taken to him and I advise you to cooperate fully, if you want to resume your travels."

CHAPTER FORTY – FOUR

Fort Granby, South Carolina, July 3, 1781

Fort Granby, the British camp near the Congaree River, protected the landing at Friday's ferry and was garrisoned by three hundred militia. While it was of strong fortification, the men there appeared to need more supplies, not unlike the Patriot forces. Francis, Lord Rawdon, had once been a formidable Irish man, perhaps not yet thirty years old, Vieve surmised, but appeared to be in declining health. She had heard some of the soldiers discussing the sickness in the South that seemed to be brought on with the warmer climate and season and the lack of proper food and sickness. She had overheard one of them say that Lord Rawdon had been stricken with a severe attack of the ague at some point. His decorated red coat and white breeches accentuated his authority, and she found the pleasant Irish brogue reminiscent of a few of the people she had known in her childhood days in the streets of London. Lord Rawdon, she had been informed, was in command of the entire British campaign in the South. He surveyed the disheveled women before him with both mild amusement and concern. Emily stood in front of the others, smoothing her dress, and trying to appear as a proper Southern lady.

"Miss Gray," Lord Rawdon began, "I am told you and your servants were found after having crossed the Saluda on horseback during the night, and that you have been evasive with my men. Perhaps you would care to speak to that concern."

"I beg your pardon, Sir," she held her head high, "but I was direct in my response by informing your men that I only seek to reach my sick uncle, who lives just a short way past this place. I am no threat to anyone, and I wish to be on my way."

"You shall indeed be on your way, Miss Gray, once you and these servants are searched by a woman who has been sent for such."

An audible gasp could be heard from all, including Emily, who flinched, her cheeks taking on a notable blush. Lord Rawdon smiled.

"Perhaps you would like to amend your story, tell us who you are going to see and where you are coming from?" He pressed his fingers on the desk in front of him, leaning forward and studying Emily Geiger. "It would be a shame to lose such a gathering of women to treason."

"Do what you must, then." She glared at him. "I have done nothing wrong and wish no part of this conflict, this war. I merely want to attend to my uncle."

As you wish," Lord Rawdon bowed his head to her, still smiling and motioning for two of the guards at the door. "Take our guests to the room above the guard house. Lock the door and see to it that no one leaves unattended for any reason. Notify me when the farmer's wife arrives, and they have all been meticulously searched."

Vieve held Maybelle's hand as they were taken from Lord Rawdon to the upstairs room. Ashwiyaa walked behind everyone, making note of all around them. Emily was secured between the two guards. All eyes in Fort Granby were on the women. Vieve knew they were all afraid, though none would show such in front of their captors. How she wished Oliver Montague was here to help them. What frightened her more than Lord Rawdon's threats of treason was the fear of never seeing him again.

When the door was locked behind them, the girls turned to Emily Geiger. All knew that she was the one most in danger of being in harm's way. The room was devoid of all but a table and several wooden chairs.

"What now?" Vieve whispered, "we have to do something."

"No," Emily whispered back. "It's me they want. But we have to act quickly. Keep a watch on the door, Ashwiyaa." She turned her back to the door and the girls, drawing General Greene's letter from her bodice. With firm strokes, she tore it into four pieces. Handing a piece to each girl, she smiled. "Now eat!"

"Eat?" Vieve asked. "Eat this?" She held her piece in the air.

"Yes. Yes, eat it now and be quick about it. They cannot hold us here if they find nothing. We need to leave this place as quickly as possible. Billy Mink may still be looking for us."

Emily watched each of them crush their piece of the letter and shove it into their mouths, chewing while making the most unpleasant of expressions.

"Tastes terrible!" Maybelle breathed, trying to swallow. "Like straw."

"Emily is right," Vieve whispered. "Better straw than treason. Chew it up."

A loud knock on the door startled the girls, who all turned to Emily, still holding her paper. Opening her mouth as wide as she could, she stuffed the remains inside and began to chew, turning away from the door as a guard pushed it open. With no warning, Emily's whole body began to shake. She groaned, covered her face with her hands, and made loud sobbing noises. The farmer's wife who had been summoned to conduct the search stared in surprise as Emily threw herself prostrate on the floor, arms in front of her eyes, the crying sounds continuing.

Vieve realized the ruse, poking Maybelle in the side, and entering the dramatic fray.

"Mistress Gray, are you alright? Mistress Gray!" She knelt before Emily, placing herself in front of the girl so that the woman could not see Emily's jawline working to chew and swallow the paper. Vieve stroked her back and whispered soothing words. "It's going to be alright, truly."

"Step aside, Miss," the older woman commanded. "You may close the door now and I will knock when I am done." She motioned to the guards to leave the room.

"Please remove all but your inner garments. Your shoes, as well. Place them on the table and stand aside." The woman was both formal and firm but emanated a compassionate countenance. "Get up off the floor, young lady. I have no intention of hurting you."

Vieve watched as Emily feigned wiping tears from her face. To her horror, she thought the girl might still be trying to swallow some of the letter.

"Please, kind lady," she attempted to get the attention of the woman. "Please understand that we are all scared of such terrible accusations. We mean no disrespect and I know Mistress Gray will do what you ask." She stared at Emily, who now smiled, having just swallowed the last of the letter.

"Yes, I apologize for my emotions," Emily replaced her smile with a penitent expression. "Search as you must. We want to be on our way to my sick uncle."

The woman conducted the search with rapid speed, shaking each shoe, patting down each girl, and rifling through the outer garments. Once satisfied that no evidence of treason was present, she pounded the door for the guards, then accompanied the accused party back to Lord Rawdon.

"Well, Miss Gray, it seems I owe you my sincerest apology. You and your slaves are free to go, with my good wishes. Your horses have been watered and are ready for you to proceed on your journey."

"Thank you, Lord Rawdon," Emily retained the feigned formality with her captor. "No ill feelings remain. We just want to reach my relatives who require my help."

"You may be on your way then, Miss Gray. Safe travels to you all."

"And to you, as well."

"I will have a scout escort you part of the way to see you in sight of your destination," Lord Rawdon continued. "That is, to the home of your uncle."

"I appreciate your generosity and help," Emily gave him the most beguiling smile she could manage, befitting of a well-bred woman. "Thank you once again. My uncle will be very grateful."

The ride from Fort Granby to the home of Jacob Geiger was not far. The girls remained silent during the short trek, as they had resumed the roles of servant and slave to Emily, who made light conversation with the soldier scout. When they had reached a fork in the wooded path just before her uncle's house, she spoke in exaggerated excitement for the scout.

"There, just up that road is where he resides with my cousin," she smiled. "I cannot thank you enough for accompanying us to safety. I am much obliged to you, Sir."

"Take care, Miss. Safe travels and regards to your uncle."

"I will most certainly tell him." Emily smirked, holding her relieved laughter until the scout had ridden out of sight. "And good riddance to you!" She clasped her hands together, looking up into the sky, as if in prayer, then back at the others. "We cannot waste any time. Billy Mink could be headed this way also. We will not stop now, but ride further to the home of a friend of my uncle's where we can get fresh horses for the last ride of the journey, then ride through the night to the encampment of General Sumter. We will have to cross the Congaree once again and navigate some swampy land. General Sumter should not be too far from that point. By the time anyone discovers the truth, we will be gone and safe in the encampment. We will stop only as long as we need for the horses to rest and get a bit of water also. You need to be prepared for a long and tiring ride.

CHAPTER FORTY-FIVE

July 4, 1781

Emily Geiger had been right about everything. They had secured fresh horses, been given nourishment and the briefest of respite before resuming the arduous journey to General Sumter. The swampland, the damp and oppressive heat, the exhaustion, the long night ride, was all as she had described. Vieve once again felt the exhilaration of the refreshing waters of the Congaree, the relief from the sweat and grit of the journey, and the reassurance of having the company of her friends. At night, in the dark when conversation was sparse and the darkness helped to hide emotions and fears, she saw the faces of those she missed and longed for their presence. Oliver Montague was foremost in her thoughts. She wondered if he knew of Lucy's death or had any notion of where she might be now. Her heart ached at the thought of how long they might be apart. Claire Whittier, too, was a constant memory. Vieve often thought of her mother, of Simon, and how they would have loved the pristine beauty of this South Carolina. But they, too, would have been indentured, perhaps not even allowed to remain together, as Maybelle's family and so many others had been brutally ripped apart. Claire may well have been forced to endure the same as Maybelle's sister, Jonsie.

"Vieve?" Maybelle whispered as the daylight began to stretch across the Southern sky, "You thinking about Oliver?"

"Yes," she looked up into the dawn, forcing back the tears, "and Lucy, Ash, my family, and yours. All that we've been through. And all that remains unknown to us."

"You think we will win this war, that Mr. Paine is right about how this country can be?"

"I do think he is right. I hope it with every breath I take. What do you think, Maybelle?"

"I want him to be right. For my people, I think freedom will be a long time coming, even so. If the Patriots win, what will happen to the slaves then, even the ones who have already received their freedom? Will I be sent back in chains to Montague Hall, or worse? Ash, too. Will your servitude be made longer if we are caught? I'm glad we did what we did. But I know that there could be serious punishment ahead."

"You know I have come to love you like a sister I never had, don't you? Oliver wants to help, and I trust him. He truly wants better for us all."

"I know that." Maybelle hesitated, "but Master Montague is still his father and the master there. Oliver may not be able to do all he wants. If South Carolina chooses to keep the slaves, it could all be as it was before or even worse. That glorious change Mr. Paine wants to see may be years and years away. Folks' minds don't change so easy after many years of believing something, even if it's wrong. Power blinds those with it to what other folks are going through. Mr. Paine said all people throughout time have done such cruelty to each other even before Jesus. That kind of thought won't change any time soon. All the slave masters and their kin have convinced themselves that they are teaching their slaves better. They believe that to ease their guilt."

Vieve thought about the truth of what her friend was saying. She knew her own London had been the same way. People had been placed on an imaginary ladder of importance. The further down one was, the less worth one had. Those at the bottom rungs, like her own family, who lived by less than desirable means, were all but invisible or like dirt under the feet of the more affluent. Vieve smiled, remembering Claire. She had fought with everything in her to provide for her and little Simon.

"Maybelle, if Mr. Paine is right, then we must fight as much as we can for that vision of this country. If that Declaration of Independence from Great Britain means anything at all, then we cannot stop. We are here! It has fallen to our lot in time to act. If those governing truly represent the people, then the people must join together, always be vigilant and care about what is happening before them. I know your people and even Ash's are not fully considered here. In truth, I'm somewhere between you and the next rung of folks above me on that ladder. But opportunity and hope have been placed in our very laps! How can we ignore that? For the love of all who came before us! For me, I choose to never lose my God-given reason and voice. I choose to use it for the good."

"You know we could be hanged or shot, or perhaps whipped, and then hanged and shot." Maybelle added. "Alright then, so be it. We don't give up, no matter what. If Oliver and Lucy could change their minds, so might others, even if it takes years."

"You two are having some deeply serious conversation," Emily commented. "You have given me much to think about, as well. Ashwiyaa, if you make it to your people who remain, what will you do?"

"That is for *Wakan Tanka* to decide, to guide me," the Indian girl said. "I want to be with my people, yes." Ashwiyaa turned from her position behind Emily to look at Vieve and Maybelle. "But you are my loyal friends. You are not so bad, for your dark and light skin ways," she grinned. "Freedom for the land and her people is a worthy fight."

"Do you remember when we put on the war paint and pledged to one another that we would be strong and remain together?" Vieve asked. "That is one of the best days I have ever had. We should make that a tradition for us, yes? And for our children, if we ever have those? I'm going to name my daughter Lucy Claire, if I am fortunate enough to be graced with a daughter," Vieve smiled.

"Lucy Claire Montague." Maybelle whispered. "It is a good name, and such a girl would be most fortunate to have you and Oliver. I can only hope that I will see Mama and Jude and Jonsie once again."

"Oh, I hope that so much for you, my friend," Vieve leaned into her friend. "Who knows, there may be a fine man in your future too. And, Maybelle, you can become a teacher! You can teach all of our children; would that not be grand?"

"Grander than you could ever imagine." Maybelle sighed.

"That's just it," Vieve responded, "I can imagine it now."

The party rode in silence as the noonday sun pushed its way through the lush verdant woods. The trees and heavy foliage provided much-needed shade to alleviate the direct rays of blazing light, but the heat of the summer season was upon them. The night ride, with the exception of the swamp navigation, had not been as strenuous as it was lengthy in duration, with no sleep. All were weary and weak with thirst and now the bearing down of the worst of the sun. Ash turned once again to face her friends.

"We must stop soon. I fear Emily is becoming too weak to ride further."

"Look!" Vieve exclaimed, pointing ahead, "They are Patriot militia, are they not?"

The young women rode toward the band of soldiers, rejoicing aloud that their mission would soon be completed. In minutes, soldiers rushed to them, removing Emily from her horse, and carrying her into the encampment of General Sumter, who was most intrigued by their presence. He knelt beside Emily, who had been placed in a chair and given refreshment.

"I am told you have a message for me from General Nathanael Greene?" He placed an arm on her chair. "He has made many requests of me. What now, and why has he sent such as you?"

Vieve smiled, watching the man General Greene had referred to as the "Carolina Gamecock." His strong resolve and aggressiveness were evident even now, without being in the heat of battle. The girls had been seated behind Emily Geiger, reassuming their roles as her servants. They watched with eager anticipation of what General Sumter would do.

"General Sumter, you must forgive me. I fear I had to chew and swallow the letter intended for you from General Greene." Emily blushed in profusion while watching the eyes of the Gamecock widen. He glanced at the other officers in the tented room, smiling with amusement. She relayed all that had happened to the stunned leader of the rebel partisan forces of the South Carolina piedmont area.

"Miss Geiger, your bravery and dedication to the Patriot cause is most admirable. You have sacrificed much for the independence of this country. Are you aware what day it is today?"

"Yes, Sir, I am. It is the Fourth of July, I believe. It has not gone unnoticed by me."

"My men will provide the best quarters possible for you to rest momentarily. You will excuse me while I address the soldiers who must move quickly to fight once more. I will return to speak with you soon."

"Thank you, General Sumter." Emily gave a grateful smile, then faced her companions.

"They must be given care, too, Sir. They have assisted me in every possible endeavor, and I am most appreciative of their dedication to me. I might request some private time to gather my thoughts, if my servants could attend to wherever you might need them to do to accommodate us for now?"

"Granted, as you ask," the Fighting Gamecock responded before rising from his place beside her and motioning to the officers to have the young women given the best of care that might be provided.

CHAPTER FORTY – SIX

"I trust your accommodations were acceptable, though meager in these times of war." General Sumter motioned for Emily Geiger to be seated before him at his makeshift desk. Vieve, Ashwiyaa, and Maybelle were seated along the side of the enclosed space, beside a few of the attending officers.

"Yes, quite suitable, given our deplorable condition after such an eventful journey."

"Miss Geiger, we will do our best to notify your father of your whereabouts and assure him that you are secure. I suggest that you remain here for a brief period to ensure your safety, as the British may well be searching for you. As soon as possible, we will reunite you and your father, or get you to safety with a family close in proximity, where you might be safe from the enemy."

"As you wish, of course," Emily responded. "We do not want to interfere with the war endeavors and will do what we can to assist in any way. We can tend to your sick or injured and mend, wash, or cook as you might need, as well. Or simply provide needed conversation, write letters for those who cannot do so."

"Indeed, I am most appreciative of your continued willingness to assist in the war effort. Very well, then. Our United States of America are most grateful to you. South Carolina is most grateful to you, Miss Geiger."

"Thank you, Sir. My efforts pale in comparison to what your soldiers and all of our fighting men have volunteered to do in the name of freedom. In that regard, I have a small favor I wish to ask."

General Thomas Sumter relaxed in his chair, propping his legs on a wooden stool that he had pulled from behind the table that served as his desk, and crossing his uniformed arms against his chest.

"What favor might that be, Miss Geiger?"

"With regard to my slaves, Sir." She motioned to the companions behind her. Maybelle reached for Vieve's hand. Ashwiyaa leaned forward in her chair, both hands resting on her knees.

"What about them?" General Sumter regarded the young women with casual aloofness, before returning his gaze to Emily.

"One of your officers graciously provided me with writing implements so that I might prepare this document. Of course, I had such a document already secured at the beginning of our travels, but, as you are aware, it became necessary to destroy it prior to our arrival. If you will indulge my request, Sir." Emily handed the linen paper across the table to General Sumter, who read, then re-read its contents.

"Miss Geiger, you are indeed quite generous in your charity. How would you wish for this to be done?"

"If you will, Sir. The Indian girl, Ashwiyaa. She is a member of the Catawba Nation and was captured by the Cherokee, who fight against us. She was traded into slavery and then bequeathed to us by Mr. Elias Montague."

Vieve and Maybelle remained expressionless as they glanced first at each other and then at Ashwiyaa, whose eyes had narrowed, her head bowed. *What is Emily Geiger doing?*

"I see," General Sumter said. "Go on."

"I wish to see her returned to her people at the Catawba Reservation."

Ashwiyaa's head made an instinctive jolt, rising in swift reaction to Emily's words. She stared ahead, not looking at her friends. Tears moistened her eyes, and she blinked them back. Emily Geiger continued.

"Yes, like the others, she has served well over the years, none more than now, and I have given this much thought."

"And these slaves, what do you wish done with them?"

Maybelle squeezed Vieve's hand. Vieve felt the trembling and responded by placing her other hand atop Maybelle's. She felt the wet tears from Maybelle's eyes freefalling to her lap.

"Yes, the others," Emily paused. "I wish to see the Negro girl, Maybelle, manumitted immediately. She has been a part of chattel slavery since infancy and has served so well, along with her family, who have remained for now at Montague Hall near Charlestown."

Vieve could hear the emotion in Emily's voice, though the farm girl fought to restrain it.

"I wish her to be allowed to do as she pleases, but would suggest that for now, she accompany Ashwiyaa to the reservation for safety."

"What of this one?" General Sumter nodded at Vieve. "What do you wish done with her?"

"She has been an indentured servant since childhood, as well. She has more than paid her dues, for which we are grateful. All have been placed in my care." Emily turned to face them all. "I wish you all to be free, manumitted as such, and able to conduct your lives from this point on, as you see fit. I thought that Independence Day might be an appropriate time for such action."

"Thank you," Vieve whispered, smiling at Emily, unable to say more.

"Also," Emily continued, facing Vieve and winking so that General Sumter did not see her face, "Vieve, your remaining brother, Oliver, will be notified of your release from indenture, and when he is able, he will come for you at the Catawba Reservation. He has joined the noble fight for independence." Ashwiyaa, too, reached for Vieve's shoulder, the understanding seeping in.

"Oliver," Vieve whispered, her eyes clouding at the thought of him engaging in battle. But it was what he had said he would do, once he had assisted in establishing Montague Hall to receive war wounded. Maybelle wrapped her arms around Vieve and whispered.

"For the good. Never give up. God bless us all."

"To be clear, then, Miss Geiger, you wish for manumission for these women, as you have written here?"

"I do," Emily smiled. "Is it possible to assist in that regard?"

I believe so, yes," the Fighting Gamecock responded. "With troops massing near Eutaw Springs, by the Santee River, it is my hope that we can effectively force the British to surrender in the South, as we have weakened their resolve. If that can indeed occur, then it will be a monumental success for us. Travel would be much safer and easier to accomplish at that time. In the meanwhile, these young women may provide care here."

"Then that is how we shall plan. That is, if you all agree?" Emily gave a wide smile to the now free young women.

"Yes," Vieve was elated. "Yes, we most certainly agree. And thank you.

CHAPTER FORTY – SEVEN

July 4, 1781

The night was deep and quiet, save for the changing of the guards to keep the Patriot garrison safe at all times. Vieve had slept for a brief period, but the gift of being able to come and go as she pleased, and all that had happened since leaving London hung thick in her memory, as the heaviness of the seasonal Southern air. She felt drawn to move about, to both celebrate the blessing of freedom and to unravel the events of her life during the past seven years; to make sense of it all. She stood at the edge of the fortress, peering out over the full moon that illuminated the calmness of the Wateree River. A pale moon it was—mysterious, splendid, glorious. Not unlike the moon she had seen on the night of little Simon's death. Her mother had held her hand, watching for the carriage that would take them back to the seedy London streets. They had waited in the cold, sad and desolate, banished from the home of Lord Carrington to be sent to an unknown life in the colonies. Yet, somehow the pale moon, rising high into the night sky, had imparted hope. Hope of redemption, of grace and glory, of the promise of new life.

Vieve let her thoughts drift back to the day that Ashwiyaa had painted the faces of each, made them all warrior-sisters, united in something bigger than each of them had been alone, and prepared to do battle at all costs. She smiled, looking up at the moon once more. What was it Ashwiyaa had said regarding her people's belief about the giant orb? That it was a guardian spirit who guides, protects, and is the keeper of time, fertility, and seasons. The moon, to Ashwiyaa's people, heralded a time for great self-examination and letting go of the past, even finding the way out of the darkness.

In her own faith, the moon, especially the rising pale moon, was as Mary had been to Jesus Christ. Vieve laughed aloud, remembering being in church with her mother, sitting in the very back, hearing a thundering priest comparing Christ to the Roman sun god, Sol Invictus. The Unconquered Sun. Christ, too, the Son, God Incarnate, could not be conquered by death, but was the hope of all salvation, with Biblical references to fire and light. Mary, then, was the bringer of dawn, the new day, whose glory was that same Son. Vieve stared at the moon, marveled at its waxing and waning, its constant change, like the cyclical seasons that passed and returned, of nature in all of its primitive beauty and savage force.

Perhaps Mr. Thomas Paine was indeed right about the vulnerability of people, of nations as they grew, the ultimate waxing and eventual waning of all civilizations of every race and creed, who had adhered to the oppression of others in their staunch refusal to change. Vieve remembered the words he had written, in his *"Common Sense,"* that had stirred her very soul.

"Should an independence be brought about, …we have every opportunity and every encouragement before us, to form the noblest, purist constitution on the face of the earth. We have it in our power to begin the world over again."

She studied the pale moon rising in the sky once more; a beacon of light in the darkness, most beautiful when it was full, such as this, in all of its magnificence. But it, too, had its seasons of incompleteness, of less light or beauty. Yet it cycled through the predictable stages each time to reach its finest version, before beginning those stages yet again.

Vieve leaned against the stark mast that held the flag of the new nation for which the bloody fighting continued. Thirteen stars encircled together next to the field of red and white stripes. She stared back at the pale moon. Thomas Paine and Maybelle were prescient in their insight—that the building of a strong and great nation, rooted in a God-given freedom for all, would take the same cyclical revolutions as the moon, perhaps over more decades, even centuries, than anyone could know. The changing of hearts, the resolve to each be better than before, would take work, forgiveness, faith, love—and hope. Always hope. And she would hold fast to that notion, pray for it, seek it, with every ounce of strength she had for the rest of her days.

Perhaps the world could indeed begin again.

Milton Keynes UK
Ingram Content Group UK Ltd.
UKHW040831071024
449371UK00007B/727